the
Ivy
Lessons

S.Quinn & J.Lerman

S.Quinn
UK

Copyright © by S.Quinn

First Edition 2012

Designed by: Page Turners
Manufactured in the UK.

For my readers

Chapter 1

Ivy: A hardy climbing vine with evergreen leaves and black, berry-like fruits that can both damage buildings and protect them from weather damage.

You've been accepted ...

I stare at the letter, and can't believe what I'm seeing. The words *Ivy College* glitter in gold at the top of the page.

... to study Creative Theatre at Ivy College, London.

The mug of tea in my hand shakes, and I feel a big, silly smile on my face.

I can't believe it. I absolutely can't believe it. Thousands of young actors auditioned for Ivy College this year. I didn't think for a moment I'd get through.

I look at the letter again, not totally sure it can be real, and think back to the day I auditioned for Ivy College.

It had been a particularly hot morning, and London's tubes were a sticky mess of people, water bottles and fizzy drink cans.

I'd only ever been to London once before, to help my best friend, Jen, find a special pair of shoes for a wedding, and that day we hadn't ventured past Oxford Street.

I'd never experienced the panic, aggression and heat of summer rush hour, and I'd felt like a little doll, being thrown back and forth.

I got lost finding the college, and when I'd asked people for help, most of them were too busy to stop.

Eventually, a man with a white beard and clipped accent offered to show me the way. He led me off the main road and past pretty townhouses, to several acres of green grounds circled by fir trees and black railings.

On the grounds, I saw red-brick buildings covered in real ivy, silver and green. The buildings were surrounded by green grass and woodlands.

'I love ivy,' I'd told the man. 'It's one of my favourite plants.'

'Enjoy it while it lasts,' the man had said. 'This college is owned by a Hollywood actor. It'll only be a matter of time before he tears the whole place down and turns it to glass and concrete.'

'Are you talking about Marc Blackwell?' I'd asked.

The man had nodded. 'I've heard nothing but bad things about him. Extraordinarily arrogant, apparently. A very cold man.'

'I heard that too,' I'd said. 'But then, I suppose he has every reason to be arrogant. He's not much older than I am, but he's achieved so much. Winning two Oscars, founding this college.'

The man had looked at me then, perhaps wondering what business someone in a faded t-shirt and jeans had with the college.

'I'm applying for a place here,' I'd explained. 'I won't get it. Not in a million years. I only came because my university tutor said the audition would be a good experience. And it's lovely to see the college. It's beautiful. There are so many trees. You could get lost in those trees.'

I remember the red-brick, ivy-covered buildings were huddled close together, like they were trying to keep warm. They'd looked like children lost in a forest.

'Well. Good luck to you.' The man had left me then, and I'd stared at the college in wonder. The buildings all had turrets, balconies and arched windows like something from a fairy tale. A princess's castle. But I'd liked the trees better than the buildings. A little wildness in the centre of London.

I'd stared for a long time, before pushing open the wrought-iron gate and heading through the grounds. I felt so tiny and plain in such grand surroundings, but I wasn't nervous. I had nothing to lose, after all, and experience to gain. I had no idea I'd be meeting Marc Blackwell himself at the audition.

Chapter 2

Somehow, I found the audition room amid the winding pathways, brick arches and corridors.

When I walked into the room, I saw two people sitting behind a long desk.

The lady on the left I recognised as Denise Crompton, an actress famous for her musical theatre roles. She smiled at me, her eyes crinkling.

When I saw who was sitting on the right, I nearly tripped over my feet. There, real enough to touch, sat Marc Blackwell. I'd seen him in the movies many times, of course. But this was the first time I'd seen someone so famous in real life.

His light-brown hair looked softer and cleaner than it did in the movies, but his blue eyes were just as intense under thick, brown eyebrows. He was wearing a black t-shirt, and I remember thinking how lean and toned he looked. I'd read somewhere that he was playing a drug addict in his latest movie, and guessed he'd had to lose weight.

His cheeks, already angular, were a little hollow, and there were smudges of grey under his eyes. His skin looked very white as usual and he was handsome, in that cold, edgy way that made him the perfect choice for all those arty films he won awards for. His leanness and the curves of his muscles made him look more elegant, somehow, and a little bit dangerous.

He wore a black shirt, and despite the hot day, it was crisp and hung perfectly on his long, lean body.

I just stood there like an idiot, staring at Marc for the longest time. In real life, he was captivating. Just captivating. I found my gaze dropping to his lips, which were a sharp red colour and looked ever so slightly amused.

Despite his handsomeness, the hard look in his blue eyes told me he didn't stand for any nonsense, and that he wasn't impressed so far.

Denise smiled at me again, but Marc's face remained serious. He didn't waste any time with pleasantries.

'This is Denise Crompton,' Marc said, gesturing to his left. His voice was deep, and each word was spoken clearly. Precisely. He had the edges of an English accent, which surprised me since I'd heard he grew up in LA. 'She teaches singing, music and dance.' Marc folded his long fingers together. 'And if you have any sense, you'll know who I am. I own the college and offer students three lectures a week. And you are?'

'Sophia Rose,' I said, feeling my throat tighten. Try as I might, I just couldn't tear myself away from his eyes. They were like a flickering candle in a dark room. There was nowhere else to look. He returned my stare, leaning forwards onto his elbows.

'Well, Miss Rose,' he said, a smile spiking his curved lips. 'Nice of you to dress up for us today.'

I looked down at my white t-shirt and jeans.

'My university lecturer told me to go casual for auditions,' I said. 'Otherwise you look like you're trying too hard.'

Marc raised an eyebrow. 'Did he indeed?'

'She.'

The smile just about reached Marc's eyes. 'Are you correcting me, Miss Rose?'

'I -'

'Let's see what you can do. Who are you playing?'

'Lady Macbeth.'

'Ah.' Marc leaned back in his chair and tapped a navy pen on his notepad. 'The evil lady of Shakespeare.'

'Oh, no.' I felt myself stand taller. 'She's not evil.'

'Correcting me again?'

'But she isn't.' I insisted. 'I don't believe anyone is wholly evil. Even bad characters have lightness in them. You just have to look for it. If I don't see the good in a character, I can't play her.'

Marc's gaze was so intense, then, that I honestly thought it might knock me off balance. His blue eyes grew darker, and his brows pulled into a straight line.

I found myself moving my feet further apart, and my shoes squeaked on the parquet floor. We stared at each other for the longest time. Then Marc sat back, and spun his pen around his long fingers.

'Well, Miss Rose. As I said. Let's see what you can do. Ready?'

'Yes.' I gave a stupid nod, shook out my fingers and took a deep breath.

I played the scene where Lady Macbeth has blood on her hands. I read from a script that I'd altered myself, and put all my passion and spirit into the performance. I felt the light and dark of the character, her hunger for power, but also her remorse and madness.

I didn't look at Marc, but sometimes out of the corner of my eye I saw his eyebrow raise and the hollows in his cheeks ripple.

When I'd finished, Denise clapped heartily. Marc watched me, stony faced, and I guessed I'd have to do a lot more to impress an Oscar-winning Hollywood star.

I stumbled on my way towards the door. 'Thank you for your time.'

'Miss Rose,' Marc barked.

My hand faltered on the door handle.

'Light and dark, is that what you believe? The good in everybody?'

'Yes.'

He gripped his pen so tight that his knuckles went white. I noticed his jaw harden, and I wondered if I'd upset him. Then he rested his pen on his note-pad. 'Thank you for your performance. I enjoyed it very much.'

Chapter 3

I think about those words as I stare at my acceptance letter. *I enjoyed it very much.* I guess he must have meant it.

I pick up my Blackberry and find Jen's number. It's sunny in Dad's garden, and I shade the screen as I press to connect. Jen is my best friend, and she's always top of my frequent calls.

'Jen. It's Soph.'

'What happened? Are you okay? Your voice sounds funny – where are you?'

I laugh. She knows me so well. 'It's okay. Nothing bad. At least, not yet. I'm just at Dad's house, taking a break from cleaning.'

'You spend *every* weekend cleaning their cottage –'

'I know, Jen, but they need my help.' Since Dad had a baby with his new girlfriend, Genoveva, their house has been in chaos. I used to live there before I started university, but now I just visit at weekends.

I take a deep breath. 'But ... I got accepted on a post-graduate course. A good one. At a college in London.'

'Accepted? To a college? I thought you were done with university and all of that.'

'It's *post* graduate. And it's a really good college.'

'Which college is it?'

'Ivy College. London.'

'Oh. My. God. You're kidding me!' Jen shrieks down the phone. 'The Marc Blackwell college? You MUST be kidding me. You told me that course had thousands of applicants. Thousands and thousands. You said you were never going to get it. You said Marc didn't like your audition.'

'I know. But I guess he did.'

'I can't believe it, Soph. I said you were good. Didn't I tell you?'

'Thanks Jen.'

'Marc Blackwell,' Jen shrieks. 'He'll be teaching you. You'll be *living* in his college.'

I put a hand to my mouth to stifle a nervous laugh. 'Mad, isn't it? I mean, I can hardly believe it.'

'Hold on.'

I hear pages rustle.

'I've got Heat magazine right here,' say Jen. 'There's an article about him. Here it is. Something about him pledging money to save some crumbling old church in London. There's a picture of him. He's *hot*. Not exactly the university lecturer type, though. I mean, he's – what – twenty seven?'

'Marc Blackwell's been acting since he was a child,' I say. 'He's been in more movies than most forty year olds.'

'Oh my God, Soph, he is *so* sexy. Those eyes ... that body ... there's something so lethal about him. Maybe it's all those gritty, martial arts movies he does. He'll be *teaching* you. *Talking* to you.'

'That's if I accept the place,' I say. 'I met him already, remember? He's kind of cold. Not exactly nurturing and supportive. Maybe it's not the right course for me.'

'Have you told your dad yet?'

I bite my thumbnail. 'No. I mean, there's nothing to tell right now, is there? I haven't even decided if I'm going to accept.'

'Are you kidding me? That's it.' The phone goes dead. I know what that means. Jen is driving over here in her new Mini.

Jen and I have been friends since primary school, but we're from totally different worlds. Her dad works for a city law firm, and her mum stays at home, ironing clothes, cleaning and generally making sure Jen and her dad are presentable.

My world is much more chaotic. When I was seven, my mother passed away, and I was raised by my father. My dad is fantastic, but he works odd hours as a taxi driver, so sometimes I go days without seeing him. I did my best to take care of the house when we lived together, but my dad is the sort of person who makes things messy just by looking at them, so it was always a struggle. I was the kid who turned up at school in a crumpled shirt with sleeves an inch too short.

A few years ago, my dad got together with Genoveva – a woman Jen calls my wicked step-mother. I don't see Genoveva that way. She's not a bad person, she just doesn't want to share my father with anyone or be reminded he had a life before she came along.

When they got together, Genoveva moved into our cottage. It was okay for a while, but then Genoveva got pregnant, and I offered to move into the annex next door so they'd have more space. I won a place at a Scottish university, but it was so obvious they needed my help that I chose a uni in the nearby town.

The annex is a bit rough and ready, but it means I'm close enough to help out, and Dad let me stay there rent free while I was studying.

I look at the cottage. I know what Dad will say if I tell him about Ivy College. Follow your heart, follow your dreams. But I also know he and Genoveva will struggle without my help.

I hear a screech outside, and the crackle of gravel tells me Jen's Mini has just skidded into our driveway. I grab the acceptance letter and run to the front of the house, waving at her.

Chapter 4

'Soph!' Jen waves back. She looks amazing, as always. Long, blonde hair lying straight as a ruler down her back. Designer jeans. Huge green eyes outlined in kohl, and cute chubby cheeks like a chipmunk. She's short and curvy, with a huge bust – just the opposite of me, with my willowy arms and legs, wavy brown hair and just-about B-cup.

'You're accepting that course,' she says, as she crunches over gravel towards me.

'Shush!' I wave my hands at her. My dad, Genoveva and my baby brother, Samuel, are all inside the cottage. I can see Dad and Genoveva through the living room window and I think maybe they're arguing, because Genoveva's hands are flying around.

Jen takes my arm and pulls me towards the annex, which sits metres away from the cottage. It's a bungalow bedsit. Kitchen, bedroom and living area all in the same space, but it's okay. It's got everything I need, and as long as I keep it tidy, I don't mind the lack of space.

We go inside, and Jen slams the door behind us.

'How can you stand this place?' She goes to the kettle. 'That woman has stolen your house from you.'

'She keeps Dad happy,' I say, wiping a cobweb from a framed photo of my mum, which sits on the windowsill. Mum smiles at me from the photo-graph. She was in our garden when that picture was taken – the sun shining on her long, black hair. 'Anyway, I like the annex. It's all mine.'

'Is this your acceptance letter?' Jen asks, taking the white paper from my hand.

'Yes,' I say. 'I still haven't read it properly. I'm in shock. I don't know, Jen. I don't know how Dad and Genoveva will cope without me. London is a long way away.'

Jen waves a hand at me as she scans the letter. 'London is half an hour by bus, then one hour by train. You can come back every weekend if you need to. Listen – you're my best friend. I'm not going to let you pass up this chance. I'm just not.'

'Just because some arrogant Hollywood star is teaching the course?'

'He's not just some Hollywood star,' says Jen. 'You said yourself, he's an amazing actor.'

'With an amazingly cold reputation,' I say.

'Okay, maybe he does come across as a bit arrogant,' says Jen. 'Apparently, he won't even *read* a script unless it's given to him exclusively. He takes it as an insult if any other actor is even *considered* for a role he's up for.'

I swallow. 'And this is a man who might be teaching me? Do you really think that would be a good idea? You know I can be sensitive.'

Jen shrugs. 'It's time you toughened up a bit. Maybe he's exactly what you need. Anyway, perhaps all the gossip is just that. Gossip. Anyone who's as successful as Marc is going to get knocked by the press. It's what they do. You can't pass up this chance, Sophia – you're an *amazing* actress.'

I sigh. 'Jen, you're biased.'

'Hello!' Jen waves the letter. 'Evidently Marc Blackwell and everyone else at Ivy College agree with me.'

'They saw one audition,' I say. 'An audition when I wasn't nervous because I didn't think for a moment I'd be accepted. They don't really know me. When they do, they might think they've made a mistake. Anyway. There are practical things. How can I afford it? Dad's got no money right now. He's too busy taking care of Genoveva and Samuel. He's already letting me stay at the annex for free – I can't ask him for anything else.'

Jen doesn't say anything. She's still scanning the letter. Then she puts the paper down.

'What is it?' I ask.

'Did you just say something about money?' Jen asks.

'Don't you offer to lend me any. You know I won't take it.'

'I wasn't going to.'

'Good.'

'I wasn't going to, because your place is fully funded. Look. It says so right here. They pay for everything.'

'What?' I take the letter. 'But ... how? I haven't applied for scholarships or anything like that.'

'You don't need to,' says Jen. 'Take a look at that.' She points to a paragraph. 'Your place is fully funded, which means accommodation and food are paid for, and they'll give you a living allowance and preparatory budget.'

'I don't believe it.' I read the paragraph over and over again. I feel like I'm going to faint. 'Fully funded?'

'Now tell me a good reason why you can't accept.' Jen takes the letter again, and carries on reading. She turns the page over and reads right to the end, her eyes rushing back and forth. 'Soph, where's the envelope?'

I shrug. 'In the garden I think. Why?'

'We'd better go get it.' She hurries outside, and I follow her past the crumbling walls of the cottage, to the lawn, flowers, trees and vegetables of Dad's garden. I say Dad's garden, but truth be told, it was Mum's garden, and now it's mine because I'm the only one who takes care of it. Not that it's a chore – I love growing things. I'd be out here all day if I had the choice.

Jen picks up the brown envelope from the garden table. 'You're not going to believe this. Stop twiddling your hair. There's nothing to be nervous about.'

I drop my hand. My hair is straight at the top, but goes wavy at the bottom, so I'm always twiddling the ends to try and straighten them – especially when I feel nervous. My hair makes me look ridiculously young, like a little girl with ringlets, but Jen always says she's jealous of my Kate Moss waves. I'd prefer her straight, blonde hair any day.

'What is it?' I ask.

'A fully funded place means your accommodation, food and living expenses are all paid for,' says Jen. 'And they'll buy all your books for you, too. But that's not all. They're giving you a one-off payment. For clothing and university supplies.' She picks up the envelope and feels inside. Triumphantly, she pulls out a cheque.

'Oh my goodness.' I take the cheque and look at the amount. It's more money than I've ever had in my life. I put my hand over my mouth.

'Do you know what this means?' Jen asks.

'What?' I ask.

'It means,' says Jen, 'we're going shopping.'

Chapter 5

Usually, going shopping with Jen is a mixed blessing. She's great fun, always making me try things I'd never dare on my own, and she has endless patience. But she also has an endless credit card, whereas I've always had to survive on minimum wage earnings from one of my many part-time jobs.

Most of the time, I can only ever afford practical things, like jumpers and jeans, and only one item a month if I'm lucky. But today, I can buy whatever I want. No checking price tags. No heading for the cheapest shops. It feels great and weird at the same time.

We pull into the shopping centre car park, and Jen sticks a parking ticket behind the car windscreen, then links arms with me.

'This is going to be fantastic,' she says. 'I've seen so many things that would suit you for autumn.'

We take the lift to the first floor – a floor I usually avoid, since it has all the shops with clothes I can't afford.

'Look, there's a sale on in that shop,' I say, pointing. I have a good eye for sales.

'Forget the sales today,' says Jen. 'They'll be selling off summer stock. You need the new season stuff. Clothes that'll make you look hot enough for Marc Blackwell to fall madly in love with you.'

I laugh. 'I can't see that happening.'

'Come on,' says Jen. 'I know exactly where we should go.'

She takes me to Brickworks, a beautiful boutique that smells of essential oils. Rails of clothes are dotted around a huge, white floor space.

I see a forty-something woman with cropped, platinum-blonde hair and black sunglasses leading around a beautiful, tall girl who I assume is her daughter. They both have armfuls of clothes, and I wonder what it must feel like to be so rich you can buy whole wardrobes in stores like this. I guess I'm about to find out.

Jen is already loading jumpers and dresses into my arms. 'This one is over-sized, off-the-shoulder. Look at that green. It'll go perfectly with your eyes. I'd *love* to have brown eyes. This is your season, you know. Autumn.'

I smile at her. 'You and your seasons.'

Jen is obsessed with colours, and matching them to people. Apparently I'm an autumn, which means I can wear oranges, soft greens and yellows. Jen wears cool colours, like silver and very pale pink.

I look at my eyes in the mirror, and suddenly think of my mother. My eyes remind me of her. Sometimes, I worry I'll forget her completely. The memories fade every year, and bit by bit she slips away. That's why I keep pictures of her all around my annex, and have a box of her things under my bed.

'And these jeans – wow. You'll look so hot in these.' Jen throws a pair of skinny jeans, tastefully ripped, and the most beautiful grey colour, over my arm. 'And jewellery! I love the jewellery here. This necklace will go perfectly.' She loops gold hoops of crinkled, beaten metal around my neck. Jen hurries me towards the fitting room, where an attendant opens a door for us and hangs the clothes on artfully twisted metal hooks.

'May I suggest a draped t-shirt with those jeans,' she says. 'You're a size eight, right?'

'She is, the lucky thing,' says Jen. 'And she still thinks she's fat.'

The assistant brings us a hanger of smooth, draped fabric in a buttery, fawn colour.

'That is just *perfect* for your skin tone,' says Jen.

'But what about the green jumper?' I say. 'I like that too.'

'Soph, my love. You're forgetting. Today you don't have to decide between things. You can buy both of these.'

'Right.' I nod and smile, realising it's true. Weird.

'Did you notice our autumn boot collection?' the assistant says.

'No, I ...'

'She'll try on whatever boots will go with skinny jeans,' says Jen, 'and some high heels for this dress.'

'But I never wear heels ...'

'Soph, you don't have to be practical today. You can buy things that are a bit silly. Things you might only ever wear once in a blue moon.'

'Where would I wear high heels?'

'My mother always says, buy the outfit and the event will come.'

'Okay, fine.' I give in.

I try everything on, and as usual Jen has a perfect eye. The soft, blue dress she's picked out sparkles under the store lighting, and clings to my waist in a way that's both classy and sexy. The high heels make my legs look terrific. I feel like I'm someone else – someone who won't look out-of-place at Ivy College.

'It all looks great,' I breathe, putting everything carefully back on the hangers. I check the price tags. 'Yikes. Jen, I don't know ...'

'Oh yes,' says Jen. 'You're taking the whole lot. New wardrobe, new life. If you don't buy it, then I'm buying it for you.'

'Okay, okay.' Jen is always threatening to buy things for me. She knows I'd never let her, but she still tries. 'Fine. I'll buy it.'

'All of it?' Jen asks. 'Jewellery too?'

I notice the sales assistant leaning in keenly.

I smile. 'Yes. Everything. Belts, boots and jewellery.'

Jen and the sales assistant both clap their hands.

'Great!' they say in unison.

Chapter 6

Seven stores later, and I'm weighed down by paper bags. I've watched countless beautiful pieces of clothing being lovingly folded and packaged in tissue paper. One store even sprayed the paper with lavender oil, and offered to carry the bags to our car. I'm used to clothing with red sale stickers on, scrunched into polythene bags.

'There's something else you need before I take us for coffee,' says Jen.

'I'm taking *you* for coffee,' I say. 'It's the least I can do. You've bought nothing on this trip. It's all been about me.'

'Soph, all the times you've traipsed after me while I've tried things on, and gone home with nothing yourself. This is a treat for me. I love seeing you get new stuff. You deserve it more than anyone. You work so hard.'

'You're such a good friend,' I say, taking her arm. 'I don't know what I'm going to do without you when I'm in London. I'm going to miss you so much.'

'I'll come down and see you all the time,' says Jen. 'I'm only ever a phone call away. Anyway, I reckon you'll have a whole new set of friends within minutes. You're so kind and thoughtful, people always want to be around you. You'll forget about me in no time.'

'Never,' I say.

She steers me towards the end of the shopping mall, where all the men's shops are.

'Where are you taking me?'

'You'll see.'

She leads me towards the bright lights of the Apple Store, its white interior glowing with tablets, laptops and computers.

'I thought this would make you happy,' says Jen, squeezing my arm.

I've always been a bit of a cyber geek, and love computers, gadgets and games. Not that I've ever been able to afford many of them, but I've always enjoyed helping Jen choose a new mobile phone or computer.

Inside the store, I approach a line of white laptops, all thin as a paper notepad.

An assistant wearing an Apple t-shirt approaches.

'Hi,' he says. 'Are you interested in a laptop?'

'That's an understatement,' I say, running a hand over a perfectly smooth Apple logo on a bright white laptop case.

'What's your budget like?'

'Um ... well, I guess ... I suppose I don't have a budget.'

'Oh. Well, we have credit plans -'

'No. I mean ...' I know my cheeks are going red. 'Price doesn't matter.' I feel embarrassed, like I'm showing off. 'At least, not today.'

He looks at me curiously, no doubt wondering how a twenty-something girl, in scruffy converse and a bobbled sweatshirt, can afford to say price doesn't matter.

'Well, is there any model that takes your interest?'

I move along to the newest Mac laptop. It's light as a paperback novel, with a battery that lasts all day. It's so weird to be heading towards the high-est-priced item, rather than the lowest. Usually, I scan prices to find the cheapest thing. It doesn't matter where I am – a restaurant, cafe or department store. I'm hardwired to look for the lowest price. It's difficult to break the programming.

'She'll take this one,' says Jen, following my gaze. 'It's the best one, right?'

'I would say so,' says the assistant. 'It literally came out last week. There have been waiting lists for it, but we restocked today and we've got two left.'

He goes to a back room and returns with a smooth, flat white box. 'Here it is.'

'If she's buying at full price, what else can you throw in?' says Jen, her eyes sharp.

The man swallows. 'Well. I suppose ... a laptop case?'

'What else?' says Jen, tapping her foot.

'And some virus software.'

'And one of those ... what are they called? Mice? Is that what you'd call them all together?' says Jen.

'You want a mouse with it?' the assistant asks.

'Yes. Add a mouse and we'll shake hands.'

The man looks uneasy, but I think he real-ises it would be stupid to argue with Jen in barter mode.

'Deal,' he says.

'Great!' Jen leads me to the till.

We leave the store with me clutching my laptop like a new baby. I love it, I love it, I love it.

Jen sees the grin on my face, and puts an arm around my shoulder. 'This has been the best day.'

Chapter 7

When Jen drops me off, I see Dad in the cottage doorway, waving at us. He comes to the car window.

'Christ almighty. Another shopping trip, Jen? How much did this little lot set your dad back?'

Jen looks at me, and we share a quiet understanding that neither of us will tell him all the shopping is mine. Dad gets really anxious about money. If I told him I'd received a huge cheque for clothing and university supplies, he'd want me to put it in a bank account and buy clothes from a charity shop. Which is very sensible, and exactly what I'd usually do. But I'm glad Jen forced me to live a little.

'Would you girls like a cup of tea?'

I glance at the cottage, trying to work out if Genoveva is home. It sounds bad, but sometimes I avoid going in if she's there because she's always bossing me around. If it's just Dad and Samuel, it's fine. I'd never admit to Dad I feel that way. It would break his heart to know we weren't all best buddies.

'Is Genoveva home?' Jen asks, always straight to the point.

Dad scratches his head absentmindedly. His hair is black and grey now, and totally bald at the back. Genoveva has bought him this hair thickening stuff he uses sometimes, that turns his scalp black. He's been bald since his early twenties. It never bothered my mum. I know the other taxi drivers tease him about it sometimes, but he can put up with teasing.

'She's taken Samuel to have his photo taken, with a friend,' says Dad.

'Didn't know she had any friends,' Jen whispers.

'I'd love a cup of tea,' I tell Dad. 'But don't worry. You look tired. I'll make it.' My dad is the sort of person who makes a mess. He doesn't mean to, but I know if he makes tea, there'll be hot water and sugar all over the counter, and it's me who'll end up clearing up, else he'll get snapped at by Genoveva.

'Thanks, but I have to get home,' says Jen, turning to me. 'Can I have your opinion about something before I leave?' Her eye twitches, and I know she wants to talk to me alone.

When Dad goes inside, she says, 'Do you think he'll be upset?'

'I don't know.' I pull hair curls down, and feel them ping back up again. 'I mean, it was always on the cards that I'd move out this year, but I don't think he'd expect me to go so far away. I think they've come to rely on me for childcare and that sort of thing.'

'He'll cope,' says Jen. 'They both will.'

'Maybe,' I say. 'And once I'm out of the annex, they can rent it and make a bit of money. So the sooner the better, really.'

'Exactly,' says Jen. 'You will tell him today, won't you? I don't want you putting it off, then changing your mind about the college.'

'I will.' I take a deep breath. 'It'll be hard, but I'll do it.'

'Good. Your dad's a soppy old so and so, but I think he'll take the news just fine. You'll see.'

She starts the engine and drives away.

I go into the house, and hear the kettle rumbling.

'Dad?'

'Do you want one of your camomile jobbies?' Dad asks.

'You sit down. I'll do it,' I say, going to the cupboard and taking out mugs. There's no need to ask Dad what he wants – it's always tea, made exactly the same way. Very white with two sugars.

'You always make it better than I do anyway,' says Dad, smiling and sitting at the dining table. The cottage is old, but Dad took out a lot of walls when he first bought the place, and everything is open plan. The kitchen and dining area open right out into the living space, and there are black wooden beams running along the ceiling. It's three times the size of my annex and always warm and cosy.

I'd never tell Dad, but the annex gets freezing at night and my bed sheets always feel damp. Sometimes, my box of Mum's stuff gets mould on it, and I have to wipe everything clean.

'Soph – I hope you don't mind me asking this, but is there something on your mind?'

'What makes you say that?' I say, a spoon of sugar hovering over his mug.

'It's just ... you seem a bit distracted.'

'Yes. Maybe I am a bit.' I drop the sugar into the tea and start to stir. 'How are things with Genoveva?'

Dad laughs. 'Oh, you know. She likes a row now and then. Nothing different than any other couple, I expect.'

Mum and Dad never used to row. They were both so agreeable, there was nothing to row about.

'But you're okay? Generally?' I ask. I don't want to drop a bombshell on him if he's had a bad day.

'Oh yes,' says Dad, staring out of the window. 'Generally okay. I wish I could let you stay in the annex for as long as you liked, but -'

'Dad. Come on. Not this again. It's fine. You've got Genoveva and the new baby to look after now. You need the rent from that place. I'm a grown up. I'll be fine.'

'I don't deserve a daughter as good as you,' says Dad, taking his mug of tea. 'There are custard creams in the tin.'

'Thanks.' I love custard creams, but right now I don't feel like eating. 'Okay.' I take a deep breath and let it out. 'I do have something to tell you.'

Dad puts his mug on the table.

'Are you okay, Soph? Is there anything you need help with?'

'No.' I shake my head. 'Nothing at all. But I have news for you.'

'Oh?' Dad tries to smile.

'Yes,' I say. 'It's great news really, in one way.'

'Well. Let's hear it.'

'I've been offered a fully funded place on a post-graduate course.'

'That's fantastic news, Soph,' says Dad. 'Really, really fantastic.' He breathes out. 'Oh, that's such a weight off my mind. I've been having sleepless nights, thinking about how you're going to get a job in a village as small as this one. Without a car, and all that. I wish I could buy you a car, but – Soph, do you need to stay in the annex a while longer, then?'

'No.'

'So where are you going to live? Your university doesn't have any accommodation for postgraduate students, does it?'

'The place isn't at my university,' I say. 'It's at a college in London.' I look into my tea, and see a grey teabag bobbing in brown water. 'I just applied on a whim, actually. It was my tutor's idea. I didn't take it seriously at all. I never thought for a moment I'd be accepted.'

Dad nods sadly. 'London's a little too far for you to come back at weekends, isn't it?'

I shake my head. 'It's only a few hours away. I can come back all the time.'

'It sounds like you've already decided to accept, then,' says Dad, with a gentle smile.

'I have. It's an amazing opportunity. Thousands of people applied. And I'm pretty sure Jen will kill me if I don't take it.' I smile.

'She's a good friend to you, that Jen.' Dad takes a sip of tea. 'Don't worry about me, Soph. I don't want you worrying about me at all. You go and enjoy yourself. Tell me about this college.'

'It's called Ivy College,' I say. 'It's owned by a famous actor. Marc Blackwell. He teaches some of the classes.'

'I've heard of him.' Dad clicks his fingers. 'From that film ... what was it ... the wheelchair one. He plays a basketball player in a wheelchair.'

'*The Windmills of Your Mind*,' I fill in. 'He won an Oscar for that part.'

'So is he in a wheelchair, then?'

I smile. 'No, Dad, he's an actor. He was just playing the role. He's able bodied. So able bodied, in fact, that they wanted him to play James Bond a few years back, but he turned it down.'

'James Bond!' Dad's eyes light up. 'You're going to be taught by James Bond?'

'He turned the part down.'

'Why on earth would he do that?'

I shrug. 'I guess he thought the role wasn't right for him. He doesn't do much mainstream stuff.'

Dad puts his tea down and throws his arms around me. 'I'm so proud of you, petal. Truly. You're the best daughter any dad could hope for. You go knock 'em dead at this place.'

Chapter 8

It's the night before I'm due to head to London, and Jen has invited me round for what she's calling 'the last supper'. She has some news for me, apparently. Some good news. And also hot chocolate, brandy, marshmallows and popcorn. Hopefully she'll serve the popcorn separately, but with Jen you never know.

I buzz her intercom three times – our secret signal – and she releases the door mechanism to her apartment block. I call her apartment the big brother house, because there are cameras everywhere. She lives in one of those brand new glass and metal blocks that are built like fortresses.

When Jen left sixth form, she didn't bother with university. Instead, she got a well-paying job in PR, and moved into this place. Her dad was furious, but Jen is always her own person. Her plan is to have her own PR agency one day.

I tried to grow some things on Jen's glass balcony so she'd have something of a garden, but they all died. Jen has many talents, but she's not green fingered.

I'm a little sad as I reach Jen's blonde-wood front door. The thought of leaving her makes me feel homesick. We've known each other long enough to practically be sisters, and shared everything. First sips of cider in the park, first crushes, first kisses, first boyfriends ... everything.

Before I can knock on the door, she pulls it open.

'Soph! Have I got news for you.' She drags me inside. 'Oh! You brought wine. Goody. Shall we have it as our starter?'

We both giggle.

Her apartment is huge, with a breakfast bar separating the kitchen from the lounge. Big glass windows look out over our local park, and Jen says that's better than having a real garden. If it's not hers, she can't kill it.

Jen opens the wine with a pop, and nods towards the coffee table, where there is a pile of DVDs. 'Can you guess what my news is?'

'Something about Marc Blackwell,' I say slowly.

I pick up the first DVD. It's *Through a Stranger's Eyes*, an arty film that never quite made it mainstream, but received plenty of critical acclaim. I turn it over, and see the handsome, teenage face of Marc Blackwell on the back. 'He looks so young,' I say. 'This must have been the first film he ever starred in.'

'Actually not the first film he starred in,' says Jen, pouring wine into shiny crystal glasses. 'He starred in some as a child. He was in adverts too. He had a very pushy dad who decided from a young age that Marc was going to be a star.'

'A pushy Dad?' I say.

Jen nods. 'Wait until you hear what else I found out about him.'

'What?'

'I got my firm to do a little digging,' says Jen. 'And apparently, he's very protective of the people he cares about – the few of them there are.'

'Oh?' I raise an eyebrow. 'And who are they?'

'He doesn't get on with his father, and his mother passed away. But he has a sister, and he's also very close to a lady called Denise Crompton.'

'His mother passed away?' I murmur, thinking how cold he was in the audition. 'Maybe that's why he isn't the warmest of people.'

'What rubbish.' Jen shakes her head. 'You lost your mum, and you're one of the warmest people you could ever meet.'

'It opened me up, in a way,' I say. 'Losing her. But I guess it can go the other way, too. It could close you down.' I swallow. 'Denise Crompton – she was at my audition. She works at the college, too.' I sit on the sofa. 'And you say he's very protective of her?'

'Very.' Jen nods. 'He's been known to have serious words with any paparazzi that bother her. And his sister, too. She has a drug problem, apparently. And a young son. He gives her money, but it all goes on heroin. The rumour mill says he punched out her boyfriend once, but paid him off so he didn't go to the press.'

'It's so weird to think I'll be in a classroom with him.' I sink down onto the sofa. 'He's so ...'

'Hot,' Jen finishes. 'What did he look like when you met him?'

'Different from on screen,' I say. 'I mean, on screen he's amazing. The way he moves, the way he becomes the roles. And all the emotion that comes from him. But in real life, he's just ... I was mesmerised. Not just because he's handsome. Which he is. Sort of, quirky handsome. All white skin and dark shadows. But there was something about his eyes. They were so strong. Like nothing could get to him.'

'But beautiful, right?'

I think about Marc in his crisp, black shirt, holding me with his eyes. 'I guess that's a fair word to use.'

'How will you learn anything? You'll spend the whole time just gazing at his face.'

I laugh. 'He's a brilliant actor. I mean, he's just amazing. He becomes the parts.'

'That's because he's messed up,' says Jen. 'The best actors always are.' She raises her eyebrow at me. 'Maybe all actors are.' We both laugh.

'Maybe he's not so messed up,' I say, feeling chills go up my arms. 'I mean, being protective of his sister, and Denise. That sounds nice.'

'You always try to see the good in everyone,' says Jen, with a smile. 'Save your opinion until I tell you what else I found out.'

'Which is?'

'He's never publically had a relationship for more than a few weeks. And no girl he's been with ever goes to the press, which is strange. He's been pictured with plenty of girls. Plenty. But none of them last long.'

'Maybe he treats them well, and they have no reason to sell a story on him.' I pick up the next film. 'I love this one. *Vietnam Bride*.'

Jen hands me a glass of wine. 'Let's watch it.'

When Jen and I watch DVDs, we hardly ever really *watch* them. We talk the whole way through. But this time, we're both silent as Marc Blackwell's face appears on screen, tanned, sweaty and dirt-marked.

He's only sixteen in the movie, and his blue eyes are just as emotionally intense, but ... different.

There's an openness and softness to his expression that I didn't see at the audition.

'He looks so cute there, doesn't he?' says Jen.

I watch Marc struggling to load a gun on screen, his young hands dropping the bullets. His cheekbones are fatter than when I met him. Less angular.

'Never held down a relationship for more than a few weeks,' I repeat, watching Marc's handsome face, brow furrowed over blue eyes, giving the most intense, amazing performance. He's full of warmth and life, and I find my gaze drifting to the DVDs that feature Marc as an adult. I realise that, as an adult, Marc has only played cold, hard roles. Action heroes. Men with terrible pasts.

'I wonder what happened to him,' I say, watching the young Marc, 'to make him so cold.'

'Like I said,' says Jen. 'His childhood messed him up. His dad sounds like a monster.'

'I guess.'

'He's hard to take your eyes off,' says Jen, drinking her wine. 'Just think, you'll be looking into those eyes for real tomorrow.'

'I doubt it.' I sip my wine. 'Tomorrow is settling-in day. It's just a chance for us to move our things into our rooms. Classes start the day after.' I put my head in my hands. 'I can't believe this is happening. It's nerve wracking, you know? I mean – look at him.' I gesture to the screen. 'He's such an amazing actor. What if I'm not good enough?'

'Don't be ridiculous. He's seen you audition. He knows you can act.'

'He's seen me audition,' I say, feeling the words more keenly than ever. 'Marc Blackwell has seen me audition. That's ... just so weird.'

'And he liked what he saw.'

My hands are shaking as I put the wine back down on the table. 'God, this is intense,' I say.

'Are you packed?'

'Yes.'

'So you're all set. I'll drive you down tomorrow afternoon, and help you unpack. I can't wait to see the college. It sounds amazing.'

Chapter 9

After spending half an hour getting lost around London's one-way system, Jen and I finally find the signs for Ivy College, and follow them until we reach the leafy grounds.

When Jen sees red bricks, curvy turrets and acres of lawn, she gives a little shriek. 'Look at this place. It's huge. Who'd have thought they could stuff all this into Central London? You'd think they'd have built a load of shops and apartments on this space by now.'

Jen drives through the open gates, and onto a gravel path that leads through beautiful manicured grounds. 'I can't believe it, Soph. This place is like a palace.'

'A secret castle, more like,' I say, pointing to the turrets. *With mysterious woodlands, and maybe even a monster.*

'Good job you don't have many bags with you,' says Jen. 'Because it looks like there are a lot of stairs.'

We follow a sign that says, 'accommodation block', and I see a gangly young man with bright blonde hair carrying suitcases out of a green Jaguar.

Jen pulls into a parking space, and we get out of the car.

'This must be where my room is,' I say, taking my rucksack from the boot and strapping it to my back. I pick up the box with my mum's things in it, balancing a few fresh potted herbs I've grown from cuttings on top.

'I can't believe that's all you have,' says Jen, taking the box and herbs from me. 'No hair dryer. No iron. Lucky you're pretty enough to carry off the crumpled look.'

I smile at her, but inside my stomach is turning somersaults. The building is beautiful. All the windows are arched, like castle windows, and they're mounted in handsome red brick.

The gangly man comes past us, but he doesn't look at me or say hello. He just takes another suitcase from his car and goes back into the building.

'I guess he must be another student,' I say.

'Nice he's so friendly,' says Jen.

'He's probably nervous,' I whisper. 'I am too.'

We walk into the building, and there's a reception area manned by a short, plump lady. She has grey hair and a few missing teeth, but a very friendly smile.

'Can I help you ladies?' she asks, her voice full of warmth.

'I'm a new student,' I say. 'Sophia. Really nice to meet you.'

'Wendy.' The woman shakes my hand. 'I've got you down right here. You're on the very top floor. The turret room. It's the nicest, I think. Certainly the biggest.' She hands me a big, silver key with a black fob.

She glances at Jen. 'I'm so sorry, but your friend can't stay. It's one of the rules. We think it helps everyone get to know each other quicker.'

I turn to Jen. She puts the box down and we give each other the longest hug.

'Take care, Soph. Ring me as soon as you're unpacked.'

'I will. Ring me to say you're home safe.'

I watch her drive away, then pick up my box.

'You can take the lift, if you like,' says Wendy, pointing down a long corridor that smells of new carpet and looks light and warm.

'Thanks,' I say, 'but I haven't got much to carry. I'll let the students with lots of luggage use it. Anyway, I've been in the car for hours. I could do with the exercise.'

I head towards a stone archway, and follow a spiral staircase up to the first floor. I see the tall, blonde student heading back out of his room, towards the lift.

'Hi.' I wave. He ducks his head and hits the lift button. I walk towards him. 'I'm Sophia.'

'Ryan,' says the student, and up close I see nervous lines around his eyes. He can't quite make eye contact, but I give him a big smile anyway. I can understand him being uncertain. Perhaps he was the first one to arrive.

'Good to meet you, Ryan.'

'You too,' he says. Then he scurries into the lift.

I head back to the stairs, up, up to the fourth floor. By the time I reach it, I'm out of breath.

No more doughnuts for you, Soph.

The door is arched oak, and studded with wrought iron. Pushing my box under my arm, I slot my key into the lock and open up my new room.

I can't believe it.

The room is amazing. Huge, beautiful and amazing. There must have been a mistake. It looks like a hotel suite.

The room is round, with a huge double bed against one of the walls, and a brand new wet room en suite built into one of the curves. There's a balcony with French windows opening out onto it, and a fireplace that looks like it might be fully functioning.

The view from the French windows is stunning. I look out over gorgeous green grounds, and see the historic buildings of London in the distance.

Wow.

I put my rucksack in the big wardrobe, and it looks lost. Mum's box goes under the bed, as usual, but not before I've taken out framed photographs of her and arranged them along a window sill. I face the pictures outwards, so she can see the gardens outside.

There's a small, neat kitchen area with a kettle and fridge, but no cooker. I'll guess I'll be eating in the college meal hall from now on, and other people will cook for me. Which is a weird thought.

A huge bunch of red and white roses sit on a table by the window, a card propped beside them. The card pictures the Old Vic, and when I turn it over I blink in surprise.

The card is from Marc Blackwell.

It reads:

'Dear Sophia, you're an extremely talented actress and I'm looking forward to working with you in the coming months.'

I put the card down. He seemed so cold at the audition, but this is such a thoughtful gesture. So considerate.

Excitement rushes through my body as I remember he'll be teaching me. I hadn't really given myself a chance to think it through before, but Jen is right – I'll be sitting inches away from one of the best, most creative actors I've ever seen on screen.

I see more cars pull into the car park below, and decide to head down and meet my fellow students.

As I run down the stairs, I bump into Ryan again, who's carrying yet another suitcase.

'Did Marc leave a gift in your room?' Ryan asks.

'Yes,' I say. 'Flowers. And a card. Really thought-ful. I thought he was sort of arrogant in the audition, but maybe I got it wrong.'

'I got aftershave,' says Ryan.

'How's your back after carrying all those suit-cases?' I joke. But Ryan doesn't laugh.

'What did your card say?' Ryan's forehead crinkles.

'Um. Something nice about my acting. He said I was a talented actress. And that he was looking forward to working with me.'

'*What?*' He throws his suitcase onto the step with a bang. 'Why would he say that about someone like you?'

'Someone like me?'

'Forget it. Never mind.'

I look at him for a long time, daring him to expand on whatever he meant. But his face clouds over, and I can see I'm getting nowhere.

'Yes, let's forget it,' I say, hurrying down the stairs. I hope the rest of the students aren't so snappy and unfriendly.

At the bottom of the steps I see a girl with glori-ous, long red hair, and square, black glasses on her white nose. She's wearing a black blazer over jeans, and grins as she looks around the entranceway.

She's standing by a man in a wheelchair who wears a black Robin Hood style hat with yellow feathers in it. The man is a little chubby, and his bright pink shirt stretches around his middle. On the back of his wheelchair is a sticker that says: 'At least I always get a seat'.

They're both talking to Wendy at the reception desk.

'I'll get your keys,' Wendy says.

'Oh. Thank you.' The red-headed girl smiles. 'My name is Tanya Holmes.' Her accent is Yorkshire and when she smiles, dimples appear in her white cheeks. 'It's terrific here, isn't it? I had no idea there was anything like this in London. Actually, I've never seen anything like it in my life.'

Wendy hands her a key, and turns to the man in the wheelchair. 'And you are?'

'Tom Davenport.' Tom takes her hand and kisses it. 'A pleasure to make your acquaintance.' His accent is clipped and perfect, and exactly what I expected an Ivy College student to sound like. In short, nothing like me.

Tom takes the key, and turns to me. 'Hello there. Are you a new student too?'

'Yes,' I say. 'I'm Sophia. Call me Soph.'

'A pleasure to meet you too, *Soph*,' says Tom, clearly fighting his conscience over the abbreviation. 'My, you're extremely beautiful, aren't you?' He takes my hand and kisses it too. 'You look to have some Italian blood in you, would I be right?'

I smile, and nod. 'On my mother's side.'

'Just so you know,' Tom says, 'if you're after any sexual experiences here at college, my door is always open.' He winks at me. 'I've already extended the invitation to Tanya here, so you'll be in good company.'

Tanya shrieks with laughter, then smiles at me. 'I'm Tanya. Good to meet you Soph. Have you been here long?'

'Just got here,' I say. 'I've only met one other student.'

'Oh?'

'He's called Ryan.'

'Well let's go grab him,' say Tanya, 'and head over to the student bar. It's gone five. That's beer o'clock, isn't it?'

Tom frowns. 'Shouldn't we unpack first, dearest?'

'There's plenty of time for that later,' says Tanya, waving a dismissive hand. 'Leave the bags in the boot and come for a pint.'

'I don't want to destroy your notions of me as an alpha male,' says Tom, 'but a gin and tonic is more up my street.'

'Double?'

'Indeed.'

'Then that's fine.'

Tanya runs up the stairs to find Ryan, but comes back alone. 'He says he wants to carry on getting his room in order,' she says, putting an arm around both our shoulders. 'Never mind. He'll catch us up.'

Chapter 10

We tread a gravel path through manicured lawns, and find an oak door facing our student accommodation. When we push it open, there's a cosy pub set up inside, with a bar serving real ales, whisky and brandies. All the stools are made out of beer barrels, and there's a thick rope nailed along the bar. I feel like we're inside a ship.

'How did you know this was the bar?' I ask Tanya.

She taps her nose. 'Let's just say I have a talent for more than just acting.' She blushes. 'Oh shit, that came out wrong. I don't mean to sound big-headed or anything. I don't mean ... I mean, I'm not saying I'm not a good actress, but -'

'There, there my dear.' Tom puts an arm around her waist. 'No need for this ridiculous modesty. We've all been awarded a place in one of the most prestigious colleges in the country. Of course we have a talent for acting. Which is not to say we don't have a lot to learn. Now. What can I get you?'

'Pint of Old Peculiar,' says Tanya.

'And you my love?' Tom turns to me.

'Um. White wine please?'

'Certainly.' Tom rings the bell, and to our surprise Wendy appears from some mysterious place at the back of the bar.

'My word, a woman of many talents,' says Tom. 'Receptionist and landlord too. How marvellous.'

Wendy gives him her toothy grin. 'I run everything round here. You'll soon learn. Well? What can I get you?'

Tom gives her the order, and we all take seats on the stools.

'I'm nervous about meeting him, aren't you?' says Tanya, holding her pint.

'Meeting who?' says Tom.

'Who do you think? Marc Blackwell of course. He was dead snooty at my audition. Told me I needed to work on my accent more. I came away thinking, what a rude so and so.'

'I liked him,' Tom declares. 'He's had a heck of a life – we can't expect him to be all hearts and flowers. I found him honest and intelligent, and I respected him. Not everyone has the courage and strength of conviction to tell it like it is. He gave me some great feedback about how to use my body. He didn't sugar coat it. He just said, Tom – you're slouching. Sit up better, we'll feel you more. Not many people say things like that to a chap in a wheelchair.'

Out of the window, we see more pupils arriving. There's a girl with icy blonde hair, and a tall, well-built boy who looks sporty.

'Of course,' says Tom, 'he has less of an allure to me than to you two girls. But ... he is certainly one of the finest actors alive today. And I was very impressed by him in *The Windmills of Your Mind*. He'd clearly done his research. So, I'm looking forward to being taught by him.'

'He *is* on the abrupt side, but I have to admit he's just so ... charismatic,' says Tanya. 'In my audition, I nearly fainted when I saw him. It's those eyes. You see the whole world in them. I bet there aren't many girls on the course who don't fancy him. How about you, Soph?'

I feel myself go red. Silly. After all, who doesn't have crushes on actors? 'Maybe a little.' When I think of Marc's eyes again, I nearly miss my lips with my wine glass. 'But he seems a bit cold.'

'He gives one million a year to charity,' says Tom. 'Maybe he keeps his nice side hidden.'

'Maybe you're right,' I say, taking a sip of wine. 'He's sent us all welcome presents. They're in our rooms. Have you seen yours?'

'No,' says Tanya. 'I haven't seen my room yet. Look – more new students.' She points to three people coming into the bar – the two students we saw arriving earlier, and Ryan.

Up close, the icy blonde girl has very pointy features, and although she's pretty, her expression isn't friendly. She's very tall, and glides to the bar beside the well-built boy and Ryan.

'It's nice to meet you all,' says Tanya, smiling her brilliant smile. 'Soph here says we've all got welcome gifts from Marc Blackwell. Isn't that amazing?'

The icy blonde girl gives a curt nod. 'He wrote us cards, too. *Mine* said he hoped I enjoyed my time at college.'

Ryan leans towards the girl. 'Cecile, that one over there thinks her card said what a talented actress she was, would you believe.'

Cecile gives a screech of laughter. 'You're kidding?' She throws her hair from one shoulder to the other. 'Why would he say that to you? Who are you, anyway? Why would he even know who you are?'

'He saw my audition,' I hear myself say.

'No, no, sweetheart,' Cecile says. '*He* was only there as head of the college. Denise was the one who picked us. I have a brother who works with Denise Crompton's husband and he gave me the inside scoop. So none of us are all that special to darling Marc. Although I'm hoping *I'll* be special to him by the end of the course.'

'It's still a nice gesture, though,' I say, thinking back to the card and wondering if I misread the handwriting.

Cecile shakes her head. 'He probably got his secretary to do it. Although I'm hoping for a rather more personal card by the end of term.'

'Marc Blackwell saw Soph's audition,' says Tanya, waving her pint so it spills. 'And if his card said Soph here is a great actor, I'm sure he meant it.'

Cecile looks me up and down. 'Why *would* he?' she says, without a hint of teasing in her voice. 'I've never seen or heard of you before, and I know anyone who's any good. You don't even look like you come from London, no offence.'

'What do you mean by that?' says Tanya.

'Children, children.' Tom wheels between the two girls. 'We should be celebrating our fabulousness. We've all been accepted at this amazing college. Which means we're all terrific people. So. Let's have a drink to terrific people.'

He raises his glass.

'To terrific people,' Tanya and I say.

'And are we all excited about meeting the man himself tomorrow?' Tom asks.

'Tomorrow?' says Tanya.

'Why, yes indeed,' says Tom. 'He'll be hosting our first seminar.'

'Will he?' Tanya says. 'What time?'

'It was in our introductory paperwork,' says Tom. 'Nine o'clock in King's lecture theatre.'

I remember the piles of paper the college sent me when I accepted my place. I didn't get to read all of it. I had so much to do before I left – making sure Dad and Genoveva had enough food in, and Samuel had nappies and giving the house a last thorough clean to last them until I could come back.

'Exciting, isn't it?' says Tom. 'First thing tomorrow, we'll be meeting the infamous Marc Blackwell.'

Chapter 11

When I wake up the next morning, I think maybe I dreamt Ivy College and Marc's card and flowers. But here I am, and there the flowers are – beautiful roses, on a highly polished table near a window overlooking the greenest of green grounds.

I feel excited and refreshed. I did the sensible thing last night and went to bed early, even though I was having fun with Tanya and Tom.

Before I went to bed, I checked the card again and sure enough – it was exactly as I remembered it. *A very talented actress.* Handwritten and signed by Marc Blackwell.

Mr Blackwell, I remind myself. *You don't know him. Just because you've seen him on the big screen, it doesn't make you friends.*

I get up and read the card again, and as I bring it closer to my face I smell something good. Like woodlands. Trees after the rain. I bring the card right to my nose and inhale. I catch sight of myself reflected in the French windows, and rest the card back on the flowers.

What on earth are you doing, Sophia? I twiddle my hair and look out over the college grounds. *Don't be a silly student with a crush. He sent gifts and cards to everyone.*

I take a quick shower, smoothing serum into my hair to make it extra shiny, deciding to let it hang loose and dry naturally. Then I dress in my new skinny jeans and high leather boots, and choose the bright green slouchy jumper that Jen said made me look beautiful. Nothing too fancy for my first day. I love performing, but off stage I don't like to draw too much attention to myself.

I'm too nervous for breakfast, so I take a walk around the grounds instead. I love being among trees and greenery – it's good for my soul. If I can't be around nature at least once a week, I feel empty.

The grounds are peaceful, and the lawns are covered in dew. It's still sunny, but the slight coolness of autumn is already beginning to take hold, and I'm glad I wore a jumper.

I take a walk through the woodlands, loving the bird song and stillness. The soil is fresh and clean, and I think maybe I could plant a vegetable patch out here. There's plenty of space between the trees, and I could give what I grow to the kitchen. I don't feel like myself unless I'm growing things.

As I pass a clutch of fir trees, I discover something that takes my breath away – a small, still lake with green reeds growing all around it. The lake must be manmade, as there are no streams or rivers around here, and the water is very clean and pure.

I breathe in cool, fresh air and wish I had time to go for a quick swim. Not for the exercise – I could cross the lake in a few strokes – but for the feeling of being in natural water, surrounded by trees.

I sit by the reeds, and pull off my shoes and socks, sinking my warm feet into the icy cold water. The bottoms of my jeans get wet, but I don't mind – I like feeling part of the woodlands.

A screeching sound sends a squirrel scampering back up a fir tree, and I snatch my feet out of the water.

What was that?

I take a few steps through the woods, feeling puffy soil under my bare feet, and realise I'm very near the college car park.

I peer through the trees, and see a black Ford Mustang screech to a halt in the car park. Brushing aside a sapling branch, I watch the convertible slide into a parking space reserved for college staff. It takes me a moment to realise I'm not breathing. The shadow in the car is tall and broad and, as I hear the door click, I grip my trainers.

Marc Blackwell emerges from the car, rests his elbow on the soft bonnet and looks over the college buildings. He's wearing a tailored black suit and shirt, and takes a cigarette from his jacket pocket, lighting it with an effortless flick of his palm.

I'm momentarily mesmerised. The way he moves is so elegant. So refined. Even the way he inhales the cigarette and blows it towards the tarmac is like a dance.

He heads towards one of the college buildings and inspects the brickwork, looking up at the tall, red walls, his eyes following a crack that runs all the way up to the roof. Then he stalks back to his car, smoking and glaring.

I watch, barely breathing, watching him smoke and frown at the ground. Suddenly, his cigarette is finished, and he stubs it somewhere inside the car and slams the door.

He takes two strides towards the college, then – to my horror – turns and looks at the woodlands, right where I stand.

I freeze, and my heart beats in my throat. I feel my cheeks colour, and realise how stupid I must look, standing there with damp, bare feet.

Has he seen me? Oh god. Yes.

He walks towards me, a little smile playing on those dangerous lips.

I want to run and hide, but his eyes hold me frozen to the spot.

He looks even better than I remember him. Tall – taller than he looked in the audition, and his long limbs move like water. His light-brown hair is a little long on top, and falls slightly over his forehead and his left eye.

'Miss Rose.'

I open and close my mouth. *He remembers me.* My teeth suddenly feel huge in my mouth.

'Good morning, Mr Blackwell,' I manage, not meeting his eye.

'What, may I ask, are you doing out here with no shoes on? Don't you realise it's autumn? You'll catch cold.'

I look at my bare feet, turning blue with cold now. What must he think of me, sneaking around in the woods, watching him? 'Um. I was paddling in the lake.'

'In the *lake*?' Marc's jaw hardens. 'It's cold in there.'

'I like the water,' I say, lamely.

Marc's brow furrows. 'I have a duty to look after my students. Don't go paddling again.' He runs a hand through his hair. 'However. I'm pleased to see someone exploring these woods. I like people to enjoy my trees.'

'They're not your trees.' I don't mean to say the words out loud, and I feel red blush spreading up my neck.

'I beg your pardon?'

'They're ... the trees. They're living things. Not yours or mine.' I feel the red reach my cheeks.

Marc stares at me for a moment. He rubs his ear with his thumb and forefinger. 'Still correcting me, Miss Rose?'

'I ... no. I didn't mean it to sound that way.'

'Just like at your audition.' Marc cocks his head. 'I'm still intrigued by what you said that day. Light and dark. Seeing the goodness in every character. I wonder, Sophia. Do you see both in me? Light and dark?'

I look up at him. It's not fair. He's holding me with those eyes again, and I'm rooted to the spot. I can't think. I can't move. I'm about to answer. To tell him yes – I see both. But suddenly he turns and strides away.

Stunned, I watch his broad back stalk across the college car park.

After a few moments, I put on my shoes, and head back towards the college.

My first seminar with Marc Blackwell. Even thinking those words is scary, but after our little encounter in the woods, the thought of seeing him again is scarier than ever.

Standing in line outside the lecture theatre, I clutch books to my chest and feel my heart beat against them.

I think over what just happened. It was so surreal. Maybe I was dreaming. *I wonder, Sophia. Do you see both in me?* Standing so close to Marc Blackwell – it's still affecting my body, even after the event. I feel wobbly, like I've just stepped off a fairground ride. I'm so nervous at the thought of him walking down the corridor. I try not to think of his eyes or his fingers or lips.

I check my watch. It's five minutes to nine, but I've been waiting outside the lecture theatre for ten minutes now. I stopped back at my room to pick up my course books, and now they're starting to feel heavy.

I can't see Tom or Tanya – I guess maybe they're nursing hangovers and will turn up as late as possible. But I see Cecile and Ryan. I smile and wave at them. Neither seems to notice me. By the sound of things, they're too busy gossiping about Marc: parts they've seen him play and newspaper articles they've read about him.

And then, I hear clipped, measured footsteps.

Chapter 12

Someone whispers: *Shush!*

I clutch my books tight and turn to see the man I just saw in the woods – the tall, dark, blue-eyed actor who makes thousands of women weak at the knees.

Those eyes. They're such a deep blue, like a Caribbean ocean, and suddenly I remember Tanya's words: *You see the whole world in them.*

I'd planned to look away from him. To pretend we didn't speak this morning. That the whole scene in the woods didn't happen. But I don't need to. He glides right past us in that agile, graceful way, head high.

I imagine he's used to getting his own way, and having people bow and scrape. He walks like a man on a mission, and his shoes smack the hard floor like gunshots.

As he passes me I smell trees after rain and remember the card. I find myself inhaling deeply.

He stops and turns then, and I breathe out quickly. I try to keep myself steady, but I can feel my books slipping in my arms.

He looks down at me. 'How did you enjoy your walk this morning?'

I swallow. 'Very much, thank you.'

'I'm glad to see you have your shoes back on.' He raises an eyebrow and gives a quirky little smile that makes my heart squeeze. My throat has gone all tight. I feel my books slip out of my hands and hear them bump to the floor.

You idiot.

I crouch down, and Marc crouches down with me. 'First day nerves?'

His face is inches from mine. The lines of his nose and chin are so perfect, and the hollows of his cheeks, so dark. He picks up the books and passes them back. His fingers touch mine, and I feel goose bumps run all over my arms.

'Don't be nervous,' he says, then turns and strides into the classroom.

Everyone follows him into the lecture theatre, but I'm too dazed to move. I feel myself knocked left and right as the other pupils flood past. By the time I've got myself together enough to go into the theatre, the only seats left are in the front row.

Oh holy Jesus.

I can feel the other students watching me, but all I can focus on is Marc. He's striding back and forth, waiting for everyone to take their seats. To put it more accurately, he's waiting for *me* to take my seat – the last student to come into the room.

I slide into a seat at the front of the class, noticing Cecile is also in the front row, a few seats away. She's smoothing down her blonde hair, and has already written: 'First Marc Blackwell lecture' on her notepad, and underlined it.

Marc closes the lecture-theatre door. Then he goes to a projection screen with the words 'Ivy College' bouncing around on it.

He is only a few feet away, and I feel ... I don't know, exposed. Although he doesn't look directly at me, I sense he notices where I'm sitting. I wish I had a mirror so I could see what my hair is doing, and check there's nothing on my face. He could notice all my imperfections if he wanted to – my small breasts, the slight kink in my nose, the spot growing on my chin.

'Well, class,' says Marc, slotting his thumbs into the pockets of his trousers. 'I imagine you've heard all about me in the newspapers. Marc Blackwell, Hollywood actor. Arrogant. Rude. Doesn't take any nonsense or suffer fools gladly. Likes to get his own way. Let me put you straight. I'm *worse* than the newspapers would have you believe.' He gives a little smile. 'I'm tough. In this class, I expect one hundred percent in everything you do. And if I don't think you're trying your hardest, you'll know all about it.'

The lecture theatre door creaks open, and Tom wheels himself inside, followed by Tanya. They look suitably sheepish, and Tanya squeezes into the only free seat, which happens to be beside me.

Tom wheels himself to the side of the row, and takes his rucksack off the back of his wheelchair. In the silence of the lecture theatre, the sound of him unzipping his bag is loud enough to wake the dead.

'You two.' Marc taps his Rolex. 'I don't tolerate lateness. Ever. Late again and you're off the course.'

Tanya's eyes grow wide. 'But we had to wash Tom's wheelchair,' she says. 'The grounds were muddy, and it got all over his wheels.'

'I don't tolerate excuses, either,' Marc snaps. 'Tom. In your audition, you told me you'd been in a wheelchair your whole life.'

'Yes, indeed,' says Tom. 'And it's never stopped me from doing what other people do.' I notice his black hat has a peacock feather in it today.

'Then you should know to leave yourself more time to get to places.'

Tom's mouth snaps closed, and Tanya whispers to me, 'Talk about strict.'

'Let me tell you what else I won't tolerate,' says Marc. 'Insubordination. You do as you're told in my class, or when I'm directing you on stage. If I ask you to do something, it's in your best interest. I know what's good for you. If you can't take instructions from me, you're off the course.'

Tanya puts her hand up.

'Put your hand down,' Marc barks.

She slides her hand back down.

'Now,' Marc continues. 'I know a lot of lecturers use their first names with students, but my name is *Mr* Blackwell. Not Marc. I'm your teacher, not your friend. You'll call me Mr Blackwell. Any questions?'

A few seats along from me, Cecile raises her hand. She looks flushed, and her eyes are shining.

Another silly student with a crush.

'Yes, Miss Jefferson?'

'Call me Cecile.' She smiles at Marc, but he only frowns back.

'You have a question?' Marc asks.

'I heard our first-term mark won't count. All we have to do is pass this term, and then our marks in the second and third terms will be the ones that count towards our final grade. Is that true?'

Marc's lips pull tight, and the hollows in his cheeks ripple. 'Not at *my* college. My students are marked at all times. Every essay and performance will count, and those not getting the grades won't stay long.'

'So, you'll be marking our performances from the very first term?' Cecile asks.

'Oh, yes.' A smile plays on Marc's lips. 'Don't think you'll escape being graded, just because you're all new. I expect the very best at all times.'

'You'll get it, Mr Blackwell,' says Cecile.

Marc turns to the projection screen. 'Let me tell you about classes this year. You'll be doing three performances, all of which will be marked. I will be in charge of choosing which parts you perform. I will do this based on what I think you need most to grow as actors.

'I made notes at your auditions, and I already have parts lined up for your first performances – which will be this week. If, at the end of that performance, I don't think you have what it takes ...' He runs a hand across the screen. 'You don't go through to the second term. My college is like the real world. If you don't perform well at all times, pack your bags.'

'Which is why getting a certificate from this college opens so many doors,' Cecile pipes up. 'That's why I'm here Mr Blackwell, to get the best drama qualification in the country.'

'I don't believe I asked for your comment, Miss Jefferson,' says Marc. 'And unless I ask for it, I don't want to hear it. If you have a question, raise your hand and I'll decide if it's worth answering or not.'

Cecile looks furious at being told off, but she's clever enough not to complain.

'So.' Marc picks up a pointer and smacks it on the projection screen.

'Your performances will prove to me you have what it takes to stay on this course. You will be performing in front of me, one-on-one. We start this week.'

Chapter 13

Marc picks up a remote control from the lecturer podium and clicks away the Ivy College screen. In its place are lists of names and plays. I watch his strong fingers grip the pointer, and he smacks it on the screen again.

'I've assigned each of you a part and pages for your first performance.'

I stare at the lists of names and realise they're *our* names, followed by the name of a character, play and page numbers for the script. I scan the list for my name. Beside me, Tanya takes heavy-rimmed black glasses from her bag and slides them on.

'Make a note of which part you're playing, and start practising,' says Marc. 'I have a library of scripts in the stationery cupboard.' He waves the pointer at a door beside the projection screen. 'You can go get your script at the end of class.'

I squint at the screen, and finally see my name, right at the bottom. My play is: *Call of the Night*, and my character is the lead, Jennifer Jones. I blink and stare. Oh my god. Jennifer Jones is a ballet dancer who seduces her theatre director. The part has been played by some amazing actresses. Nicole Kidman. Meryl Streep. There's no nudity, but the role is very femme fatale.

Beside me, Tanya groans.

'Who did you get?' I ask.

'Bianca, from *The Taming of the Shrew*,' she says. 'About as different from the parts I usually play as you could get.'

'Quiet now,' says Marc, silencing the grumblings in the room. 'The point of these parts is to stretch you as actors. To take you into territories you haven't been before. I want you to go away and practise. Then, each of you will come and see me in the theatre room and perform. If you pass the performance, you get to stay on the course and try out for the next one. It's that simple. Got it?'

I see nervous nods around me, and feel myself nodding too.

'For those of you performing scenes with two people, I'll be performing the other part. Some of you just have monologues. So.' Marc strides along the front row, and I hold my breath. 'Any complaints about my teaching methods?'

There is silence.

Marc stops right in front of me. 'Good. Because have no doubt. If you don't like the way I do things, you've got one option. Leave.'

I grab my pen and start twiddling it. I don't think I can do this. I don't think I can play the part of Jennifer Jones in front of anyone, let alone Marc Blackwell. It's too ... I don't know. Jennifer Jones is supposed to be really attractive and sexy, and I don't see myself that way.

Marc opens the cupboard beside the projection screen, and waves his hand to welcome us into it. 'The scripts are all in there. Help yourselves. And remember. The mark of a good actor is their ability to take on any role and make it their own. I hope you're ready to impress me.'

We get up from our seats, and crowd towards the stationery cupboard. I hold back. When the scrum is over, I go into the cupboard and find *Call of the Night* beside a pile of Oscar Wilde plays.

When we take our seats again, Marc is standing behind the lecturer's podium.

'Go away and rehearse,' he says, 'and I'll see your performances this afternoon, and tomorrow morning. I'll put times up on the notice board outside in one hour.'

'Today and tomorrow?' Cecile asks. 'How are we going to learn our lines in that time?'

Marc glares at her. 'It's only a few pages. Enough for you to get a feel for the part. I don't expect you to follow the script exactly. A good actor understands the character, and improvises when necessary.'

'But it's so soon,' says Cecile.

Marc frowns. 'You'll find the real world of acting isn't as precise and organised as you might like it to be. Auditions come out of the blue. Think of this as experiencing a little of what that's like. You want control? Then become a teacher.' He checks his watch. 'I'll see some of you later today, in Queen's Theatre.' With that, he strides out of the room, leaving all the students chattering nervously.

We file out of the classroom, and Cecile waits for me by the door. 'That was a clever little stunt,' she says. 'Dropping your books like that.'

'I didn't do it on purpose,' I say.

'I'll bet.' She walks off.

Chapter 14

Tanya appears beside me, smiling. 'You want to get a coffee while we wait for the times to go up? Practise our parts?' She lowers her voice to a whisper. 'Have we got some news about our new teacher.' She waves at Tom, who is wheeling himself out of the theatre. 'Coffee?'

'Oh my word, that's exactly what I need,' says Tom, putting a hand to his head. 'This hangover is monumental.'

'News?' I ask. 'About Marc?'

'Well. Scandal really. So? Fancy a coffee? Or would you rather go rehearse on your own?'

'Not at all,' I say. 'I'd love to have a coffee with you.'

'He's a bit on the strict side, don't you think?' Tanya whispers,' looking over my shoulder as if Marc might magically appear. 'I mean, today was like ... whoa! If we step out of line, just a tiny bit, we're off the course.'

'He's ... intriguing,' I admit. 'He comes across as so cold, but at the same time I get the feeling he really does care about us.'

'He's deep alright,' says Tanya. She grins. 'Aren't all the best actors?'

We head to the college cafeteria, where I see trays of eggs and bacon laid out, left over from this morning's breakfast.

'I'm starving,' I tell Tanya, picking up a plate. 'I was too nervous to eat anything this morning.'

'Me and Tom were too hung over,' says Tanya.

'Do you guys want any breakfast?' I ask, picking up a tray.

'Not for me, darling,' says Tom. 'Delicate goods today.'

'Just coffee for me,' says Tanya.

I pile up the plate with eggs, bacon, tomato, hash brown and toast. We all get coffees and take a table by the window. There's a fir tree outside, magpies hopping between its branches.

'So,' I say, unable to contain my curiosity any longer. 'What's the news?'

Tom pulls the Daily Mail from his khaki rucksack. 'Check out page four.'

I flick the pages, and see a headline: *Blackwell Sister Deals Drugs*

The pictures are all grainy black and white, but I see the outline of two silhouettes on a dark street – one small and female, appearing to hand something to a taller figure.

I scan the article, and read that Marc's sister, Annabel, was caught selling heroin, and faced a prison sentence. Marc hired one of the best solicitors in the country to keep her out of jail, and told the court he was committed to her continued drug rehabilitation.

'Poor Marc,' I murmur. 'It must be awful to have someone you care about wrecking their life like that.'

'She's lucky to have a brother like him,' says Tanya, looking over my shoulder. 'Plenty of famous people wouldn't want to be associated with a family member who's a drug addict. It's pretty brave to go to court in person, too. He must have known it would go to the press.'

'Not quite as cold as he seems then, ladies?' Tom says, with a light smile. 'I'm telling you, there's more to him than meets the eye. I'm an excellent reader of people.'

At the end of the article, I read:

'This fresh Blackwell scandal comes after recent speculations about the star's sex life.'

'What speculations?' I ask Tanya.

'Oh, *that*,' says Tanya. 'Rumour is, our Mr Blackwell likes to be in charge in *every* way. The Celeb Focus website says he uses ropes and paddles in the bedroom.'

'Everything on Celeb Focus is unsubstantiated,' says Tom. 'Anyway, what he does in his private life is his own business. Don't we all have our sexual preferences?' He wiggles his eyebrows. 'I'm sure you girls have got up to plenty of things.'

'Not me,' I say. 'I'm twenty two and haven't done anything more than sex in a double bed with the lights off.'

'No!' Tom laughs. 'A lovely thing like you? It doesn't seem right. You need to get out more.'

'I know,' I say. 'But there was so much to do at home. Cleaning, looking after my dad and my little brother. And working. I didn't have time for anything much.'

'Hopefully you'll meet some handsome young man here who shows you a great many variations,' says Tom. 'And if you can't find a handsome one, I'm always willing to step in.'

'You are handsome,' I tell Tom. And I mean it. Okay, he's a little overweight, but he has lovely green eyes, dark black hair and tanned skin, and his personality is as large as the cafeteria.

I think about Marc taking care of his sister like that. Hearing about this side of him, this protective side, makes me feel a surge of warmth. Then I think of what Tanya said, about Celeb Focus and Marc being in charge, and my skin feels like it doesn't fit my body quite right.

'So does he have a girlfriend, or something?' I ask, feeling like a stupid, jealous schoolgirl.

'He doesn't have girlfriends, does he?' says Tanya. 'Isn't that what the magazines always say? He's photographed with different women all the time, but he never dates anyone for long.'

Chapter 15

When the paper goes up on the notice board, it's immediately surrounded by jostling students.

I wait at the back, trying to stay calm. Will my performance be today or tomorrow? It almost doesn't matter. Whether it's sooner or later, I just don't know if I can perform this part, especially in such close proximity to Marc.

Tom waits with me, but Tanya manages to squeeze through.

I hear Cecile say, 'Oh *great*,' and push through the crowds in a huff. When she reaches me she hisses, 'I have my own books to drop, you know. Don't think you've won.'

'I'm not trying to win anything,' I say.

'Well, *I'm* going to be spending time alone with Marc in the theatre this afternoon, and I intend to make every second count.' She storms off.

I move closer to the board. 'Oh shit, shit, shit.' My name is right at the top. I'm first. I'm performing at one o'clock today.

Tanya appears beside me. 'I was trying to find you,' she says. 'Sorry for the bad news. But at least you get it over with. Me and Tom are today too. Not long after you. What did Cecile just say?'

'Oh, she thinks I dropped my books on purpose earlier. I dropped my books and Marc, I mean, Mr Blackwell picked them up. But it was an accident.'

'She's an idiot,' Tanya snorts.

'I'm *first*,' I murmur to myself, blinking in disbelief. I look again, just in case I've misread it, but there I am. Sophia Rose. Right at the top. I'm seeing Marc in less than two hours. 'Oh *shit*. I'd better start practising. See you later.'

I hurry back to my room, where the roses are perky and beautiful by the window. The card is still propped beside them.

I look over my copy of *Call of the Night*, and flick to my scene. We checked over our scenes while we were having coffee, and I was relieved to find mine isn't too bad. It's the scene where Jennifer talks to her theatre director about giving her the role. Just talking. It doesn't escape my attention that I'll be talking to Marc, but as Tanya said, it's still easier than a monologue.

I power up my laptop, and look up a plot precise for *Call of the Night* online. I'm familiar with the story, but not that familiar. I haven't looked at this particular play since school.

I find a website that summarises *Call of the Night*:

Jennifer Jones, a young ballerina, is desperate to succeed at any cost. To win the lead in The Nutcracker, she seduces her elderly theatre director and gets the role. However, the public don't warm to her, and when she is booed off stage, Jennifer commits suicide. The play explores issues of age gaps in relationships and female empowerment.

I look at myself in the mirror. My lips are big – true. And my eyes are okay. A nice brown colour, with really long eyelashes. But I'm not stunningly beautiful, like Jennifer is supposed to be.

I know I should go back to studying the play, but my fingers stray to the keyboard, and I find myself Googling: *Marc Blackwell girlfriend.*

Images come up of beautiful Hollywood women, linking arms with Marc at various premiers and parties. They're all truly stunning. Straight, white teeth, glowing skin, shiny hair and gorgeous clothes.

I read the articles, and they all talk about Marc being seen 'partying all night' with someone, or 'leaving a hotel'. But none talk about a girlfriend.

If all these beautiful women can't make him commit, I guess there's no hope for anyone, I think, and with a sliver of annoyance, I realise I'm disappointed.

Why, Sophia? Did you think you'd win him over, because he remembered your audition?

Of course not. And yet, when we spoke in the woods this morning ... about light and dark ...

I shake the thought from my mind. Marc Blackwell is not interested in a young student from a farming village.

I check my watch and realise, with a stomach flip, that it's nearly time for my audition.

Chapter 16

The Queen's Theatre at Ivy College was built in honour of Dame Gabriela Knight. I know this because outside the red-brick theatre building, there's a gold plaque telling me about the esteemed actress who made the theatre possible.

It tells me something else too. The theatre was commissioned last year and finished just three months ago. Which means we'll be the first students to use it. In fact, it's entirely possible I will be *the* first student to use it. Which does nothing for my nerves.

I think about the old man I met on my audition day, and what he said about Marc turning the whole building to glass and concrete. This theatre has been built to look exactly like the other buildings. Which suggests Marc isn't out to ruin the look and history of Ivy College after all.

I push open the double doors, which are arched like everything else around here, and find the theatre in darkness and silence.

To my left, I find a white panel of light switches and flick them all on.

Rows of plush, red-velvet seats appear, lined up in front of a curved stage made from highly polished wood. The stage itself is bright now, and seeing it makes my heart leap. I love stages. I love being on stage. I love looking out at the darkened faces of the audience, hearing their reactions as I perform.

My romance with the stage chases away my worries, and all I can think about is going up those steps. I just *love* performing. I become myself on stage. My true self.

Hanging from the ceiling are dozens of lights that I'm guessing cost thousands each.

Everything is in place, but there's no Marc. I suck in my breath and venture further inside.

As I reach the stage, I hear the door slam and clipped footsteps. I spin around.

Marc Blackwell walks towards the stage. He's wearing a black short-sleeved t-shirt that's tight against his shoulders and pale biceps. No jacket. Black trousers. His long, white fingers are curved around a laptop case handle.

It's cold outside, but Marc seems completely oblivious to the temperature.

He sees me, but doesn't say a word at first. Instead, he walks right to the front row and takes a seat.

'Hel-lo.' I stammer.

'Good afternoon, Miss Rose.' His voice is so deep, I feel it all the way to my feet.

'After seeing your Lady Macbeth, I'm very keen to see what you'll do with this role. As I'm sure you'll have guessed, I picked a part I thought would challenge you.'

I swallow. 'Yes,' I say. 'Thank you.'

He stares at me intently, a devilish smile pulling at the corners of his lips. I feel my face freeze, and my limbs become awkward. Why do I get so self-conscious around him? He's only my teacher. I've had teachers before. But the way he looks at me – I feel naked. Not just naked, totally exposed. Like he's taking in everything. Every mark and flaw, and there's nowhere to hide.

'Well?' he says eventually.

'Well what?' I ask.

'What are you waiting for? Get up on the stage.'

'Oh. Right. Sorry,' I murmur, finding the three wooden steps up to the stage. I stumble on the first one, and catch myself on smooth wood.

'Nervous?' Marc gets to his feet.

'Yes,' I admit.

'Don't be.' He takes my arm and helps me up. I feel his warmth against my skin and smell that woodland smell again, mixed with soap and cigarette smoke. It's intoxicating and I find myself breathing it in.

'What you asked before, about light and dark,' I say. 'You didn't give me time to answer.'

Marc raises an eyebrow. 'That's because I didn't need an answer. It was a rhetorical question. I was asking myself, as much as anyone. On the stage, Miss Rose.'

I climb up on stage, and clear my throat. I'm not going to let him get away with that. He asked me the question, and I have the answer for him. 'My answer is, I see light in you hidden by dark. You want people to believe you're nothing but dark. But you're not. Everyone has light in them.' I look at the floor.

Marc steps back, his eyebrows pulling together. 'Not everyone.'

'Everyone,' I say.

Marc turns away. I catch his expression in profile, and his eyes look momentarily lost. There's a long pause. Then Marc runs a hand through his hair, and turns to me. 'Let's begin,' he says, his voice softer than before. He opens his laptop case and pulls out a script. 'Here we are. *Call of the Night*. Our femme fatale, Jennifer. Persuading Jonathan to give her the part.'

I clear my throat again, and head to the centre of the stage. 'I'll try my best,' I say. 'But it's so different from the parts I usually play.'

'I know,' says Marc. 'That's why I selected it. I looked over your CV, and the notes I made at your audition. You were ... bewitching. That's the word for it.' His eyes drift to the script, and he says, '*Dangerously* bewitching. I've never pitied Lady Macbeth before, or felt protective towards her. But when you played her ... quite a gift you have. But from what I can see, you've never played anything too provocative. All very nicey nicey parts, and usually naive young girls. I want to see your sultry side. Jennifer knows what she wants. She uses her body and brain to succeed. Let's see what you make of her.'

'Right.' I take the play from my pocket, but Marc bounds up the stage steps and takes it from my hands.

'No,' he says. 'Why do you think I gave you so little time to practise? I'd like to see you feel the part. To use your subconscious and your imagination to become the character.'

'But I really don't know the character too well.' I can feel the heat of his body. He's too close. It's making me dizzy, and suddenly there's a magnet in my chest and he's metal. I'm being pulled towards him. I can't handle it. I take a step back. 'Mr Blackwell, I don't think I can do this.'

'You can.'

'I need more time,' I say. 'I'm not good enough to play this part right now. I need to practise -'

Marc shakes his head. 'Don't be ridiculous.'

I feel tears coming, and am annoyed with myself. Why do I have to be so sensitive?

'Look at me,' he whispers.

I do, and see his eyes searching mine. Warmth rushes into my chest.

'You can do it,' says Marc. 'You are what you believe you are. If you believe you're not good enough, then you'll fail. Here, in my college, I make sure everyone believes in themselves. You're a good actress. I've seen you perform. You can do this. I'll start reading as Jonathan, and you jump in, okay?'

He steps back, and begins pacing around the stage.

'Okay.' I clear my throat again, and try to make my body feel more like Jennifer. But I'm so uptight. So rigid. Fear is holding me captive. I shake my arms.

Come on, Sophia. Get a grip.

'Ready?' Marc asks.

I give a little nod. 'Ready.'

Chapter 17

'Thank you for your time, Jennifer,' Marc begins, his posture and voice changing to that of an older man. It's amazing, seeing him transform like that. Everything about him is different – his voice, his posture, his eyes. 'I've seen enough for today. I'll let you know.'

I swallow, thinking of the script. The words buzz around my mind, tripping over themselves and confusing me. *He wants me to ad lib*, I think. I try to let it all go. Instead of feeling fear, I try to feel what Jennifer must be feeling, as the type of person she is. Angry. Frustrated. To have worked so hard for a part, and not be given it.

'Oh, I don't think you've seen enough at all,' I say, feeling my shoulders pull back, and my hips sway to the left. 'I really do have so much more to show you.'

Something flashes in Marc's eyes. He's pleased.

'No, we're finished,' says Marc. He's such an amazing actor. I feel like he's aged ten years right in front of me, and yet he's still so charismatic. So captivating. His posture, his voice ... amazing. 'I have many more dancers to see today.'

'Really?' I raise an eyebrow and step towards him. 'Because I think maybe, if you can postpone them, I can win you over.'

I'm doing it, I'm doing it, I think. *I'm becoming Jennifer. Just keep going. Keep it up.*

'Oh?' Marc asks.

I know the words I want to say. The words the character should say. But they stick in my throat.

'Well?' Marc cocks his head.

I shake my head. 'I know what I want to say, but ... it's hard to get the words out.'

'Okay.' He jumps down the theatre steps, and takes a seat. 'I was pushing you. That was the idea. But this is definitely an area you need to build on. If you can't play a provocative role, you'll always be limited in how open you can be with the audience.'

A provocative role. I feel myself shiver at those words. How can he say them so easily, whereas I can only *pretend* to play a femme fatale for a few minutes? I feel pathetic.

'I can't honestly say this was as impressive as your last performance,' says Marc. 'Nowhere near, actually. We'll see.' He folds his fingers together. 'Okay. Performance finished. Let the next one in, would you?'

I freeze on stage.

'Let me try again. I can do this.'

Marc looks up from the script. 'Perhaps,' he says. 'But I don't give second chances.'

I nod and swallow, knowing my eyes are pulling down with disappointment. I walk down the stage steps, past Marc and along the seating aisle. At the door, I turn back.

'I feel like I've let you down,' I say. 'I should have been able to play that part better.'

We stare at each other, and I feel something pass between us. Electricity. A connection. It's the strangest feeling, and when I look at Marc, I know he feels something too. His mouth opens, just a little, then he turns his head away, and the connection is gone.

'Yes, you should have,' says Marc. The hardness is back in his voice.

What does that mean? I think. *Was my performance good enough to pass or not?*

Outside the theatre, Ryan is waiting.

'Dropped any more books recently?' he says.

I ignore him.

Chapter 18

In the cafeteria, there are comfy looking red sofas and armchairs away from where the food is being served, and Tanya is curled up on a chair, studying *The Taming of the Shrew*. She stares intently at the pages. She'll probably do a great job of her performance.

The thought depresses me. Have I failed? What if I'm out? I sink into a comfy chair beside her, thinking I might treat myself to a cheer-up hot chocolate.

I think of how, moments ago, I was standing so close to Marc and feel my chest grow tight. And that look we shared ... was the look on his face just recognition that yet another woman had a crush on him?

'Hey Tanya,' I say.

'Hey,' she says, pushing her glasses up her nose. 'How's it shaking? How did the audition go with Mr Big?'

'I don't know. Not great, I guess. He didn't care about me using lines from the play. He ... he wanted me to ad lib.'

'I'm terrible at ad libbing,' says Tanya. 'My worst skill. Still. It'll be good practise. You don't look so happy.'

I nod. 'It was ... strange. And so hard. I just crumpled under the pressure.' I put my head in my hands. 'Maybe I don't deserve to be here after all.' Tanya comes and puts her arms around me. 'He's making it tough, but it's good for us,' she says.

'Think how amazing it is that you got to perform in front of an Oscar-winning actor. Don't beat yourself up. It's only the first performance.' Tanya checks her watch. 'Yikes. I'd better go. Wish me luck.'

'Break a leg,' I say, managing a smile.

Now I'm alone in the cafeteria. All the other students must be in their rooms, practising. I decide to phone Jen. My insides feel like a washing machine full of clothes, spinning round and round, muddled and confused.

I order a frothy hot chocolate with whipped cream and marshmallows, and dial Jen's number on my iPhone – the latest model, thanks to my scholarship.

'BABE!' Jen screeches down the phone. 'I was waiting for your call. I didn't want to bother you while you were settling in, but I'm DYING to know how it all is. What's he like?'

I don't need to ask who *he* is. 'He's ... interesting.'

'Oh?'

I tell Jen everything – the class, the performance and Marc saying he hasn't seen the best of me. I haven't quite figured out a way to explain the look we shared, and now I'm no longer with Marc, I wonder if I imagined the whole thing.

'Wow,' Jen says, when I'm finished. 'Difficult first day. Trial by fire, and all of that. But it sounds like he's a good teacher. I mean, that's what he's supposed to do, isn't it? Stretch you and challenge you?'

'I suppose.'

'And he's right. You do usually play nicey nicey parts. So. Is he as cold as you remember?'

'In some ways,' I say. 'But I think, deep down, there's a warmth to him. I felt it today. I think.'

'I guess everyone has a nice side.'

'I feel so frustrated with myself, right now,' I say. 'I won't find out if I passed until tomorrow afternoon at the earliest. That's when we have a lecture with him again. What if I'm off the course?'

'You won't be,' says Jen. 'I know how good an actress you are. Wow. You've just had a one-on-one with Marc Blackwell. Intense Marc Blackwell.'

'He's that alright,' I say. Suddenly, the newspaper article about Marc's sister spins through my mind. 'Jen, did you see the paper this morning?'

'I didn't get round to it yet. But wait, I have a whole pile of them here. Which one?'

'Any of the tabloids,' I say.

There's a rustling, then silence. 'Poor guy. Wow. If she's dealing drugs, then no doubt she's taking them too. It must be hard, having a drug addict in the family.'

'The article I read mentions a scandal about his sex life,' I blurt out.

Jen laughs loudly. 'There are *loads* of scandals about Marc Blackwell. Which one?'

'Tanya read something online. About him liking to being in charge in the bedroom,' I say. 'And using ropes and stuff.'

'Sounds about right,' says Jen. 'He comes across as very domineering. Why – are you thinking about ending up in a bedroom with him?'

I know she's joking, but my silence tells her all she needs to know.

'*Sophia*!'

'No,' I say, far too quickly.

'At least ... what would be the point? He'd never be interested in a girl like me.'

'Why not?' Jen shouts back. 'A beautiful, talented, sweet girl like you? Who wouldn't be interested?'

Suddenly, I hear something. I see Cecile by the coffee counter.

'Jen, I'll call you back later, okay?' I whisper, and hang up the phone. I don't want her to overhear our call.

'Hi Cecile,' I say.

'How was your performance?' Cecile asks. 'Was it as *intimate* as you wanted it to be?'

'No, not at all,' I say. 'Really. I didn't want it to be ... intimate. I just want to learn how to be better.'

Who are you kidding? says a voice in my head.

I try to change the subject, and say the first thing that comes to mind. 'Did you see the newspapers this morning?'

'Of course I did.' She takes a black coffee from the counter and stirs in sweetener. 'Our darling Marc has a druggy sister who he wastes his time looking after. Put me off him a little bit. The fact he mixes with that sort of person. But not enough for me to give up the chase.'

'I think it's nice he cares about his sister,' I say.

'I'm hoping it's *me* he'll care about most this term,' says Cecile. 'And I intend to tell him so during my performance. I can't wait to be alone with him. One-on-one. Only half hour to go now.'

She lets the words hang in the air, and I realise I really don't like the idea of Marc alone with Cecile. I shake my head, trying to push the thought away.

Don't be stupid, Sophia. Why should you care? A man like Marc would never be interested in you, anyway.

Chapter 19

When Cecile leaves for her performance, I want nothing more than to be by myself.

I head up to my room, and sit on the balcony with a mug of tea. The warmness of summer still lingers, and I stay out there, thinking about Marc and my performance, until dusk falls.

I know I should go to the meal hall and have something to eat, but I feel too anxious. If I'm off the course, I don't know how I'll handle it. I have nothing to go back to really, except Jen. This course means everything to me, now. Everything.

I crawl under my duvet and try to take a nap.

'Soph?' It's Tanya's voice, outside my bedroom door. 'Are you in there?'

'Yes,' I say. 'I'm not feeling too good.'

'Really? I was hoping we could catch up about our performances. I just talked to Cecile and ... well, I just wondered if we could talk.'

Talk? About Cecile's audition?

I climb out from under the duvet and open the door.

'You look pale, love,' says Tanya, putting a hand to my forehead. 'Shall I make you a cup of tea?' She's dressed in a brown leather jacket, with an autumn-red scarf and her long, brown hair is tied up in a bun.

'No, honestly I'm fine,' I say. 'Just tired after today.'

'Can I come in?'

'Sure.'

I open the door wider, and she steps into my room. I'm aware my rucksack is on the floor with exploded clothes all around. I'm used to mess after living with my dad, so hanging clothes wasn't a priority, but I'd still rather they were all tidied up.

'Wow.' Tanya looks around. 'Look at your view. It's amazing.' She moves across the room. 'And you've got a balcony!' She puts her face against the glass door. 'Oh my god, you can see the whole of London from up here.' She turns to me. 'Sorry. You said you were tired. Listen to me, all high octane. So I was going to tell you about the performances.'

'Let's go out on the balcony,' I say, opening the glass door. 'It's still warm enough.'

We walk outside, and look over the grounds.

'Cecile was *furious* after her performance,' says Tanya.

'She was?' I ask, trying to feign disinterest. 'Why?'

'I don't think it went so well. Marc said she wasn't playing the part as it was supposed to be played. He said she was just reinventing the role she played at her audition.'

'How do you know?'

'Tom had the audition after her. He got there early. He opened the theatre door a little to see what was going on, and heard it all.'

'How did your performance go?' I ask.

'I don't know,' says Tanya. 'That's what I wanted to talk to you about. It was so confusing. I have no idea how I did. I tried to ad lib, and he just gave no expression of how well I was doing. He told me to play the part how I felt it. Then he watched me for five minutes or so, and said, Okay, that's it. Thanks very much. I felt like maybe I did something wrong. How do you feel about your performance, now?'

'Confused,' I admit. 'I know I stuffed up. So ... I don't know. I just have no idea if I passed or failed.'

'I'm glad you feel confused, too,' says Tanya. 'Hey – look!' She points across the grounds. 'There he is.'

I look down to see Marc Blackwell striding along a gravel path. It's hard to take my eyes off him. His nonchalant walk, his toned body under his t-shirt, the way he looks so purposeful and determined. He moves like a jungle cat – lean, elegant and strong. It's still cold out, but he strides along in his t-shirt as though it were a summer's day.

Watching him gives me goose bumps, and I find myself wishing he'd look up and notice me.

He heads to the car park, and I hear tarmac smack under his feet. For a moment, I think he's heading straight for his car. Then, very slowly, he stops, turns around and looks to where I stand.

My chest turns to melted butter as our eyes meet.

I can't read his expression. His brows pull together, then he turns away, pulling a cigarette from his jacket pocket, lighting it, and unlocking his car.

My heart is pounding, but he doesn't look at me again.

I watch him jump into his car and speed through the college gates.

'Probably off to some party in the city,' says Tanya. 'I hear he has a town house near here – some million pound London pad. Look – there's nothing left to do today. Let's you, me and Tom hit the town, have something to eat, start spending our scholarship – what do you say? Tom knows all the best places.'

'Okay,' I smile. *Anything to take my mind off getting my grade tomorrow.*

Chapter 20

Our night out is fun. Tanya, Tom and I go to an Italian restaurant that Tom says has 'fantastic parmesan' and does. Actually, all the food is fantastic. Then we have cocktails at a bar in Soho. Tom is fairly confident about his performance, although he says the same as Tanya – that Marc was inscrutable. We decide on an early-ish night, and agree to meet up tomorrow over breakfast, an hour before our first lecture with Denise Crompton. But when I get back to my room, I can't sleep.

After an hour of tossing and turning, worrying about tomorrow's result, I decide enough is enough. The moon is huge and silver, and throwing so much light over the grounds that the woods look bright and alive. I decide I'll go for a walk to get rid of my worries and tire myself out.

I get up, put my furry slipper boots on and head towards the woods in my pyjamas and dressing gown. I know lots of people are scared of the woods at night, but not me. I love being among the trees when it's dark.

Everything is so still and peaceful that I almost feel the trees and I can talk to each other. There's a little magic in the air, as there always is in dark woodlands.

I hop over gnarled tree roots in my furry slippers, enjoying the silver canopy of leaves above me and breathing in the fresh air. If I don't sleep after this, then there's no hope.

I find myself, as I knew I would, heading towards the lake.

I take off my slippers and sink my feet into the water, feeling the sting of ice on my bare skin. I roll up my pyjamas and push my feet in deeper, reeds and mud squelching between my toes.

I love how the lake looks – dark, but lit up by the silver moon. It's so mysterious. There could be all sorts of fish and frogs in the water, but they're all hidden in darkness.

It's heavenly, being part of nature like this, and I stand and walk a few steps into the dark water.

I'm enjoying myself, singing a little, when a sharp stone throws me off balance. With a gasp, I tumble shoulder first into the water. I take a deep breath at the wrong moment, and cough as water splashes into my throat. My eyes sting as my body goes under, and I see a world of murky green and blue shapes, creeping and waving.

I flail my arms. Something warm catches my wrist and I stop failing, biting my lip in shock.

Suddenly I see moonlight, and I'm coughing – big wracking coughs that make my ribcage tremble.

I shake water from my hair and eyes, not knowing which way up I am, only knowing that I'm somehow not in the water any more.

When I open my eyes, I stare through watery eyelashes, not believing what I'm seeing. There, inches from my face, are the stormy blue eyes of Marc Blackwell.

Marc carries me from the lake. His arms are steel under my body, and I find myself clinging to him, shivering.

'What on earth were you playing at?' He's angry. No, *furious*. His jaw is set into a hard line, and I can see the soft brown stubble along his cheeks rippling with annoyance.

'I ... nothing. I didn't mean to fall.'

Marc frowns. Silently, he carries me between the trees.

'What the hell were you doing out here at night? You could have drowned.'

I'm shaking now, as my skin reacts to cold night air and icy water. My cotton pyjamas and towelling dressing gown cling damply to me, dripping water over the woodland floor.

'How did you know I was out there?' is all I can manage to say.

'I was in the theatre building. I heard someone prowling around out here and thought it was an intruder. I never for a moment imagined it would be a pupil idiotic enough to go midnight paddling.'

'I didn't mean to fall in.'

Marc doesn't answer. Instead, he carries me out of the woodlands to the car park, where his Ford Mustang is parked. He opens the passenger door.

'In here. You'll warm up much quicker in the car.'

'But Marc ... I'm drenched. I'll ruin your seats.'

'I don't give a damn about the seats,' Marc snaps. 'All I care about is stopping you from getting hypothermia. Christ, what were you thinking? If I hadn't of been there ...'

'I'm glad you found me,' I whisper.

Marc lowers me onto the passenger seat, and I feel my soggy clothes squelch against the leather.

Oh no. I'm getting water all over his seat.

He leans over me and slots a key into the ignition. Then he turns the car on and winds the heater dial right up.

I watch his long arm stretch past my chest, and can't help noticing how perfect it is. He's wearing the short-sleeved black t-shirt from earlier, and there are water droplets on his pale skin. His arm is strong and muscular, but elegantly shaped. He doesn't seem to be noticing the cold at all, even though there's a big damp patch on his t-shirt from where he's carried me.

'Take your clothes off,' Marc barks.

'Wh ... what?' I stammer.

'Your clothes. Now. Before you catch your death. I have my running clothes in the trunk. You can put those on. Don't worry. I won't watch.'

He goes to the trunk, and returns with a thick grey sweatshirt and jogging bottoms.

'Put these on.' He slams the passenger door closed and stands outside the car with his back to me.

I look at the clothes, then at Marc's broad back through the passenger window. The college is totally dark. No one will see me get changed, and Marc's right – I'm freezing in my night clothes. My hands have turned blue.

I struggle out of my dressing gown and pyjama top, and pull Marc's sweatshirt over my head, smelling a delicious mixture of cologne and woody, leafy something or other. God, it smells good. I'm lost for a moment in the smell, but then I come to my senses and struggle out of my pyjama bottoms, dumping them in the foot well next to my gown and top.

My underwear is still damp, but there's no way I'm taking that off with Marc standing outside, so I pull the grey jogging bottoms over my wet panties.

Once I've got the bottoms on, I look down at myself, taking stock. My body is lost in the huge clothing, and I don't even want to think about what a mess my face and hair must be.

I look through the passenger window at Marc, and – I guess sensing I've stopping wriggling around – Marc turns his head just a fraction. He must be able to see I'm dressed out of the corner of his eye, because he walks around the car and jumps in the driver's side.

'Better?' he asks, tapping each heater duct to check they're blasting out hot air.

'Yes. Thank you.' I'm still shivering, but my body is calming down a little now.

'Would you like to tell me what you were doing, paddling in the lake at gone midnight?'

'I couldn't sleep,' I say. 'I ... was nervous about my audition result.'

My fingers are still shaking in my lap, and I see Marc watching them. He picks up my hands and holds them against the heating duct.

I flinch at his touch. It's so unexpected.

He frowns at me. 'I just want to warm you up. Rub your fingers together.'

I do, glancing at him as my cold fingers feel the heat.

'You must think I'm such an idiot,' I say.

Marc moves his hands to the steering wheel. 'No. I don't think you're an idiot. I understand why you love walking in those woods. I love them too. Just don't go to the lake on your own again. Okay?'

'Okay.' My fingers are turning from blue to red. 'I'm so sorry about your car.'

'I told you. I couldn't care less about the car. I care about you.' He clicks on the stereo, and the Kinks 'Sunny Afternoon' comes on.

'You like the Kinks?' I say.

'They're good story tellers.' Marc stares out of the windscreen.

Even with the music on, I feel the weight of the silence between us. I scrabble around my brain for something to say – anything to ease the discomfort.

'Lucky you were working late,' I say.

'Very lucky.'

'You must care a lot about teaching. To work so hard.'

'I care a lot about my *pupils*. Not teaching.'

Suddenly a wave of tiredness washes over me. I yawn, and quickly put a hand to my mouth.

'Tired?'

I nod.

'I'll take you back to the accommodation block.' Marc looks down at my soggy clothes in the foot well. 'I'll have those taken care of and brought back to you. But you might want to take your accommodation key, if it's in one of the pockets.'

'Yes.' I stoop down and fish my key and card from my dressing gown.

'Wait there,' says Marc. He opens the driver's door and climbs out. I watch him walk around the car, his lean, agile body so relaxed and purposeful.

Then he opens the passenger side and lifts me into his arms.

'I'll carry you,' Marc says. 'There's too much cold gravel around here for you to walk on in bare feet.' He kicks the car door closed and carries me towards the college.

I watch the moon sway back and forth above me, trying not to notice Marc's perfect skin and cheekbones, or the warmth of his arms under my body.

When we reach the main door to the accommodation block, Marc takes a card from his pocket and scans open the door. Then he shoulders it open, and lets me down onto the carpet inside.

'So,' he says, scratching his ear. 'Sleep tight.' He hesitates for a moment, then turns to leave.

'Mr Blackwell?' I say, the words blurting out of my mouth before I can stop them.

He turns to me. 'Yes?'

'I ... thank you. For saving me.'

'Don't mention it.'

'And ...' I look up at his face and our eyes meet. His gaze is so intense that I feel I might be knocked over.

'Yes?' he says again.

'I saw a lot of light in your just now.'

He gives a cynical smile and looks away. 'Then I guess I'm having an off day.' He turns and marches away.

The next morning, I wake up in bed wearing Marc's grey joggers. I look down at myself, stunned.

Oh my god. Last night really did happen. I really did fall into the lake, and I really did sit with Marc in his car.

Embarrassment sets in.

I saw a lot of light in you just now.

What a stupid thing to say. And ... on no. I got water all over Marc's car. What must he think of me?

Okay, okay. No point dwelling.

I dress and try to push aside memories of last night. Both kinds of memories – the embarrassing memories of me being an idiot, and the nice memories of Marc's arms, and his hands holding my fingers. There's no point dwelling on either. And anyway, there are more important things to think about – namely our audition result.

Once I'm dressed, I head to the cafeteria. I take a small bowl of muesli and sit near a window, staring out at the grounds. Tom and Tanya should be here soon, and I wonder if I should tell them about last night.

I see Cecile and Ryan at a nearby table, and she's gushing over him. I guess she needs an ego boost now she's been rejected by Mr Blackwell.

When Cecile notices me, she says. 'Just to let you know, if we're having a competition over who gets Mr Blackwell, I win.'

'There's no competition,' I say, although the words catch a little in my throat.

'The performance yesterday. Let's just say I got pretty close to him.'

'That's not what I heard.'

I take a seat, and wishing Jen were here.

Tom and Tanya arrive, and I feel immediately better.

'Hey guys,' I call out.

'Soph!' shouts Tanya. They grab breakfast – an apple for Tanya, a fry-up for Tom – and join me.

'Ready for Ms Crompton, Ms Rose?' Tom asks.

'I'm looking forward to it,' I say. *Anything to put off seeing Marc again.* 'I've never seen her perform, but I've heard loads about her. All good.'

'She's absolutely wonderful,' says Tom. 'I've seen her dozens of times – I love West End musicals. Such an amazing voice. I saw her just a few years ago in *Monty Python and the Holy Grail*. She played the Lady of the Lake. Amazing. I still have a signed programme from her somewhere – when you're wheelchair bound, you get treated like a VIP. All I have to do is make myself sound extra pathetic and disabled, and whoosh! I'm wheeled backstage to meet the cast.'

'Didn't she have something to do with Marc, when he was a teenager?' Tanya asks. 'I'm sure I read somewhere that she brought him up for a while.'

'Really?' I ask.

'Yes,' says Tanya. 'He had a difficult childhood, and he lived with her, I think. And now he's hired her as a lecturer here. So I guess that's his way of thanking her.'

'I guess so.'

Chapter 21

Denise's lecture is in a small classroom in the east wing – nothing like the big lecture theatre Marc used.

When we turn up outside the classroom, most of the students are already there.

'I guess Marc's lecture about lateness paid off,' Tanya whispers.

I clutch my books.

'You won't be needing those for this class,' says Tanya, glancing at my books. 'Denise Crompton is all about feelings.'

The class shuffles forwards, and I see the classroom door opened by the large, cuddly lady I met at the audition. She's wearing flowing, flowery robes and has blonde-grey hair. Her tiny blue eyes radiate warmth.

'Come in, come in,' she calls. 'I promise my classes are great fun. I'm looking forward to getting to know all of you better.'

As students pass her, she welcomes them by name.

'Cecile! I loved your audition. Very clean and poetic. Welcome, Ryan. A very powerful actor. I see great things in you.'

As we draw near, I realise I don't know anything about Tanya's audition, or Tom's. I wonder what plays they performed. I soon find out.

'Tanya!' Denise calls out. 'A very determined young lady. You really made *The Vagina Monologues* come to life. I can see the passion when you perform. You make everything so real.'

Tanya grins from ear to ear.

'Tom Davenport.' Denise bends down to shake Tom's hand. 'Such an elegant voice and manner. The perfect *King Lear*. You command attention. I could watch you all day.'

'And Sophia.' Denise smiles warmly. 'So humble. So charming. You draw us all in and make us love you.'

I'm dumbfounded. I give a half smile, and mutter thanks, then walk into the room, where there's a horseshoe of chairs facing a whiteboard. Tanya and I take seats at the end, and Tom wheels himself beside us.

'I can't believe she remembered all our performances,' says Tanya, watching eagerly as Denise comes to the front of the class.

'Command attention,' says Tom, banging a fist to his chest. 'I am deeply in love with this woman.'

Denise clears her throat and holds up her hands for silence. 'A very big welcome to you, class. And congratulations on being the chosen few. The UK's finest new talent. We expect big things from all of you.'

Cecile and Ryan exchange smug glances.

'Feel free to call me by my first name,' says Denise. 'I know Mr Blackwell likes to retain authority, but I can't pretend I have any. I'm a push over, which is why I teach university students, not school kids. They'd eat me up and chew me out. And on the subject of Mr Blackwell, you should all know his bark's worse than his bite.'

There are a few uneasy murmurs of laughter.

'I'm serious,' says Denise. 'I practically brought him up when he was a tearaway teen, and he's got a softer side. Softer than he shows. He'd kill me for telling you, but Marc cares about each and every one of you, that I promise. His strictness is his way of showing it. Of getting the best out of you.'

Suddenly, she blurts out a set of scales: 'La, la, la, la, la, la, laaa.' Then she walks around the horse-shoe, her fingers on her chin. 'Mmm. Who will I pick on first?'

Everyone shuffles in their seats.

To my horror, Denise stops right in front of me.

'Sophia. You go first. They say singing reveals the soul, don't they? Let's see what your soul sounds like.'

'I'm no singer,' I insist. 'I'm hoping you'll teach me.'

'Nonsense!' says Denise. 'Everybody can sing. Just give me a few short notes. La la la la la la laaa.'

I know I've gone bright red, but Tanya and Tom are looking at me encouragingly.

I clear my throat. 'La la la la la la laaa,' I croak. I know I sound terrible. Not out of tune – I know the basics. But just ... I don't know. Sort of thin and girly.

'What a lovely soul you have,' says Denise, smiling.

'But I have no power in my voice.'

'Singing isn't all about power,' says Denise. 'It's about feelings, too. *You* put feeling into your voice when you sing, and you sound beautiful. We just have to work on the technical parts – volume, pitch, and most of all, confidence, if you can call that technical. You need to feel more comfortable, exercise your vocal chords and you'll be there.'

'Really?'

'Really.'

I love the rest of the singing class. Denise shows us old movie footage of her favourite singers, and we sing along to *The Sound of Music* and *Mary Poppins*. She gives us vocal exercises to practise on our own, too.

'You can practise in your rooms,' she says. 'In the shower. Anywhere private really, to build up your confidence.'

When we leave the lecture theatre, Tanya puts a hand on my shoulder.

'Marc Blackwell soon,' she says. 'Grade time.'

Chapter 22

I'm early for Marc's lecture, of course. Crazy early. The door to the lecture theatre is open, so I go in. I slide into the front row, taking the same seat as last class.

I flick through books, and doodle on my notepad, and a few more students arrive. After drawing little flowers over my reading list, I sense someone watching me and my neck prickles.

I look up. There, three feet away, is Marc. When I look up, my eyes meet his and for a moment I feel like I'm falling into him. His eyes are clearer and bluer than I've ever seen them. Marc snatches his gaze away and strides to the podium, his laptop case under his arm.

I watch him take out papers and sort through them. He studies the pages intently, and I see the hollows in his cheeks ripple as his jaw tightens and releases.

Over the next few minutes, more students filter in. Tanya and Tom sit next to me – on time today – and Cecile sits a few seats down, as close to Marc's podium as possible.

Marc bangs his laptop case closed.

'Good afternoon class,' he says, his head snapping up. 'Some interesting performances yesterday and this morning.' He doesn't look at me. 'I'm feeling comfortable that I picked the right people for this course.'

The right people ... I feel my whole body sag in relief. Oh, thank goodness. I didn't mess it up too badly. Even if he does think I'm an idiot after last night. It's okay. It's okay.

'However, you all have things to work on. I want to bring out your hidden talents. The things you've kept secret, even from yourselves. You need to work on your discipline, too. As actors, we control our emotions. Hence, my insistence that you follow my rules and arrive on time. If you can't be disciplined, you have no future as an actor.'

He strolls back to his podium. 'If I teach you anything, it's that discipline and craft go together. Without discipline, researching the role, learning a character's life and habits, we have nothing. But if there is only discipline alone – if we don't let go, and let our own instincts and feelings work with the character – we have nothing either.'

Marc walks past the blank white board. His gaze falls on me, but he quickly pulls it away. 'I was like all of you, once. Nervous. Afraid. Out of control. As a young boy, I was very fearful, as a matter of fact. And it made me deliver some spectacular performances. So don't feel too bad about being afraid. But you must master it.

'All your experiences, good and bad, can be drawn upon, when you master your emotions. Your father beat you? Use your humiliation, your pain, your sense of injustice, and bring it to a character who requires those emotions. You have bad habits? Use your sense of shame and self-loathing to bring depth to a misunderstood character. Acting is a wonderful profession. We can turn our greatest pain into our greatest triumph.'

Your father beat you?

The way he says those words, I feel he's talking about himself – his own experiences. And bad habits ... yes, I know he must have those too.

At the end of the class, Marc announces we'll be performing again in a few weeks' time. Oh good god. Just when I thought we'd got past the stress of the first performance, already we have another one to think about.

My heart flutters in my chest, and I feel my stomach tighten. Another audition. After I made such a mess of the last one. I can't do it. At least, not without help. I need Marc's help. I need him to show me where I went wrong, and help me put it right.

All the other pupils filter out, but I stay behind. I can see some of the students giving me odd looks and nudging each other.

I wait until the last pupil leaves the room, and then walk round to where Marc is putting papers in his laptop case.

He doesn't look up, but he glances sideways at me. 'Can I help you, Miss Rose? Not planning any more midnight swimming sessions I hope?'

I smile. 'No.'

'Well?'

'Can I ... Mr Blackwell, I think I need extra help. Before the next audition.'

Marc snaps his laptop case closed and looks up. 'Extra help? Sophia, listen. You're a promising actress. Very promising. And there's something so ...' He spreads out his hands, and looks at the ceiling. 'It's hard to put into words. I don't know. Unaffected. Genuine in your performance. Like nothing, no one I've ever seen before. But ... I'm being totally honest with you here. I've been thinking. I had high hopes for you, but maybe I gave you a challenge too far. Let's just stick to the nice young lady parts for now, and see where they take us.'

'But I want to challenge myself,' I say. 'I want to fulfil my potential. That's why I'm here.'

'Well.' Marc picks up his laptop case. 'That's admirable. But sometimes in life, we have to accept our limitations, as well as trying to overcome them. Let's take a step back. I have something a little easier planned for your next performance.'

'Wait,' I say. 'I want to be challenged. I want to try again. I don't want to be held back. I'm here to try my best.'

'It's good to hear that. But I think ... extra help in your case may not be such a good idea.' He checks his watch. 'I'd best be going.'

'Please,' I call out. 'You're my teacher. If I can't ask you for help, who can I ask?'

He strides to the door, but when he reaches the doorway, he stops. He places his hand onto the doorframe, and I see his chest move up and down. He turns around.

I see his jaw ripple, and his teeth are a little gritted. 'You're right. I am your teacher.' He closes his eyes slowly, then opens them again. 'I'm on campus tonight until seven thirty. Queen's Theatre is free all evening. Meet me at seven, and we'll see what we can do.'

He strides out of the room.

Seven o'clock tonight. I'm meeting Marc Blackwell at seven o'clock tonight. Alone. Oh good god, what have I got myself into?

Chapter 23

It's still light when I arrive at Queen's Theatre that evening. I'm dressed in jeans and a loose cashmere jumper, and shiver a little in the cold air.

The door is locked, so I lean against it and wait.

At exactly 7.30pm, I see Marc strolling towards the theatre. Suddenly I don't know what to do with my arms. I wrap them around myself, and pretend to be studying the arched doorway intently.

'Miss Rose. Nice and punctual I see. Very good.'

I manage to give a little nod.

'Well.' He reaches past me to unlock the theatre doors. Then he flicks on the lights. 'Let's go inside. After you.'

I wander into the theatre, ever aware of Marc's sharp footsteps behind me. It's a little chilly inside, and dust spins around under the lights.

'Shall I go straight up on stage?' I ask, turning my head. Marc is walking with his shoulders pulled back, like he owns the place. Actually, now I think about it, he does own the place.

'Yes, go on up,' says Marc. 'Are you ready to try again as Jennifer Jones?'

'Yes,' I say, walking up the theatre steps.

'Good.'

I clear my throat and head to the centre of the stage. 'The same scene as before?'

'No,' says Marc. 'Let's try another. I'm guessing you're reasonably familiar with the play?'

I nod. 'I read the whole thing before my performance with you.'

'Okay. So pick a scene.'

'How about the final scene, when she leaves the auditorium and -'

Marc cuts me off with a shake of his head. 'Too easy. At least, for you it's too easy. I've seen you do melancholy.'

'Okay,' I say. 'How about the scene when she seduces the male ballerina in the play.'

Marc frowns. 'Maybe *too* much of a challenge. Antonio is a seductive character in his own right. Jennifer has to hold her own.'

'I need a challenge, Mr Blackwell. I need to do better. That last audition -'

'Okay, fine. I'll play Antonio.'

I take my script from my jeans pocket, but Marc shakes his head.

'No script, Sophia. We're going to ad lib. Like before. You have a feeling for the character. You remember the scene. So go with your instincts. It's much more believable that way.'

'Is that what you do?' I ask. 'When you act in movies?'

'Always,' says Marc. 'But only after I know the script like the back of my hand. I spend weeks memorising movie dialogue. I could quote you any scene from any movie I've starred in.'

'Wow. That's very impressive.' I raise an eyebrow, and to my surprise, Marc's lips twitch into a smile.

'Why thank you, Miss Rose. I like to think so.' Marc's smile vanishes. 'You look far too tense.' He walks towards me and I feel myself growing even more rigid. He takes my hands, and shakes my arms.

My upper body relaxes a little, but I'm keenly aware he's holding my hands. I find myself staring into his eyes.

He drops my hands and looks away. 'Better?'

I nod. 'Thank you.'

'Don't try to remember the scene,' says Marc. 'You don't need to. I know it very well and I'll lead. Try to feel what it is to be Jennifer at this moment. She's just found out her director beau is sleeping with another young ballerina, and that she may lose her part. She's looking for comfort. And reassurance that her sexuality can still get her what she wants. What would you be feeling if you were her?'

'I'd be angry,' I say. 'And scared.'

'Okay. Good. What else?'

'I'd feel powerless. Humiliated. And I'd want to take some power back. Have some power over someone else.'

'Very good. How would you show that in your body?'

I feel myself standing taller, looking him dead in the eye, a hand falling to my hip. My eyes narrow and my lips part a little.

'Excellent. Let's start.'

I nod. 'You're an extremely talented dancer, Antonio.' I stroke my hair. 'I imagine you've known a lot of leading ladies in your time.'

'A few,' says Marc, with a quirky smile. Once again, I'm amazed by how he manages to transform, just like that. I feel Antonio's youth and muscular energy.

'Oh?' I say, with a smile. 'How *well* have you known these leading ladies?'

'Some of them *very* well,' says Marc.

'Perhaps you'd like to get to know me better too,' I say, coming closer. Our torsos are inches apart, and I can feel the heat from his chest. *Wow.* That tug again. Can he feel it too? Like a magnet, and it frightens me because I can barely stop myself throwing my body into his arms. And that isn't what a student should do with her teacher.

I move closer, not because of the tug, but because I'm Jennifer, and this is what she would do with Antonio.

Chapter 24

If Marc is feeling our bodies pull together, he's not showing it. He's Antonio through and through. Calm and in control.

I walk in a circle around him. Marc – or rather, Antonio – watches me keenly until I come to a stop in front of him.

'Do you like what you see?'

'Very much.'

I pause. I know what Jennifer would do and, from what I remember of the script, is roughly what she *does* do. But I don't know if, feeling what I'm feeling, it would be a good idea. I take a deep breath.

'Keep it going,' Marc says. 'You're doing well. Don't let it go.'

I nod, and make myself tall again.

'Perhaps you'd like to see more?' I turn around, slide my jumper down over a shoulder, and look back at him with a little smile.

'Very nice.'

I slide the jumper across and over the other shoulder. 'Could you help me unlace this costume?'

Marc comes to stand right behind me. He pretends to undo laces from my shoulders to my lower back, and I feel a shiver down my spine. I pretend to climb out of my costume.

I go to him, and wrap an arm around his neck, looking fiercely into his eyes. I whisper, 'I'm yours if you want me.'

Feeling his chest against mine feels so good. My insides feel soft, and the low-lit theatre rushes around me like a train. All I can see, feel and hear is Marc.

He returns my gaze with equal ferocity, and I feel his arms coming around me, leaning me backwards. 'I do.'

I hear a little sigh escape my body, and smell that smell again –a dewy morning in the woods. It makes me feel so safe. Warm and protected.

I know what should happen next. The couple freeze on stage, and then break apart for a scene change. The sexual experience between them is left to the imagination of the audience. I remain still, his arms around me, unable to break away from his eyes, even if I wanted to. I don't want to move. I want to stay like this forever.

I hear his breathing. Thick and heavy. His chest heaves back and forth against mine.

My senses come back to me, and I remember I should be Jennifer – seductive, powerful and confident. It's not in the script, but Marc told me to ad lib. So I lean forward and kiss him on the mouth, my body swaying slightly in his arms. It's a stage kiss, light and innocent, but I try to fill it with Jennifer's power and sexual energy.

I'm about to pull away, when Marc pulls me into his body, and presses his lips against mine.

Oh my god.

The theatre disappears, and it's just the two of us, our lips together. Nothing, no one else matters.

My heart pounds. He puts a hand behind my head, and pulls me tighter against him, pushing his lips and body into mine. I feel his strength as he brings me into him.

I close my eyes and let the sensations wash over me. The softness and power of his lips. The strength of his fingers. The heat of his body. Our mouths blend together, and we're no longer two separate people. I hear myself sigh again, and feel his hands tighten around me at the sound.

Then he pulls me upright and we break apart.

I stare at him, not knowing what to say or think. That kiss was real. Not to Jennifer. To me. To Sophia. He was kissing Sophia.

I want him to do it again. Over and over again. And more. But as I stumble back, he strides away down the theatre steps.

He turns and holds up his watch. 'There's somewhere I need to be.'

'Marc -' I venture, not sure how I'm going to finish the sentence.

'It's ...' He puts a hand to his forehead. 'I hope this evening was helpful.' He turns his back.

'Thank you,' I stammer, feeling like an idiot. Dazed by his kiss. Suddenly, I'm a silly pupil again, with a crush on her teacher.

'I don't think you need any more extra help for now,' he says, walking away, and my stomach begins to churn. 'Let's stick to the classroom.'

'Marc.' I mean Mr Blackwell, of course. But I can't bear the formality of it. I'm losing him, and I can't stand it. That kiss, those few moments together – it wasn't enough. I have to have more. 'What do you mean?' Is it my acting? Have I let him down? What just happened between us?

He still has his back to me, but he stops walking. He sighs, and I see his taut shoulders move under his shirt. 'One-on-one tuition like this ... it isn't a very healthy dynamic.'

He turns around then, and his eyes burn into me. 'This isn't about you, Sophia. It's about me. Me and what I'm capable of.' He strides down the aisle, and out of the theatre.

Chapter 25

I sit on the stage, dumbfounded. That kiss was real. I felt it. But ... it shouldn't have happened. We both know that. He's my teacher. And more than that, he's a beautiful, intense, famous Hollywood actor, and I'm a twenty-something unknown from a small village. It's silly to think I'll ever have more than that kiss. Marc's reaction says it all – it was a mistake. And I don't want a mistake to ruin our teacher student relationship.

Suddenly, I'm on my feet, running down the aisle and out of the theatre.

I see Marc walking across a trimmed lawn, the fluttering of cigarette smoke floating from his hand.

I run up to him.

When he sees me, his eyes soften and his lips pull tight.

'I want to talk to you,' I say. 'I'm sorry about what happened just then.' I don't want to cry, but I can feel the tears welling up. 'It wasn't professional and it won't happen again.'

In a nearby tree, a few birds take flight.

Marc closes his eyes and shakes his head. 'It wasn't you. You didn't do anything. I just ... I think I've taught you enough, now. I'll see you in class.'

'But I haven't learned nearly enough,' I say. 'Didn't you see how much I improved, with just half an hour of you teaching me? Your teaching is so good for me. There's so much inside I want to bring out. I need you to help me -'

Marc shakes his head. 'It's not a good idea.'

'Please -'

'Don't you get it Sophia? Don't you understand? Do I have to spell it out?'

'Look, I'm so sorry I kissed you -'

'Back there,' Marc interrupts, 'I might have ... I could have ... I'm usually so in control. But with you it's ... different. It isn't healthy for me to be around you like that. Not one-on-one.' He looks at the dark sky, and I see tumbling pain in his eyes. 'Christ, for me to lose control like that.'

I twiddle my hair. My stomach is lurching all over the place. 'What are you saying?'

'I'm saying,' says Marc, turning to me, his voice practically growling, 'that if I spend any more extra time with you, I might not be able to stop myself taking things further. Am I making myself clear?'

I swallow, my heart pounding. I can't take it all in. 'I don't want to lose you as a teacher,' I whisper. 'Please don't say you can't teach me anymore. Marc -'

'God, this is so wrong,' says Marc. 'I'm always in control. One hundred percent. But since your audition ...' He runs his hand through his hair again, and looks away.

I swallow hard, and can barely squeeze out the next words. 'If there's something about me that may compromise your position as a lecturer, you can't punish me for that. I've been selected to be on this course. There are times when I'll need one-on-one tutoring. It's not fair to penalise me because of ... whatever happened just then.'

Marc's jaw clenches and unclenches. 'You're right. I'll get someone else to teach the course. I'll step aside this year, and find someone else to teach you.'

I stare at him. 'You can't do that. You're the reason most of the pupils here are on this course. They auditioned because of you. You're their hero. Their star. They want you to teach them. No one else.'

Marc looks at me, and there's a long pause. 'This situation ... if I remain a lecturer here this year, it could become unbearable.'

I look at my trainers, and see the wet grass has stamped damp patterns onto the cloth.

'Why?' I hear myself say.

Marc moves his face closer to mine, and his blue eyes are fierce. 'Because I can't have you. And wanting something you can't have can be a very difficult thing to handle. Especially if you're used to getting whatever and whoever you want.'

'You ... you want *me*?' I stammer. 'But I thought ... I mean, I'm just some girl from a village. And you're Marc Blackwell.'

'Are you trying to make this more difficult than it already is?' Marc says. 'You know full well I *can't* have you.' He takes a deep breath and lets it all out. 'I'm your teacher. And you're my student.' I feel his stare, burning holes in me.

'Who says you can't?' I stammer, trying to get my head around that sentence. 'You must know I want you too.'

'It doesn't matter what you feel for me,' says Marc, his voice stormy. 'I'd be taking advantage of my position. You're younger than me. Vulnerable. And I'm supposedly mature. And if anyone found out, your reputation could be ... compromised. The press would hound you. I protect my students. I don't ... Christ.' The pained look returns.

I stand there, my mouth opening and closing. 'But if we both want to -'

'This can't happen,' says Marc. 'Not with you. You deserve better. God, if you knew what I was in to ... don't you read the papers? You don't want me, Sophia. Believe me. Stay away. It's for your own good.'

He strides away across the grass, and although every bit of me wants to run after him, I know it's a bad idea. I think about what he meant by 'what I'm in to.' Did he mean that comment on Celeb Focus? I don't know how I feel about that at all. Frightened. Excited. And way out of my depth. Not that any of those feelings matter, because Marc has just told me nothing can ever happen between us.

I turn and walk the other way, towards the accommodation block.

The next morning, I wake up more confused than ever. I water my plants, brush my teeth and am about to pick out something to wear, when there's a pounding on my bedroom door.

Rubbing sleep from my eyes, and checking my pyjamas are keeping me decent, I open it. Tanya and Tom are on my doorstep. Tanya's glasses are slightly wonky on her face, and Tom has no shoes on and a blanket bundled around his shoulders.

'What's wrong?' I ask, feeling my stomach shrink. 'Has something happened?'

'It's Mr Blackwell,' says Tanya.

'What about him?' I hear my voice rise.

'He's ... left.'

'Left? What do you mean?'

'He's gone,' says Tanya. 'Left the college.'

'Gone? Where?' I'm beginning to panic now. I notice Tom shivering under the blanket. 'Come inside, both of you. It's cold out there.'

They walk and wheel into my room, and I head straight to the French windows to see if Marc's Ford Mustang is in the car park. It isn't. The empty space makes me feel sad and lost.

'They said he's gone to visit his sister,' says Tanya, sitting on my crumpled duvet.

'His sister?' My shoulders relax, just a fraction. 'When will he be back?'

Tanya shrugs. 'The rumour is, maybe a week or so.'

'A week?' I rub my forehead. *Maybe it's for the best. It would have been so painful to see him today. And so embarrassing.* 'But he's coming back, right?'

'I don't know,' says Tanya. 'I got the feeling Wendy was just guessing. Tom and I are gutted. We all came here to be taught by Marc. And now ... who knows what's happening? It's enough to drive you to drink.'

'Which doesn't take much, in your case,' says Tom.

I sit on the bed beside Tanya, digesting the information.

'Are you okay, my dear?' Tom asks. 'It's quite a shock, isn't it?'

'Yes,' I admit. And I feel a dark stirring in my stomach that tells me maybe, just maybe, Marc has taken a break because of me.

Tom pats my knee. 'Hey. Let's not get too gloomy. We've still got Denise. And breakfast waiting for us. Life isn't too bad. I'm sure Marc just has family business, and will be back before we know it.'

'Yes,' I say, with a sharp nod. 'He'll be back.' I want to believe it's true. We all do.

The rumour about Marc leaving has already rocketed around the cafeteria by the time we arrive. We learn that Marc left late last night – apparently to drive to his sister's home. But there's nothing in the newspapers, no other news to confirm or deny the rumour.

Our first class that day is with Denise, and I think we're all hoping for an explanation about Marc when we arrive.

'Oh *dear*,' says Denise, as we take our places in the horseshoe of chairs. 'What a sorry bunch you are this morning. I'm guessing you've heard about a certain gentleman's departure?'

There are nods.

'Well. Not to worry. We have a wonderful lecturer to take Marc's place. Alberto Adami – a very fabulous stage actor.'

'Alberto Adami?' Cecile scoffs. 'What's he even famous for? He's been in a few plays. So what?'

'He's a fine actor,' says Denise. 'And he'll teach you a great deal while Marc's away.'

I raise a hand, and notice my fingers are shaking.

'Yes, Sophia?'

'Um. When will Marc – I mean, Mr Blackwell, be coming back?'

More wrinkles appear around Denise's eyes. 'I'm not certain as yet. He's having family troubles. They can take some time.'

'Oh.' My heart sinks. Okay, it's probably for the best not to see him. But that doesn't mean I don't *want* to see him. An uneasy voice at the back of my mind whispers, *Did he leave because of you?*

We finish Denise's class with a round-robin chorus that puts us all in a good mood.

As we're leaving, Denise takes my arm.

'Sophia my love, can I have a quick word?'

I look at Tanya and Tom, who look back at me quizzically.

'Sure,' I say.

She waits until all the pupils have left the room, then closes the classroom door. It's very warm in her classroom. Almost stuffy, but not quite.

'I noticed you weren't quite yourself today.' She goes to a kettle by the window and switches it on. 'I know it's a strange day for all of us, but you seem to be taking it particularly hard. Tea?'

'Oh. Yes please.'

'I only have herbal, I'm afraid. The milk goes off in here. Take a seat.'

I sit down.

'I hope I don't sound too big headed,' says Denise, putting teabags into cups, 'but I'm quite an intuitive sort, and I know when a pupil of mine isn't feeling good. If you ever need to talk, I'm right here. I'm a very good listener. We're one big family at Ivy College. Marc and I both care a great deal about our students.'

'Thank you,' I say. 'Marc – I mean, Mr Blackwell, has already been really kind. He gave me a personal coaching session last night.'

'Very kind,' says Denise. 'Yes, Marc's a good man.'

'I hear ... he's very protective of you,' I say, hoping Denise might tell me more about Marc.

'I've known him since he was a boy,' says Denise. 'I was like a mother to him for a while. I still am, when I can be. He was a troubled boy, but he's turned into a fine young man.' Denise gives me a sideways glance. 'Oh, I know he can seem cold. Even arrogant. His manner might ruffle some feathers – he takes no prisoners, and he doesn't suffer fools gladly. But he won't let any harm come to anyone he cares about.' She pours water into the cups. 'So, Sophia. You're interested in Mr Blackwell? Both in and out of the classroom – am I right?'

My blood runs cold. She really *is* intuitive.

Denise hands me a cup. 'It's not my place to ask anything personal, but I can promise you, if you wanted to get anything off your chest, it would be absolutely confidential.'

'Thank you,' I say. 'I appreciate that.'

Denise's eyes crinkle into a smile. 'When he told me last night that he was leaving, I felt it wasn't just because of family.'

My eyes widen.

Denise pats my hand. 'As I say, I'm a very intuitive person. I can feel things clearly that most people are blind to. And I feel ... when you told me just then that you and Marc met up last night, perhaps a piece of a puzzle fell into place.'

I take a sip of hot tea and burn my tongue.

'Did something happen last night? Between you two?'

'I ...' Tears start to fall, and I can't stop them. 'No, nothing ... I mean, not really. It was all so confusing.'

Denise nods. 'Nothing with Marc is ever straight forward, where women are concerned. He's so scared. So frightened that if he cares about someone, he'll let her down or lose her. His mother died when he was very young and he still blames himself. I think that has something to do with it.'

I wipe away tears. 'That's awful.'

'I know you lost your mother too,' says Denise. 'In fact, that's part of the reason I wanted to talk to you today. I wanted to put myself forward as someone you could confide in. If you needed to. A mother for you here at the college, if you like.'

'How did he lose his mother?' I ask.

Denise's expression darkens. 'It was his father's fault. But Marc blames himself. Even as a young boy, Marc appointed himself family protector. He was such a clever little lad, when I met him, but sad. He could memorise a script within hours and take on the emotions of any part, but he had the weight of the world on his shoulders. At the age of eleven, he felt responsible for his father and his sister. Quite a burden, at that age.'

Denise's eyes twitch into a smile. 'He spoke about you, you know. After your audition. We were having a meal, and ... he's never spoken about an audition out of context before. I should have guessed then that something was out of place.'

I shake my head. 'It isn't. Nothing's out of place. There was a silly incident last night, but it's all over now. When Marc comes back, it'll be like nothing happened.'

Chapter 26

Days turn into weeks, but still Marc doesn't return. My life at Ivy College settles into a comfortable routine of lectures, and meals and nights out with Tom and Tanya. Our new lecturer, Pablo, is just fine. He's no Marc, but we all like him and are learning a lot.

Every morning before breakfast, I walk around the college grounds and tend to a little vegetable patch I've created under a clutch of fir trees. I've planted garlic and winter lettuce, and today I've brought some asparagus seeds to plant. People say it's a tough vegetable to grow, but I always believe you can grow anything if you understand what it needs.

It's sunny today, with a sharp edge of autumn cold, and as usual I'm enjoying being among the trees. Squirrels scurry over dew-damp soil, and I sing a little – practising, as Denise tells us we should.

I finish planting my asparagus and head back towards the college, feeling pretty pleased with myself. Everything's growing really well.

I'm tramping over the undergrowth towards the car park when I notice something – ivy, growing along the woodland floor and snaking up around an oak sapling.

The oak's leaves are far too brown and yellow, even for this time of year, which means the ivy is doing damage.

I go to the tree trunk and carefully pull ivy away so the tree has a fighting chance of survival. I'm careful not to hurt the ivy too much, and pull it around and along the earthy ground, so it can grow in a way that doesn't hurt the oak.

Suddenly, a shadow falls over me and I hear a deep, gravelly voice that rumbles all the way through my torso.

'Not keen on ivy?'

I turn and see Marc, tall and handsome, standing over me. He's wearing a dark grey v-necked t-shirt and thin black trousers.

My heart begins to pound.

'I ... I love ivy,' I say. 'It's one of my favourite plants. But it was hurting this tree. So I was retraining it. Setting it on the right path.'

Marc's eyebrow rises. 'Setting it on the right path?'

'So it doesn't hurt things.' Having him so close is making me unsteady. I wobble a little on my haunches. I stare at him, and add pathetically, 'You've come back.'

Marc nods. 'Yes.'

I can't take my eyes off him.

'So, you like plants?' Marc says.

'I love them.' I say, amazed my voice isn't shaking too. 'I ... kept my Dad's garden back home.' I'm still staring at him, not quite believing he's here. Eventually, I say, 'Did you leave because of me?'

'In part.'

'You needn't worry. It'll be like nothing ever happened.'

'You promised me you wouldn't go to the lake again.'

'I haven't,' I say, dusting my hands to brush off loose soil. 'I was planting vegetables.' Just the sight of him is making me feel weak. 'Are you ... have you come back for good? To the college?'

'Yes. I'll be taking your class today. You should go inside, Sophia – you'll freeze out here.'

It's true – I am a little cold in just a jumper and jeans. But Marc is wearing far less than me.

'I was just heading in.' I smooth my hair down and stand up. 'So. We have a lecture soon? What are we going to do? I mean ... are we just going to ignore each other?'

'That's what I was planning,' says Marc. 'I'm sorry. I don't mean to be hurtful or cruel. I'm dealing with things as best I can. I'll take you inside, and then I think we should keep contact to a minimum.'

He's not looking at me.

'You don't need to take me inside,' I say, hoping my bruised heart doesn't show on my face. 'I can make my own way in.'

Marc looks at me, shivering a little in my jumper, and shakes his head. 'Let me help you,' he says softly.

'No,' I say. 'You're right. We should keep away from each other. I'm fine.'

I get up and march back to the college, not turning to see if Marc is following.

By the time I've washed all the mud off and fixed my hair, the whole campus knows Marc is back.

Before our first lecture, I catch up with Tom and Tanya outside the classroom.

'Where have you been, little miss lie-in?' Tom asks.

'Oh, just ... messing around with my plants.'

'Ah ha.' Tom raises an eyebrow. 'You're usually here before us. You're not messing around with some fellow we should know about, are you?'

I smile and shake my head. *I wish.*

The sharp smack of leather on concrete tells us Marc has arrived, and he sweeps past us all into the lecture theatre.

I shiver as he passes, but I'm determined not to look at him. I stare at the floor and try to rub away the goose bumps that have grown over my arms.

We head into the lecture theatre, taking the seats we've grown used to at the front of the class. I watch Marc take papers from his laptop case. There it is again – the familiar achy feeling that comes from being close without being able to touch him.

Marc's lecture that morning is about stage presence. How some people are born with it, but how it can also be cultivated. How we can practise to achieve it. It's interesting, but my hands are too shaky to make notes. I spend the whole class watching Marc, waiting for something, anything, to show that I didn't dream what happened all those weeks ago. That he's drawn to me like I am to him, even if nothing can come of it.

Marc barely glances at me. He doesn't meet my eye as he passes me a handout. He asks questions throughout the class, and although I'm often the first to raise my hand, he never once picks me for the answer.

At the end of class, all the other pupils filter out, but I stay behind. Tanya gives me a funny look when I tell her and Tom to leave without me, but she's too nice to ask nosy questions.

I wait until the last pupil leaves the room, and then I walk around to where Marc is putting papers in his laptop case.

He doesn't look up, but glances sideways at me. 'We've said all we need to say to each other, Miss Rose.'

That throws me. To be so dismissed. It hurts. I pull out the last of my courage.

'No,' I say. 'There's something I need to say to you.'

He snaps his laptop case closed and looks towards the back of the classroom.

'Please, Sophia, don't make this harder than it already is.'

'This isn't fair,' I say. 'You ignored me all through class. I'm here to take this course just like anyone else. I haven't done anything to you -'

'I thought it for the best,' says Marc. 'I thought you'd be pleased I'm acting professionally. Properly.' His voice falters on the last word.

'I don't want you to ignore me,' I say.

'Yes, you do. You just don't realise it. Believe me, Sophia – if you had any sense, you'd be running out that door.'

'Please,' I say. 'Even if nothing can happen between us, can't we just try and act normally?'

'I don't think that's possible,' says Marc.

'Why not?'

He looks at me then, and as usual I'm nearly knocked over by his eyes.

'You really want to know?'

'Yes. After your talk a few weeks back about managing your emotions, I'd really like to know.'

He gives a curt laugh. 'That's exactly what I *am* doing. Managing my emotions.'

'By ignoring me?'

'Yes. And if I didn't ignore you ...' He looks out the window.

The words hang in the air.

'What?' I ask.

He looks me dead in the eye. 'It's going to be hard to stop myself.'

'From what?'

'From crossing the line.'

For a moment, I feel like he's playing a part. I remember seeing him in one movie – a futuristic apocalypse-type film – where he talks like that to the leading lady. But this is no movie. We're right here in the middle of the lecture theatre, and this is the real Marc Blackwell. Talking to me.

My heart starts hammering away, and I blush from my neck all the way to my forehead. He's scared he'll cross the line. I know, as my knees turn to warm syrup, that I want him to cross the line with me. But another part of me objects to his arrogance. The fact he thinks if he crossed the line, I'd be a willing partner.

'Who says I'd agree to that?' I say.

A pained look flashes in Marc's eyes. He puts his hands in his pockets, and leans his head back to look at the ceiling. 'I do.'

He's right, of course. I want to touch his lips. To be held in his arms again. To be kissed in that strong, merciless way that left my lips throbbing. Every bit of me wants to be connected to him. And I guess he must know that.

There's a noise in the corridor – the squeak of shoes – and Marc turns to the stationery cupboard beside the projection screen. He opens it, and I see the shelves of scripts, paper packets and boxes inside.

'In here.' I feel his large hand on my wrist. 'Now.' He pulls me inside the cupboard and closes the door. 'I don't want people gossiping.'

The cupboard is warm and smells of dust. There's a little white desk and chair against one of the walls. Marc still has his hand on my wrist. He's holding it tight.

'Are you trying to torture me?' he says. 'Staying after class, making this so much more difficult than it already is?'

'Of course not,' I reply.

'You don't know what it means to be mixed up with me.'

'True,' I say. My stomach is tight, and my legs can hardly hold my weight. 'But ... maybe I'm willing to find out.'

'If anything happens between us – it would damage your reputation.'

'And yours,' I say.

'I couldn't care less about me,' says Marc, frowning. 'I have enough money to never work again. People – newspapers – talk about me all the time. I'm used to it. It doesn't bother me. But you're not part of that world and I don't want you to suffer its ugliness.' He shakes his head. 'I can't do that to you. It wouldn't be right.'

'But it *feels* so right,' I hear myself say. 'You must feel it too. That there's something pulling us together.'

He runs a hand through his hair, and a thick strand falls onto his forehead. Then he puts his hands on my shoulders. 'Yes. I feel it.' His eyes flash with emotion. Anger, confusion, fear – there's a whirlwind of feelings dancing around in blue, and I'm swept away.

Oh my god.

He puts his hands under my backside, and lifts me onto the desk. 'Are you sure this is what you want?'

'Y ... yes,' I stammer, holding onto his shoulders.

Our eyes meet and he kisses me, hard.

I'm lost in him. Totally lost. He moves his mouth to my neck and murmurs, 'I've never lost control like this. Never.' Then he pushes my legs apart with his knee.

'Wait.' This is all moving too fast.

'I can't wait. You want this. I know you want this.' With a deft flick of his fingers, he undoes my jeans, and I feel cool air on my bare legs.

I should tell him to stop, I know I should. This is real. It's really happening, and it can lead to no place good. But I can't. Desire has overtaken me, and I'm his. All his.

He finds my underwear – thank *god* Jen made me buy new underwear. I'm wearing a sky-blue g-string of thin, elastic strips. He winds his finger around the elastic, pulling it tight so it cuts into my skin.

Then he slips his hand around my neck and pulls my hair tight. I gasp.

'Call me sir,' he whispers into my ear.

Chapter 27

'What?' I murmur, and feel him pull my under-wear to one side.

'I know you,' says Marc, winding his hand tighter around my hair. 'When we were in the theatre, I knew I needed to take charge of you. To dominate you.'

'I don't want you to dominate me,' I say.

Marc laughs. 'You do.' He moves his body between my legs.

'I don't think I'm ready for what you're asking,' I whisper. 'I'm not very experienced, and -'

Marc draws back. He lets go of my underwear. 'You're not ready?' His grip in my hair loosens. 'Then I was wrong. I'm moving too quickly.' He picks my jeans up off the floor and hands them to me.

I take my jeans and swallow hard. 'Perhaps I should go.'

'Yes.' I see Marc's chest pulling up and down, and his lips form an 'o' shape as he tries to control his breathing.

I pull on my jeans.

'I'm so confused,' I say, opening the cupboard door. 'I don't know what just happened.' *But maybe I'd like it to happen again ... depending on what you mean by 'dominate'.*

I walk into the lecture theatre, and see Cecile in the doorway.

Oh shit.

'I heard Mr Blackwell was in here,' she says. 'I wanted to talk to him.'

Marc appears behind me, the picture of cool, adjusting a cufflink. His loose brown hair looks perfectly in place, and his posture is relaxed in that Marc jungle cat way.

'Mr Blackwell,' says Cecile. 'I wanted to speak to you about my performance. But I see you're busy.' She throws a poisonous glance at me, then marches off.

'Marc -' I turn to him, my eyes wide.

'She doesn't know anything,' says Marc. 'Look, I rushed things back there. I'm sorry. You're ... pretty irresistible to me. I was hoping you'd be ready, but clearly you're not.' He lets out a long breath. 'I can go slower. If you really want to do this. Do you really want to do this? Do you really want to find out what I'm all about?'

I nod.

'Then I'll be in touch.'

'When?'

'Soon.'

That afternoon in singing class, I can't think straight. There are so many thoughts running around my head. And against all of them, there's Marc's face, Marc's hands, Marc's lips. I feel him kissing me and sliding off my jeans.

In the evening, I have dinner with Tanya and Tom – a delicious looking steak and chips that I barely touch – and wander back to my room at a stupidly early hour, refusing Tanya's kind offer to take me to the campus pub.

I find a film website on my laptop, and watch movies of Marc – one where he plays a martial arts champion out for revenge, and another where he loses his memory and doesn't know who to trust. They're both typical Marc Blackwell pictures – moody, atmospheric and intelligent, and without the traditional Hollywood ending.

I watch his lean, taut torso throwing kung fu punches and marvel at the discipline of a man who can learn a whole fighting technique for a movie. His eyes are hard and powerful, and his performance leaves me breathless. Even so, I find myself thinking of the younger Marc I saw in the war movie. His eyes were softer, then. More afraid and more vulnerable. I liked them better.

I watch Marc's movies until one in the morning, then make myself a hot chocolate and sit on the balcony with my duvet wrapped around me. A cold breeze blows against my bare feet.

The campus is beautiful in darkness. Soft, yellow lights pick out shadows on the red bricks, and the ivy looks haunted and alive. I turn and see my mother's face through the glass – her picture resting against the window. She's smiling under a large sunhat, and looks far too summery for this winter weather. I head inside, take off my scarf and wrap it around the picture frame to keep her warm. Then I come back onto the balcony.

Everything is totally still and quiet.

Then I hear a knock at the door. The sound takes me by surprise, and I grip my hot chocolate mug and look back into the bedroom. I'm guessing it must be Tanya or Tom, or maybe both of them. I hope they're okay.

I kick off the duvet, put down my mug and walk into the bedroom.

The knocking is a little louder now.

'Tanya?' I call, but there's no answer. 'Tom?'

I put my hand to the door handle, then hesitate. It's late at night and I'm all alone. If it's not Tanya or Tom, maybe it's not sensible to open the door. But the college has excellent security. All the gates are locked at night and manned by security guards, and no one can enter the accommodation block without an electronic key.

I open the door, and am totally unprepared for what I see.

Marc Blackwell is standing in the doorway, shadows cast over his taut, pale face. His hair is uncharacteristically ruffled by the wind and his eyebrows are pulled together in a frown.

He has one hand against the door frame, and is leaning against his forearm. 'I saw your light on.'

I stare at him, open-mouthed.

'Can I come in?'

'Of course you can.' I open the door wider, and stand back.

As he walks into my bedroom, I notice the mess of clothes and books scattered around the place. The hot chocolate carton is open, and a milky spoon sits next to it. I hate the room being a mess like this, but I didn't have the energy to tidy up today – not after what happened with Marc. Now he's going to think I'm a total slob.

I hurriedly pick up clothing and stuff it into the wardrobe.

Marc glances at the crumpled duvet on my bed, then marches through the open French windows onto the balcony. He looks out over the campus.

I follow him. 'What ... what are you doing here?'

'You kept my flowers,' he says.

'Yes. They were beautiful. So was the card.'

Marc nods, looking distracted. 'Believe me, Sophia, I had no idea when I sent those flowers ... I hate myself for feeling this way, but ... I have to have you. There's no other way of staying sane.'

I feel that tug again. It's so strong. Being with him wakens all my senses. I smell him in one great rush. I see him in so many colours and from so many angles, it's like I was blind before I met him. And I hear him all over my body, right down to my toes.

'I need to know what experience you have,' says Marc. 'Have you had boyfriends before?'

I feel myself going red. 'Yes.'

'Tell me about them.'

'Nothing big. Just a couple of boys at college and university. Nothing serious. Just, you know. Teenage stuff. I've been working too hard to have time for a social life.'

'Did you have sex with them?' Marc asks.

'Yes,' I say, going redder. 'One of them.'

'What kind of sex?'

Chapter 28

I blush again. *What kind of sex?* 'I suppose the usual kind,' I say. 'How many kinds are there?'

Marc's lips tilt at the corners. 'Lots and lots of kinds. I think I can teach you a lot. In fact, I'm sure I can. Things you'll like. But I have to know what I'm dealing with. What you might be ready for.'

'And what if I don't agree to that?' I say, the words a little shaky.

'For this to work, you have to accept that I'm the one in charge,' says Marc. 'You need someone who knows what's best for you, sexually and otherwise.'

I think back to that afternoon. It was probably the hottest few minutes of my whole life. The way he took charge of my body. I've never experienced anything like that before. I want it again.

'I need you to make a decision,' says Marc. 'You'll either let me take charge of you in the way I want, or I'll leave the university. Being around you and not having you ... it's not going to work.'

'We've been through this,' I say. 'You can't leave. It wouldn't be fair.'

'That's our situation, Sophia. I can't stay here, not being able to touch you, teach you and discipline you in the way I want.'

'Discipline me?'

'Exactly right. If I take charge of you, I need to discipline you. If you step out of line, you'll be punished.'

I swallow hard. 'I'm not sure I like that idea.'

'If you want hearts and flowers, walk away right now,' says Marc. 'You're a beautiful, innocent young girl who any man would kill for. If I were you, I'd run a million miles from a man like me.'

'What do you mean by punishment?'

'I need to be in control,' says Marc. 'That's who I am. That's how I was made. Which means if you step out of line, I have to discipline you. Maybe I'll spank you. Maybe I'll tie you up and fuck you until you can't bear any more. It really depends how you step out of line.'

Oh my god. I squeeze my knees together. How can I be turned on by what he just said? It's so strange. So cold. But my god, it's so hot.

'Come inside. It's cold out here.' Marc strides into the bedroom. He pats the mattress beside him and I follow him in, closing the French doors and sitting beside him.

His nearness is doing things to me, and I put my head in my hands. This is too hard. I still don't really understand what he wants from me but, by the sounds of it, it's some kinky, spanking type stuff that I am in no way ready for.

My heart beats hard in my chest, and tells me to run away. Fast.

I look up. 'Maybe ... if you take things very slowly. Maybe I could ... try.'

'How many times have you had sex before?' he asks.

Must he ask me questions like this? 'I haven't kept count,' I say. 'But not a lot. Maybe five or six times. With my boyfriend at university.'

'Sophia, I'll never hurt you or let anything happen to you. You'll be safer with me than anyone, I guarantee that. But I will test you. I'll challenge your boundaries, and help you explore new parts of yourself. Are you ready for that?'

I want to kiss him so badly. I feel myself leaning forwards, but he takes my face in his hands, holding me firm.

'I have to have a decision from you, Sophia. Can you accept what I have to offer?'

'I need time to think,' I murmur. I lie on the bed, wishing I was wearing something sexier than pyjamas.

Marc stares at me, and his jaw ripples again. 'Let me show you how good I can make you feel. If I hurt you, tell me and I'll stop. Do you trust me?'

'I trust you,' I say, and realise it's true.

He stands up and paces back and forth, watching me.

'Take off your pyjamas.'

'I need more time -'

'No you don't. Not for what I have in mind. Take them off now.'

I slide the pink t-shirt over my head and slowly peel off my pyjama bottoms. Then I lie back in just my underwear – a white bra and panties.

'It had to be white, didn't it?' he says.

He goes to the French doors and closes the curtains, then takes off his jeans and t-shirt. He's wearing boxer-briefs, and I see a hard outline pushing against the fabric. It's huge.

'Are you ready for your first lesson, Sophia?' he says, coming to the foot of the bed. He grabs my ankles and flips me onto my stomach. Then he spreads my legs open, and I feel the flat of his palm moving back and forth between them.

'*Oh,*' I murmur into the pillow.

'I'll stop if and when I feel like it,' Marc whispers. 'You'll do what you're told, and feel what I want you to feel. I'm in charge.'

A shiver passes through me. Why is this so sexy? I can't resist being carried along with the tide.

His hand carries on moving, and I feel the heat building. Then he stops.

'Please don't stop,' I murmur.

He slaps me between the legs, and I jump.

Ouch.

'That's a warning,' he says. 'Tell me what to do again, and I'll teach you a real lesson.'

Oh god.

He puts his hand back again and begins to rub.

Oh god, oh god.

'I don't want you to come yet. That's an order.'

I feel the heat building, and I can't help myself.

'Oh Marc,' I say out loud. 'Oh, that feels so good.'

His hand is unrelenting, and as I try to squirm away, he pulls me back onto it.

'You have to stop,' I beg, feeling fiction turn to unbearably pleasant heat. His response is to rub harder and harder, until my whole body grows tense.

The world turns into coloured spots, and a wave of pleasure flows over me, from my navel to my legs.

I feel myself sink deeper into the bed. I hear Marc's footsteps, then feel a duvet laid over my body.

Marc whispers in my ear. 'I told you not to come. And Monday morning, I'm going to punish you.'

Oh good god. I'm not ready for anything like that. I'm really not. What have I got myself into? And yet, I can't walk away from him. I know I can't. Whatever journey we're on, I have to see it through to the end.

'Trust me, Sophia,' says Marc, stroking my hair.

I hear him stepping into his clothes and murmur, 'You're not staying?'

'I can't stay here,' Marc whispers, pressing the duvet around my body. 'People can't see me leave in the morning. I told you I'd protect you, which means protecting your body *and* your reputation. I won't have people gossiping about you.'

'I wish you could stay.'

'So do I. Monday.'

'But ...' I realise it was Friday when I went to bed, and now technically it's Saturday morning. 'That's two days away.'

'Monday,' he replies. With that, he's gone.

Chapter 29

I wake the next morning from an amazing night's sleep, and my heart shivers as I feel cold sheets beside me. Did it really happen? Did Marc Blackwell really come up to my room last night?

I smell him against my duvet, and know it's true. He really did knock at my door in the middle of the night, and he really did say on Monday he was going to punish me.

My stomach turns over as I think about that. He says he'll protect me, but punishment isn't protecting someone. Yet I have to admit, when he talked about spanking me and tying me up, I felt ... excited. Okay, more than excited. But imagination and real life are two very different things.

I check my watch. It's noon and it's Saturday. Noon! I don't think I've ever slept in so long. I'm used to working most days of the week, and when I'm not, I'm taking care of Samuel or cleaning.

I sit bolt upright. I should be getting the train back home to see Dad and Samuel today. I promised to visit. I pick up my phone and dial Dad's number.

He picks up straight away. 'Hello love. How are you?'

'I'm about to come down to visit,' I say. 'But I'm running a bit late -'

'Don't be silly.' He cuts me off. 'This is your first month at college. Get settled in. Get used to your new room. Spend time with the other pupils. I wouldn't dream of you coming home.'

'Okay,' I say. 'Thanks Dad.'

What's everyone up to this Saturday? I have no idea, but I need to do something to take my mind off Marc.

I send Jen a text: *I've just had a window into your life, Saturday with nothing to do! xx*

She texts back straight away: *You've only just woken up? Welcome to my world! MISS YOU BABES!! xxxx*

I smile, and head towards the cafeteria, but there's something going on in the campus square. Students are dressed in bright wigs, painted like clowns and handcuffing themselves together.

I see Tanya among them, and she comes running up to me. 'Sophia! We were just about to come and get you.'

I see Tom behind her wearing a bright blue fright wig. 'Fetching, don't you think?' he says.

'Very,' I laugh, with a yawn. 'Sorry. I just woke up.'

'We've got one for you,' says Tanya, running to a cardboard box and returning with a bright red wig.

'What's this all about?' I ask.

'Student Rag week,' says Tom. 'Raising and Giving. Which means we all dress up like arses, and roam the streets asking for money. Tied to each other.'

I smile. 'Sounds like fun.' And a great way to distract myself from Marc.

Tanya waves the wig at me. 'A new hairstyle for you.'

A silly, vain part of me is glad Marc isn't accommodated on campus. I'd be embarrassed if he saw me wearing this wig, but he's not here, so when in Rome ...

'Thanks,' I say, tugging on the wig. 'I guess I'll be needing some make-up too.'

'And a beer,' says Tom, reaching into a cooler box and throwing me a can of Fosters.

'At midday?'

'You're a student now,' says Tom. 'Prepare for alcoholism. This is just breakfast.'

He opens my can. 'Drink, drink, drink!'

'Okay, okay.' I take a sip.

Ryan comes over with a bottle of evil looking red liquid and a plastic shot glass.

'She needs a shot, too,' he says.

'She's only just woken up,' says Tom. 'Give her a chance, she can probably still taste the toothpaste.'

'*You* just gave me a beer,' I laugh.

'Sophia, my love. It's Fosters. It's practically a soft drink.'

'Take a shot,' says Ryan, pouring red liquid into the shot glass. He fills it so high that liquid spills onto the floor and stains the concrete.

'I'm surprised smoke isn't coming off the floor, the look of that stuff,' says Tanya. 'Ryan, it's too early.'

'No, she needs a shot,' says Ryan, pushing the glass towards me.

I sigh. 'Fine.' I take the glass and down it, swallowing quickly so it doesn't come back up. Part of me wants to get a bit drunk today. Anything to forget about Marc and last night. My body is aching for him, but I know I won't see him until Monday.

And then, I don't know what side of him I'll be seeing ...

I feel wobbly as the red liquid takes effect, and Ryan smiles. 'There's a good girl. Take your medicine.'

Cecile comes marching up to him. 'Ryan, what are you doing?'

'Giving our little star pupil a shot. A little bit of truth serum. Maybe she can tell us what's going on with her and Mr Blackwell.'

'What?' I say, feeling cold.

'Cecile saw you coming out of the stationery cupboard, isn't that right?'

'What are you talking about?' says Tanya. 'Are you trying to start some horrible rumour? Why don't you two just grow up?'

'I saw her,' says Cecile, with a smug smile. 'She came out of the stationery cupboard, and Mr Blackwell was right behind her.'

I stand there stupidly, not knowing what to say.

'So?' says Tanya. 'What are you implying exactly?'

'What do you think I'm implying?' says Cecile. 'Small-town Sophia is up to no good with the teacher.'

'Which is exactly what you'd like to do, given half the chance,' says Tanya. 'You said as much on our first night here. You're just jealous because Marc sees something in Sophia that he doesn't see in you. Or maybe any of us. She's got something – any idiot can see that.'

'We've all *got* something,' says Cecile. 'That's why we're on this course. Why Mr Blackwell would favour her, unless she's doing something she shouldn't -'

'Stop trying to start rumours,' says Tanya. 'There are plenty of reasons to go into a stationery cupboard. You're letting your imagination run away with you.'

'Yes, stop being ridiculous Cecile,' says Tom. 'You're just jealous.'

'Of *her*?' Cecile practically spits the words. 'Miss sweet and innocent? I don't think so. Come *on*, Ryan.' She pulls him away.

Chapter 30

A tall female pupil with blonde hair shouts, 'Okay, gang! Time to get tied up.' She comes through the crowds with a box of plastic handcuffs, giggling and passing them out. She pulls students back and forth, handcuffing students together, the slaps a sticker on each handcuffed student – one sticker says slave, the other says gladiator.

'What's going on?' I ask Tanya.

'The theme is gladiator and slave,' says Tanya. 'Which means whoever you're handcuffed to is either in charge of you, or you're in charge of them.'

I feel a ripple of something in my stomach and between my legs, as I think of how Marc took charge of me last night.

'So how does it work?' I ask.

'Whoever the gladiator is, they decide everything – where to go to raise money, when to stop for breaks, when the slave can go to the toilet, everything. But if you raise the least amount of money, then the gladiator gets thrown to the lions, as it were. They have to drink a gallon of beer in one go. Oh. Looks like I'm up.'

Tanya turns to the smiling, blonde student, who pulls Tanya away and handcuffs her to Cecile. Neither of them looks happy, until Tanya is given a sticker saying: gladiator. Then she smiles from ear to ear and winks at me.

I stand close to Tom, hoping I'll be handcuffed to him, but the blonde student is doing a good job of mixing everyone up. To my horror, she drags Ryan through the crowd and grabs my wrist.

'I saw him chatting you up earlier,' she says with a wink. 'I always like to play matchmaker.' She hands a fundraising bucket to Ryan, and adjusts his wig.

Through the crowd, I see Tanya laughing and shaking her head. Cecile looks furious.

I expect Ryan to complain. To say he doesn't want to be near me. But he doesn't say anything.

The blonde pupil handcuffs us together. 'There. You make a lovely couple. Now. Who should be gladiator and who should be slave?' She looks from one of us to the other. 'Oh wait – you're the girl with a crush on Mr Blackwell, right?'

'Why do you say that?' I ask, going pale.

'Cecile's been telling everyone that you won't leave him alone. But I don't blame you. I mean, who doesn't have a crush on him?'

I look at the floor. I guess it's better that people think I'm some crazy, love sick pupil than know the truth.

Tom is handcuffed to a short, black-haired girl who looks smiley and good fun, and the two of them are soon chatting away, Tom roaring with laughter.

I turn to Ryan, wondering what on earth we're going to say to each other.

'This is a turn up for the books,' he says, an unpleasant smile on his lips. 'I bet you'd prefer I was Marc Blackwell, though.'

I take a sip of beer, not knowing what to say.

'So it's true then?' says Ryan. His face is broad and flat, and for the first time I notice tiny gaps between his straight teeth.

'What's true?' I ask.

'That you're obsessed with Marc Blackwell? That you have a crush on the teacher.'

'I'm not obsessed with anyone,' I say, but I know I'm lying to myself. All I've been able to think about since I got here is Marc, and thoughts of last night still send trembles down my legs.

The handcuffed couples ahead start walking off campus.

'Come on,' says Ryan, tugging hard at my wrists. 'We don't want to be left behind, and I'm determined to win this. I won't be the loser. The couple who raises the most money wins free drinks at the campus bar.'

'I don't think I need any more to drink,' I say, still feeling a little giddy from the shot.

'You take the bucket, slave,' says Ryan. 'I'll hold your beer.'

'Fine,' I say, passing my beer over. The charity bucket feels nice and light, but I know it'll get heavy soon.

Ryan tugs at my wrists. 'I think we should go on the tube. Ask commuters for money.'

'While we're handcuffed together?'

'Don't answer back, slave. It'll give us the best chance of winning.'

'You're taking this whole gladiator thing too seriously,' I say. 'Isn't the tube a little bit unsafe?' I want to add: *since we're tied together and you're clearly drunk.*

'It'll be fine.' Ryan downs my beer, and shouts at the blonde pupil, 'Rachel, another beer. I'm dry.' He throws the empty can on the floor.

'Please would be nice,' Rachel says, throwing him a beer from the ice box.

'One isn't going to last me five minutes,' says Ryan.

'Alcoholic in the making, I like it!' says Rachel, handing him another beer. Ryan stuffs it in the pocket of his cargo trousers.

'Okay, team,' says Rachel. 'Let's get going.'

Ryan drinks half the new can in one go, and I notice he's swaying slightly.

'Do you think you'd better take it easy?' I whisper.

'No I don't,' he says, chugging more beer, and pulling at the handcuffs.

I follow him and the other couples through the campus grounds, and onto the streets of London. We walk past Great Ormond Street Hospital, and reach High Holborn where crowds flow back and forth.

Ryan is unsteady on his feet, and nearly pulls me over a few times. I'm left scrabbling to stay steady as he walks without the slightest regard for the fact he's attached to someone.

'Wait, please, you're going too fast,' I say, the bucket swinging in my hand.

'If we're not fast, we won't win,' says Ryan. 'Where's your killer instinct?'

'I don't have one,' I say. 'We're raising money for charity, not running a marathon.'

'Well I want to win,' he says. 'And I'm in charge of you. So you'll do as I say and walk at my pace.'

I stumble behind him. When he sees Holborn tube station, he drags us towards the steps that say: 'No Entry'.

'Get out of the way,' he shouts, as streams of passengers emerge from the dark mouth of the station. 'We're on student rag week. For charity.'

He pulls me down and through the crowds, but I trip and fall on the first step, and tumble down the rest, landing on my rear end at the bottom. The bucket clatters away.

'Ouch,' I say.

'You dropped the bucket,' says Ryan, dragging me across the floor.

'Wait,' I shout. 'Let me stand up.'

Chapter 31

Some passengers come to my defence, and I hear an elderly woman berating Ryan for going after the bucket.

'Let her stand up, young man. Can't you see you're hurting her? And what are you doing drinking at this time of the day? You should be ashamed of yourself.'

Ryan looks at the woman with angry, red-rimmed eyes. 'Mind your own business.'

'Are you okay dear?' the woman asks, as I struggle to my feet. My ankle feels sore, but okay.

'Just a little bump,' I say. 'I'm fine. Really. Thank you.'

Ryan uses his oyster card at the tube barriers, then bundles us both through. The gates catch on my arm. Double ouch. I never knew they shut so hard.

'Don't drop the bucket,' Ryan shouts.

The gates open again, sensing an obstruction, and I'm pulled towards the escalator by an unsteady Ryan. I hold on tight to the moving handrail, and when we reach the platform, a train is just about to leave.

'We can make it,' Ryan shouts, tugging me behind him.

'No, please Ryan. Wait.'

'Do as you're told.' He mounts the crowded tube train and tries to pull me on, but the doors are closing. There are tuts from passengers as Ryan jostles them aside.

'Just climb on the bloody train,' Ryan says. 'You're so slow. I'm not going to lose.'

'Ryan, *please*. There's no room.' I'm terrified the doors will shut between our arms, and the train will carry Ryan away on one side, and drag me along on the other, ripping off my arm in the process.

'I'll make room,' says Ryan, pushing people out of the way, and pulling me onto the train just as the doors close.

The doors slam into each of my arms, but I grip the bucket tightly this time. Then the doors reopen and I squash myself into the other passengers, apologising the whole time.

'Rag week,' Ryan shouts. 'Give us your donations.'

Not surprisingly, no one is happy to part with any money after what they've just seen, especially since it's so clear Ryan is very drunk.

We wander up and down the train for the next hour, but Ryan certainly doesn't have a winning manner and every time I ask anyone for money, he shouts, 'Be quiet, slave.'

When Ryan's beer runs out, he drags me up to the street so he can find a supermarket.

He's pleased to see a Tesco Metro, and pulls me into the cold drink aisles, throwing cans of Stella into the crook of his arm.

'I need the toilet,' I say. 'Can we find somewhere nearby?'

'What are you drinking, slave?'

'Just a coke,' I say.

'I order you to drink something alcoholic,' says Ryan.

'Well I won't,' I reply.

'Fine. If you won't get drunk with me, no toilet breaks.'

'Oh, for goodness sake,' I say. 'Don't be ridiculous.' I tug at the plastic handcuffs but they're surprisingly firm. I'd need a pair of pliers to break them open.

'You're stuck with me,' says Ryan smugly. He pauses for a moment, and blinks in a languid, drunk way. Then he appears to have a change of heart. 'Okay, fine, have a coke.'

'Can we find a toilet after this?'

'Yes.'

He takes the drinks towards the till, then pulls me into a nearby pub and up some stairs to a ladies' toilet.

'This is embarrassing,' I mutter, going into a cubicle and closing the door over the plastic handcuff chain.

'I won't peak, I promise,' says Ryan.

I hear two drinks being opened, and roll my eyes. 'Ryan, we're never going to win if you're falling all over the place.' This is awful. It's like being chained to a six year old child.

There's a fizzing sound, and I wonder if Ryan has spilt his drink.

'Are you managing okay in there, one-handed?' Ryan asks. 'You don't want me to wipe for you?'

'Oh, be quiet,' I say, pulling up my jeans and flushing the toilet.

I wash my hands, and then Ryan hands me my coke.

'Thanks,' I say, noticing he's opened it for me. 'That's the first thoughtful thing you've done all day.'

Chapter 32

Half an hour later, I'm not feeling good. Ryan's dragged me up and down Oxford Street, thrusting the charity bucket in people's faces. We've seen a few of our fellow students, their buckets rattling with money, but we've barely collected anything.

My heart is pounding, and I lean against a wall. 'Wait,' I say. 'Please, Ryan, I'm serious. I need to rest.' The world begins to spin, and my head hurts.

Ryan looks at me strangely. 'What's wrong?' he asks. 'Aren't you feeling good? You should be.'

I sink to the floor against a brick wall, not caring where I am or who's looking at me. The pounding in my heart is overtaking everything and I feel frightened.

'You're bleeding,' Ryan says.

'I am?' I say, dazed. 'Where?'

'From your nose.'

I put my hand under my nose and see blurry blood on my hand. Then I pass out.

When I wake up, I see a white ceiling. I look down and discover I'm under green bedclothes. My body aches and my head hurts. I try to sit up, and see a large lady in a nurse's uniform come towards my bed.

She takes my hand. 'You're alright. You're just in A&E, that's all. Nothing to worry about.'

'What happened?' I ask.

'You tell us,' she says, with a knowing smile. 'You've taken something you shouldn't, and it had something nasty in it. Nothing too harmful, we don't think, but better we keep an eye on you.'

'Taken something?'

The nurse raises an eyebrow. 'You may as well be honest about it, love. The more honest you are, the more we can help you.'

'But I didn't take anything,' I say. 'I had a shot and half a beer, but that's all.'

'We see it all the time on student rag week,' says the nurse. 'Alcohol poisoning, usually, but the odd idiot like you takes something stronger. You were lucky.'

'But really, I didn't,' I say, feeling on the verge of tears.

'Maybe you'll remember better later,' the nurse says with a wink. She turns around. 'Oh! My word.'

I close my bruised eyes, wondering what's bothering her. When I open them again, I see the tall, shadowy figure of Marc Blackwell approaching my bed. He looks pointedly at the nurse, who hurries away. Then, he swishes the hospital curtain around us.

Oh my god.

'What are you doing here?' I gasp.

'What happened to you?' he asks softly, taking my wrist. It's covered in bruises from the handcuff. His eyes flash as he examines my blue-brown flesh. 'Who did this to you?'

'No one,' I say. 'It's student rag week. I was handcuffed to another student.' I'm too weak to worry about what I must look like.

Marc raises an eyebrow. 'Male or female?'

'Male.'

'Who?'

'Ryan.'

'I'm taking you out of here. To a private facility. They say you took something.'

'But I didn't,' I say. 'Truly I didn't. Maybe it was something I ate. They said I'm going to be okay,' I say. 'I just need rest.'

'Well, I'd rather be safe than sorry. I have an ambulance waiting outside, and I've arranged for you to be taken to a facility in West London.'

'The nurse doesn't believe I didn't take anything,' I say, feeling tearful again. 'But I really didn't.'

Marc doesn't say anything.

Chapter 33

My private hospital room is full of roses – pink, yellow and red blooms on every surface. Marc was beside me in the ambulance, but he didn't say a word. He stared straight ahead, his forehead creased, his lips tight. As I'm wheeled into the private room by a hospital orderly, Marc helps me onto the bed.

'I'm feeling much better,' I croak, although my eyes still ache.

'Rest here,' says Marc, marching towards the door. 'I've hired people to take care of you around the clock. I'll be back, but there's something I need to do first.' At the door, a pretty brown-haired nurse in a white uniform is waiting.

'Give her anything she wants,' says Marc, 'and be very careful when you take her blood. Her wrist is badly bruised.'

He marches off, and the nurse comes into the room.

'I'm Trinity,' she says. 'Marc hired me to be your personal nurse. I need to take some blood from you, and then I'll make you comfortable. Bring you whatever food you like and set up some movies.'

I notice a flat screen opposite the bed, and see green bushes and trees outside the window.

She takes my blood very carefully, and I hardly feel the syringe at all.

'Well, now,' she says, when she's disposed of the needle and packed up the blood sample. 'What can I get you to eat? Marc's given me specific orders.

Any meal you like from any restaurant in London. You can have Gordon Ramsey himself cook you something, if you like. He's a personal friend of Marc's.'

I smile at the thought. What would Jen think if she could see me now? I decide I won't ring her or my family from the hospital. They'd only worry.

I feel my stomach grumble at the thought of food. 'Actually, the thing I'd most like is pizza,' I say. 'Followed by ice cream.'

'Your wish is my command,' says Trinity. 'Marc's bought you some sweatpants and t-shirts to help you get comfortable. He really does care for his students, doesn't he?'

Perhaps more than he should, I think, finding it hard to get a grip on everything that's happening. I appreciate Marc taking care of me, and bringing me to this fancy hospital where they can run specialist tests. But would he do this for all his students? If he wouldn't, it isn't fair. I want Marc so badly, but I don't want special treatment. I don't want favouritism.

I find myself watching the door, hoping Marc will come back. It's been such a whirlwind so far, I haven't thought about much but Marc's body and the things he's done to me. But I am his pupil, and he's my lecturer. He's in a position of authority and he's not supposed to abuse it. I'm so confused. The only thing I know for certain is that I want to see him again. Actually, not just see him. I want him to touch me again.

After a while, Trinity returns. 'We got your test results,' she says. 'Marc made sure everything went through extra fast.'

Which I guess means he paid a lot of money, I think, feeling uncomfortable.

'What did they say?' I ask.

'You took something with rat poison in it. But you'll be absolutely fine. It was a very low dose, and the body has excellent ways of getting rid of poison.'

'Rat poison?' My stomach lurches. 'But how?'

'It's something we often find cut with hard drugs.'

'But I haven't taken any hard drugs.'

'Who were you with today?'

'Another student called Ryan.'

'Was he taking anything?'

I think back to Ryan's bleary eyes and agitated manner. I thought he was just drunk, but ... 'Maybe,' I admit. 'It's possible.'

'And could you have taken something by mistake?'

Then it hits me. The Coca Cola. In the toilets. He opened my drink for me. It was such a strange thing for him to do. So unlike him to do something thoughtful.

'Maybe he put something in my drink,' I say.

Trinity nods. 'Sounds like the most likely explanation.'

Chapter 34

A few hours later, I'm eating pepperoni pizza and watching *Shakespeare in Love* on the flat screen TV. When the pizza is finished, I start on a tub of cookies and cream ice cream. Trinity brought me three flavours, just to make sure she picked one I liked. She needn't have worried. I like all ice cream.

A few specialists have come to see me, checked my temperature and asked me questions. But otherwise, I've been on my own.

I have to admit, hospital or not, I'm having a good time, except for the aching feeling I have when I think of Marc. Aside from wanting to see him, I'm embarrassed he might think I took drugs with Ryan.

A tall shadow falls over the glazed door, and my spoon pauses over a square of frozen cookie.

The door opens and my throat goes tight.

It's Marc.

'Sophia.' He closes the door behind him. 'How are you feeling?' He's wearing his usual black, fitted suit and black shirt, the top button undone. I'd never thought about it before, but I've never seen him wear a tie. I notice the bumps of his sharp collar bone, and the round muscles of his shoulders under his suit jacket.

His brown hair is loose, as usual, with a wave falling across his forehead.

'Much better,' I breathe, putting the ice cream on the side table, the spoon clattering inelegantly.

Marc picks up the doctor's board by my bed and scans the medical data. 'Good. You've had all the tests. Excellent.'

I smile. 'I looked at that board too. It made no sense to me at all.'

Marc frowns. 'I've been in a few hospitals in my time. And I have a good memory. I made it my business to learn all I could.'

'Oh?' It feels strange to think of him hurt. Vulnerable. 'You've been in hospital?' I think of his martial arts movies, and wonder if he was injured doing stunts.

'Not me,' Marc says, absently. 'My sister.'

I want to ask him more, but I sense he'll close down, so instead I say, 'Thanks so much for everything you've done for me. But I want to pay for all this -'

Marc holds up a hand. 'Don't be ridiculous. I want to take care of you.'

'I don't want any favouritism,' I say. 'Just because we've ... things have happened, doesn't mean I should get any special treatment.'

Marc raises an eyebrow. 'You think this is special treatment?'

'Isn't it?'

'I'd do this for any of my pupils,' says Marc, the skin around his blue eyes tightening. 'And I'm a little offended you'd think I wouldn't.'

'Oh. Sorry.' I swallow ice cream that has suddenly become a bit too sickly. That put me in my place. I'm not so special after all.

'You look much better,' says Marc. 'I was worried about you. When I heard you were in hospital – I'm furious with myself for letting this happen.'

'You didn't let anything happen,' I say. 'It was an accident.'

'An accident that could have been avoided.'

'You believe I didn't take drugs on purpose, don't you?' I say.

Marc nods.

'I think I know what happened,' I say tentatively.

Marc holds up his hand. 'I know, too,' he says. 'Your friend Ryan spiked your drink with what he thought was cocaine.'

'How do you know that?' I say, my mouth falling open.

'I spoke with Ryan earlier. He admitted everything. People don't tend to lie to me.'

'For the record,' I say. 'He's not my friend.'

'I guessed that,' says Marc. 'But I think he'd like to be. From what he told me, I think he'd like to be more than your friend.'

'What?' I shake my head. 'Not Ryan. He hates me. He and Cecile both do.'

'Some people just find it hard to express themselves when they feel something very strongly,' says Marc. 'He's been captivated by you from the first moment he saw you. Just like I have.'

My stomach flips at that last comment. 'But he's so ... rude. And mean.'

'Like I said. Some people have a hard time expressing themselves.' Marc turns the television off and sits on the bed. My stomach buzzes just to have him near me. 'The doctors have given you the all clear, but I think it's best you stay overnight. Just in case. You can leave tomorrow morning. Sunday,' he adds softly. 'In time for your class on Monday morning.'

I swallow, remembering what he said about punishing me. 'What's going to happen on Monday?'

'You'll have to wait and see.'

'Will you punish me for this, too? For ending up in hospital?'

Marc shakes his head. 'Sophia, this isn't your fault.'

He gets up and locks the door.

Chapter 35

'What are you doing?' I say. 'What if the nurse needs to come in?'

'She won't,' says Marc. 'I've told all the medical staff not to disturb you while I'm visiting.'

'Won't the newspapers have something to say about that?' I ask.

'One of the joys of a private facility,' Marc says, 'is that money buys you confidentiality, and they wouldn't dream of selling anything to the press here. The only story the press have is that I visited you in the other hospital. And they can make of that what they like – it proves nothing more than I care about my students. Which I do.'

Carefully, he peels the crisp, white sheet from my body and nods in approval when he sees I'm wearing the sweat clothes he bought me.

'I want you to get to know your own body better,' he says, sliding off the sweat pants. I nod stupidly, watching the way his jaw clenches as he runs a hand down my thigh. 'Do you masturbate?'

'No,' I lie. Why can't I ever answer honestly to that question?

He raises an eyebrow. 'Don't lie to me, Sophia. I'm an actor too, remember?'

I blush. 'Okay. Sometimes I do.'

'I thought so. I'd planned not to touch you until Monday, but seeing you here ...'

He slides off my panties and throws them to the floor. I see the shape growing in his trousers, and I can't help but stare. He spreads my legs apart and takes out his iPhone.

'What are you doing?' I ask.

'Taking photographs of my star pupil,' he says, directing the phone between my legs, and snapping a few shots. The flash lights everything, and I feel more naked than I've ever felt in my life. 'I'll use them later, for my own amusement.'

'Oh.' The idea both terrifies and thrills me. The fact that Marc Blackwell could want pictures of me makes me feel amazing. But on the other hand, having him able to see naked parts of me up close is terrifying.

'Trust me,' Marc whispers, running a hand up and down my thigh. 'I'll keep them totally safe. Completely protected. You have my word. You do trust me, don't you?'

'You know I do,' I say. The way he's cared for me has been amazing. And it's more than that ... despite who he is, and how awkward I feel around him sometimes, there's something between us that's the same. Our bodies speak the same language, even though his words sometimes scare me.

'I wanted to ask you something,' I say. 'About a newspaper article I saw a few days ago.'

Chapter 36

'Ah ha,' says Marc. 'So you're listening to tabloid gossip now? Don't believe everything you read, Sophia.' He looks at his phone, using his finger to flick through pictures. 'Very nice. Very nice indeed. A model pupil in more ways than one.'

'The paper said something about your sex life,' I say. 'Something about allegations ...'

'Yes,' says Marc. 'Let's just say that newspapers have a way of twisting the truth.'

'So there's no truth in it?'

Marc puts his phone down. 'The latest set of allegations? It was a set up. For money. Okay? I should have known better, but when the scenario presented itself, I ... I couldn't help myself.'

'You couldn't help yourself? What scenario?'

Marc looks away from me. 'That didn't come out right. Of course I could have helped myself. But ... I didn't that day. It's not like with you. I was in control. It was all my choice, the whole way through.'

'What happened?'

'I'd been playing a very tough role that day. The woman in question had a minor role in the movie we were making, and in the bar at the end of the night she told me she'd been a bad girl and wanted me to spank her. So I did. I guess she somehow knew I like to be in charge and set me up. All that happened months ago, before I met you.'

I feel a sliver of something unpleasant. Jealousy. I don't like the thought of him with another woman.

And spanking her ... *Good god, Sophia, what have you got yourself into? Don't fall in love with a movie star who likes to be in charge and spank people. It can only ever end in tears.*

'Touch yourself,' says Marc, holding up his iPhone.

'Marc -'

'That's an order.'

What is it about Marc that makes being told what to do so sexy? I put my hand between my legs.

'Hot,' he nods.

He moves the iPhone closer. 'Very hot. Put your fingers inside yourself.'

I reach my other hand down and do as he says.

'You look beautiful,' he breathes, moving the iPhone around to get the best angle. 'Keep going. I want to film you come.'

Suddenly, embarrassment takes over. 'I can't,' I say. 'I'll feel stupid with you filming.'

'Count this as another lesson,' says Marc. 'Getting comfortable with your body being on show. The more comfortable you are, the more sexual enjoyment you'll get. And the better actress you'll be.'

'Okay.' I have to admit, it is kind of hot having him film me. I begin moving my hands again, and he slides his fingers up my thigh. Then he pushes my top up, still filming with his free hand, and runs his fingers over my bra. Goose bumps stand out on my arms, and he smiles. Then his fingers reach my neck and chin, and he slides a thumb into my mouth.

'Suck it,' he says, filming my face. I'm still moving my hands, and having his thumb going in and out of my mouth feels really good.

The warm feelings are building up, and the more he slides his thumb in and out of my mouth, the better I feel.

'Mmm,' I mumble.

He films back down between my legs, and I notice a large swelling in his trousers.

This is really turning him on.

I reach towards him, but he moves back so I can't touch him. 'No, Sophia. This is about you.'

He pushes his thumb further into my mouth.

I suck harder, licking around the edges, and pulling it further in.

He groans then, and I try to touch him, but he's too quick for me. He snatches his thumb back, then puts a hand onto my breast, pushing me into the mattress. His jaw has tightened, and he's looking at me so fiercely that I almost feel frightened.

'Keep moving your hand,' he says, and I can hear his voice is strained. He's fighting to stay calm. To stay in control.

He pushes my legs open with his free hand, and inserts two fingers inside me, pushing hard so my body moves up the bed.

I can't help myself. Warmth travels up from between my legs, up my navel and down my thighs, and I shout his name.

'Marc, oh Marc.'

He films the whole thing, and I love it. It feels so good being at the centre of his camera lens. It's only when the wave of pleasure has passed that I come to my senses, and realise there's now film footage of me having an orgasm.

'I feel embarrassed you have that footage of me,' I tell Marc, sinking back into the bed.

'Do you want me to get rid of it?' Marc asks.

'Um ...' I sort of like the idea that he'd want to watch me.

Marc grins. 'Thought not. I'm glad. Me having this footage will help you let go of your inhibitions.'

'I don't think I'm all that inhibited.'

Marc laughs. 'You're joking? You're inhibited, trust me.'

'Next to you, maybe.'

'Oh, I have my own inhibitions. When it comes to real intimacy ...' He puts his face by mine, and strokes my cheek. 'I'll take good care of this, Sophia. And if you ever want me to delete it, I will. Now. Give me your phone number.'

'Why?' I ask.

'After today's little escapade, I want to make sure I can always get in touch with you.'

I don't like that reply, but I do like the idea of him having my number, so I read off the digits. He enters them into his phone, and I feel a swell of excitement at the thought of him calling.

He lays the sheet over me. 'Monday,' he says.

Chapter 37

I leave the hospital on Sunday morning feeling great. For breakfast, I have a delicious hospital breakfast of strawberry smoothie, toasted pumpkin seed porridge and freshly baked rye bread with unsalted butter.

Trinity asks if I need a taxi to get back to campus, but I tell her I'd rather walk and explore London. She gives me a fold-up map, and I set off into the sunshine.

I soon find myself walking through Sloane Square, past designer clothes shops and red-brick apartments. There are all sorts of delicious-looking cafes and restaurants dotted around, and I stop for a hot chocolate at an Italian deli, taking a table on the street so I can watch London life go by.

I take out my phone and see five missed calls from Jen. I call her back, and am rewarded with her screeching down the phone.

'Sopheeee!'

'I think you just deafened me.'

'Where are you?' Jen asks. 'I'm on your campus. I came down for a surprise visit, but you're not here. Are you being a dirty stop out?'

You have no idea.

'I'm just in West London,' I say. 'Near Sloane Square. At somewhere called Antonio's.'

'Will they mind me parking at your college if you're not there?' Jen asks.

'I doubt it,' I say.

'Then stay where you are – I'm coming to meet you.' The line goes dead.

Half an hour later, I'm about to order another hot chocolate when Jen comes bounding up to the table. She throws her arms around me, and I hug her back.

'She'll have a cappuccino,' I tell the waiter, 'no chocolate on top.'

'And she'll have another hot chocolate,' Jen tells the waiter. 'As much whipped cream as you like – she thinks she's too skinny.'

We grin at each other.

'Well?' says Jen. 'What are you doing in this part of London so early? Did you stay out with someone last night?' She leans closer.

I look at my hot chocolate. 'Yes and no,' I say. 'I was in hospital.'

'In hospital?' Jen's hand shoots to her mouth. 'Oh my god, Soph. What happened? Why didn't you call me?'

'It was all so quick,' I say. 'It was nothing serious, in the end. Ryan put something in my drink, and it gave me a funny turn.'

'He did *what*?' When Jen gets angry, she gets really angry. 'He put something in your drink? Wait until I get a hold of him.'

'He's just an idiot, Jen, don't worry about it.'

'I am worried,' says Jen. 'You're always seeing the best in people. Too much, so. That horrible stepmother of yours ... Anyway. He's not going to get away with this.'

'I don't think he has,' I say. 'Marc Blackwell had a word with him. I imagine he's suitably chastised.'

'Wow.' Jen flicks her blonde hair from shoulder to shoulder. 'Marc Blackwell stepped in and talked to him? What a great guy. Hey – speaking of which, you'll never guess what I found out on the PR grapevine.'

'What?'

Jen leans closer. 'That sexual scandal about Marc Blackwell? Ropes, paddles and all of that? Well, apparently he's into a bit of spanking too.'

I nod.

'Do you think it's true?'

'I'm positive it's true,' I say.

'How come?'

Jen's cappuccino arrives, and I don't answer for a moment, waiting for the waiter to leave.

Then I whisper, 'Because he told me.'

'He told you?'

'When I was in hospital, he came to see me,' I say. 'And he had me transferred to a private place in West London. He got me my own nurse. And he came to visit me there.'

Jen's eyes grow wider as she picks up her cappuccino.

'And ... we've ... things have happened between us.'

Jen puts her cappuccino back on its saucer with a clatter. 'Something happened *between you and Marc Blackwell*!'

'Shssh!' I look around. 'Yes. Something is ... well, happening I guess.'

'I want to know *everything*,' Jen leans closer.

'It's ... complicated,' I say. '*He's* complicated.'

'I'll bet. What with the spanking and everything. Has he done that to you?'

I shake my head. 'But I think he wants to.'

'And how do you feel about that?'

'It's hard to know what to feel. This is all so new for me – all of this. I've never felt this way about anybody, but then there's all this weird stuff that goes with it. I mean, you know me. I'm hardly experienced in ... well, anything. What if I can't handle what he wants to do?'

'Then just say no.'

'It's not that simple. He tells me to do something, and I want to do it.'

'Then what's the problem?'

'What if he only likes me because I'm his pupil? What if that's his thing? I mean, he's a good person, before you say it. He knows it's not right for the lecturer to be doing anything with a student.'

'And what have you done, exactly?' Jen asks.

'A few things,' I say. 'But we haven't had sex yet.'

Jen shakes her head. 'Wow. Well, I'll try and find out as much as possible about him through my agency. Forewarned is forearmed.'

'Thanks Jen.'

'I know he's hot,' she says. 'But ... well, morally speaking he shouldn't be messing around with his students.'

'I know,' I say. 'But he didn't want to. He tried to walk away. He'd leave the college if I let him. It's me. I can't bear the thought of walking away from him. Just being near him feels amazing.'

'I bet it does.'

'But I know it isn't right, the way things are happening. Or at least, it's not *normal*.'

'Soph. You worry too much. If you've got something going with Marc Blackwell, just enjoy it for what it is. And you can look back when you're happily married to some nice, normal guy and think, I had a fling with that hot actor when I was younger.'

'But what if I want it to be more than that?'

'Ah.' Jen takes a sip of cappuccino. 'Well, that's your problem. Look, he's obviously got commitment issues. No long-term girlfriend. Likes to be in control. Wants everything on his terms. Soph, you can't expect to have a usual sort of relationship with a man like that. Just enjoy it for what it is, and try not to get too hurt when it ends.'

'You're right,' I say. 'I know you're right. But then ... if it's going to end, maybe I should get out now before I get hurt.'

'Maybe you should,' says Jen. 'But you're only human. And I know you. You come across all softly, softly, but you've got a steel hand under that velvet glove. When you want something, you don't care what anyone tells you. And you want him, right?

I smile at her. 'I think we both know the answer to that.'

She nods. 'So. Enjoy it right now, and prepare yourself for heartbreak down the line. That's life. You can cope with heartbreak. It won't kill you.'

'I don't know about that.'

'So, what are we going to do today?' asks Jen.

'I could show you around the campus,' I say. 'Introduce you to the other students.'

'For a creative person, you can be very unimaginative,' says Jen. 'We're in the middle of London. There are a billion things to do. I've got a guidebook and ringed the things we should try out. Are you ready? It's going to be fun!'

Jen and I have a great day. We visit Harrods, and buy picnic food to eat in Regent's Park. A few tough, city squirrels try to steal our food, and we end up running away, screaming and laughing.

We see a movie in Leicester Square, and finish our popcorn walking around in the sunshine, watching the tourists and Londoners shop in Covent Garden.

Predictably, Jen has armfuls of shopping by the end of the day, and we head back to campus to order a takeaway in my bedroom.

Jen wants to find Ryan and slap him around the face, but I persuade her not to.

I invite Tom and Tanya over, and all four of us eat Chinese food, drink red wine and watch the sun set over the campus. We watch the *Star Wars* movies and Jen asks Tom and Tanya endless questions about their backgrounds.

Tom tells us he's from London originally, so knows the city like the back of his hand. He went to a London boarding school from a very young age. At weekends, he and his friends visited the theatre and he always did amateur dramatics in his spare time. His parents are actually a Lord and Lady, I'm surprised to hear. It's true that Tom is well spoken, but he's really down to earth.

Tanya tells us her parents are divorced, and she spent her teenage years in a custody battle between the two of them. She ended up living with her mum, falling out with her, then moving in with her dad when she was at college.

She's been to university, but quit because she took the wrong course. She's always loved drama, but her dad wanted her to be a lawyer. Two years of law told her that's not what she wanted, and now she's over the moon to be studying at Ivy College.

Tanya and Tom ask me what happened on Saturday, and I tell them I had a funny turn and ended up in A&E. Jen glares at me, willing me to tell them about Ryan, but I feel so sorry for him. Marc has already confronted him, after all.

We're having a great time, but my thoughts keep drifting to Marc. I think of him and, more specifically, his iPhone and the pictures and film footage of me.

Just as we put on *Return of the Jedi*, my phone rings, showing a number I've never seen before.

Chapter 38

My heart begins to pound.

'Back in a sec,' I mutter, running out to the balcony. I take the call.

'Hello?'

'You're not alone.' It's Marc's voice. My stomach turns over.

'No, I'm not. How did you know that?'

'Because I'm on campus, watching your window.' I look over the dark grounds, but I don't see anyone.

'I can't see you,' I reply.

'I can see you right now on your balcony. And I see your friends in the background. I wish you were alone.'

'You do?' I feel myself smile.

'Yes. But right now, I just wanted you to know that I'm watching over you. And. I've been watching you all day on my phone. Ve-ry nice. Very nice indeed.'

'Thanks,' I stammer.

'I'd like to take more footage of you. Perhaps tomorrow.'

I swallow tightly. 'Marc, I'm nervous about tomorrow. I don't know what you mean about -'

'I want you to arrive for class twenty minutes early,' he says. 'Your class tomorrow will be different from everyone else's. Don't wear any underwear.'

With that, the line goes dead.

The next morning, my room smells like takeaway and my living area is a mess. Empty wine bottles and glasses, takeaway containers ... I wish I'd accepted everyone's offer to help clear up last night.

I shower, wash up and bag rubbish. As I head down to the recycling area in the sweatpants and t-shirt Marc bought me, I see Ryan loitering in the reception area by the post boxes.

'Hello,' I say coldly. 'What are you doing up so early?'

'Sophia ...' He looks startled. 'I have to say sorry to you. I never thought anything like that would happen. I just wanted you to lighten up and have fun with me.'

I think of what Marc said, about Ryan liking me.

'Just don't ever do anything like that to anyone again,' I say.

'Mr Blackwell has already read me the riot act.'

'He told me you ... have feelings for me,' I say softly.

'What does it matter?' Ryan snaps. 'You're already goo goo over Mr Blackwell, just like every other girl on the course.'

'I honestly thought you hated me,' I say.

Ryan laughs. 'Hated you? I do in a way. It's hard, seeing someone you like and not being able to have you.'

'I guess it is,' I say.

Chapter 39

When I return to my room, there's a text message waiting. I catch my breath when I see it's from Marc.

Don't forget. No underwear.

I think over the message, and what Marc said on the phone last night. All this stuff about punishment and telling me what to do. When Marc tells me to do something, it's hot. And him asking me to wear no underwear to class is hot. But that doesn't mean I'm going to do it. Or anything else he asks me to.

I take off the sweatpants and t-shirt, and examine myself in the bathroom mirror. I have a skinny, pale body, no question about that. Not very womanly. A small waist, which is nice, and a weird gap between my thighs, which is not so nice.

My breasts are okay. Nothing special. Same with my bottom, although boyfriends have always complimented me on it. So. What does he see in me? Youth? We're only a few years apart in age. The whole pupil, teacher thing? Perhaps. But there are plenty of pupils he could have chosen, many of whom are far more beautiful and experienced.

Underwear or not? I take off my underwear and catch a glimpse of my naked body. I'm very natural looking. Jen is always going on about bikini lines, but I can't bear to tear hair out of myself, and I kind of like everything as it should be.

Dressing in jeans and an off-the-shoulder silk top, I realise I've chosen badly. The jeans cut into me, and the silk top shows my breasts a little too clearly. I choose a thick, sequinned blue jumper instead, and team it with leggings and ankle boots. No one can see anything that way, and I'm comfortable.

I check my watch and, realising it's nearly half an hour before class, I grab my bag and head towards the lecture theatre.

Marc is waiting for me when I arrive, perched on a desk wearing a pin-striped suit. No tie, as usual, and his top button undone. His hair has been combed down, and looks soft and touchable. He raises an eyebrow when I appear in the doorway.

'Glad to see you on time. Underwear?'

'No,' I squeak, feeling very exposed.

'You're familiar with the stationery cupboard,' he says, walking to the cupboard and opening the door. I watch his long fingers turn the handle, and the strong tendons stand out on his hands.

'You know I am. Marc, about this punishment. There are certain things -'

'You're about to get more familiar with it,' says Marc. 'In you go.'

I walk into the cupboard, but I'm prepared to tell him where to go if he suggests doing something I don't like.

Inside the stationery cupboard, I see something that makes me stop dead. There are two small metal hoops screwed into one of the shelves above the desk. A length of rope runs through them.

On the desk sits a bamboo cane – the old-fashioned kind you see in Victorian classrooms. I stare at the little joins along its length.

'What's that for?' I ask.

'You'll speak when you're spoken to,' says Marc. He turns me around so my back is against his chest.

'Marc -'

'Trust me, Sophia,' Marc whispers, shutting the cupboard door. 'You can stop any time. Just tell me. But right now, I think you're going to enjoy this. What I'm teaching you today is self control. You'll learn to control yourself. You'll learn that sometimes you can't come until I tell you to.'

He pushes me forwards until I'm pressed against the desk, and ties my hands in front of me with the rope. Then he pulls the rope tight, and my hands shoot into the air.

'Oh!' I say in surprise, and Marc ties the rope into a complicated knot. 'Wait. I'm not sure I like this.'

'If you want to be released,' he says, 'just pull this part of the rope, and the knot will undo. This is one hundred percent consensual. I know you want this. I hope you're able to admit you want me to keep you in line.'

Do I? It really depends on what the punishment is. But I'm glad I can pull the rope down.

Marc rubs his palm around my buttocks, and moves his lips to my ear. 'This is what happens when you disobey your teacher,' he says. 'Discipline is good for us. It makes us strong.'

He pulls my leggings halfway down my thighs, and carries on caressing my buttocks with his hand.

'Good girl. No underwear.'

He pushes up my jumper and ties a knot in it so my buttocks are exposed.

'You're about to learn how pleasurable it can be to be disciplined,' he murmurs, picking up the cane.

He tests its springiness in his hands, then swishes it back and forth and my stomach goes weak.

'Don't hurt me,' I say.

He rubs it back and forth over my buttocks, and I feel its smoothness, and the little bumps of its joins. It's torturous, not knowing if he's going to whack me with it, and I think he knows it.

'Are you going to hit me?' I ask.

'Do you want me to?' He pulls the cane back.

'Maybe,' I admit, feeling hot between my legs. 'But not hard.'

He brings the cane towards me, but stops an inch before my buttocks.

'Oh,' I moan, leaning into the ropes.

He puts the cane down. 'Right now, I have a class to teach. You'll wait here until I'm ready to deal with you.'

'You're going to leave me here?' I ask.

'I told you. You'll wait here until I'm ready for you.'

'But the class will arrive.'

'Then you'd better be quiet.'

With that he leaves the room, slamming the door behind him.

Moments later, I hear pupils arriving and taking their seats. I can't hear what anyone is saying, but I can hear the low hum of conversation.

Against it, Marc's deep voice resonates in my stomach. I feel the nakedness of my backside and ache for him to come back and touch me. How long does he plan to leave me here?

The conversation lowers to silence, and I hear Marc talking to the class. This is torture. I want him to touch me so badly, and – I have to admit it – use the cane like he threatened. I see it there beside me and feel so turned on. But now I'll have to wait until class is finished. Or will he leave me here even longer? I won't stay if he does.

Suddenly, I hear a creak of hinges and see the door handle turning.

Oh my god.

I see Marc in the doorway. No one from class could see me unless they walked right into the cupboard.

Marc closes the door behind him.

Chapter 40

'What are you doing?' I whisper. 'The whole class is out there.'

'Be quiet.' He picks up the cane. Holding it high in the air, he smacks it on my buttocks. There's a tiny 'thack' sound, but not loud enough to be heard outside.

I gasp, and bite my teeth together to stop from crying out – not from pain, but from pleasure. The line where the cane hit tingles, and my stomach turns over and over. I want him to do it again. So badly. And he does. Once. Twice. Three times. I hear a light swoosh as the cane flies through the air, and my knees go weak.

Marc puts his hand between my legs and rubs back and forth, then lets his fingers slip inside me and out again.

'Don't do that,' I beg. 'Please. I can't bear it.'

'This is what you get for misbehaving,' Marc whispers. 'Open your legs,' he instructs, standing back and sliding the cane between my thighs.

'But the class are outside,' I whisper.

'Do as you're told.'

I move my feet apart.

'Good girl. Now bend over the desk.'

Oh god. His words are making me crazy. I bend forwards, my wrists pulling against the ropes.

He slides the cane inside me, and moves it back and forth.

Oh no. I can't make a sound. This is torture.

Then he puts the cane on the desk with a clatter, and walks out of the room, banging the door closed behind him.

I hear Marc talking to the class, and feel my body ache for him. I hear the zip of the projection unit, and then the drone of a movie being played.

The cupboard door opens again, and Marc slams it closed and strides towards me.

'Are you sorry for misbehaving?' he asks.

'I didn't misbehave,' I say.

He rubs my buttocks again with the flat of his palm.

Oh that feels so good.

'Say you're sorry, or I won't fuck you,' he says.

'You'd do that with the whole class outside?' I whisper.

'Most certainly I would,' he says. 'And you won't make a sound the whole time. An excellent lesson in self control, don't you think? So. If you want me to fuck you, say you're sorry.'

'I'm sorry.' The words spill out of my mouth.

I see a smile playing on his lips. 'So you want me to fuck you?'

'Yes,' I stammer.

'What's the magic word?'

'Please,' I say.

'Good girl. Spread your legs again.'

I do, and gasp as I feel him against me, hardness against my buttocks.

He slides two long fingers inside, and I want to cry out with the pleasure of it, but I can't and it's agony.

With his hand, he rocks me silently back and forth, and it's so hard not to make a sound. Again and again, he rocks me back and forth, but then suddenly he withdraws.

'Don't stop,' I beg. 'Please don't stop.'

I hear him breathing heavily. He paces around for a few seconds, then walks out of the room, closing the door behind him.

Now I see what he means about punishment. Having him turn me on like this, but not being able to have him, is utter torture. And I can't leave until the class finishes.

I hear Marc's low voice talking to the class, and I can't bear it. I almost pull the rope to set myself free, but where would I go?

I stand and wait, thinking maybe Marc has a point about self control. He obviously has amazing self control, being able to turn himself on and off like that – enough to walk outside and take a class. And he's the most amazing actor I've ever seen. I mean, he just becomes the roles.

I've never felt this way about anyone before, and suddenly it strikes me as unfair that I have to fall so badly for someone like Marc. But maybe that's exactly why I've fallen so hard. Because Marc isn't like the other people I've dated. He's in charge, and it makes me stronger. Maybe he's what I need.

After an agonising wait, I finally hear the clatter of feet on the floor, conversation and papers shuffled and stuffed into bags. I bet Tom and Tanya are wondering where I am. They'd never guess in a million years that I'm a door away, my buttocks exposed, tied to a shelf and waiting for the teacher to come and fuck me.

Hurry up and leave, I think. God this is torture.

When silence falls, I hear the creak of the door handle and turn to see Marc.

'Well, Sophia. I hope you've learned an interesting lesson today.'

'I have,' I say.

'And it was good for you, wasn't it?'

'It felt good,' I murmur, ever the obedient pupil. 'But at times it was torture.'

'Light and dark.' He picks up the cane, and bends it between his fingertips. 'You've been silent when you had to be, but can you be silent when you don't have to be?'

'What do you mean?' I ask.

'I'm going to fuck you now,' he says, 'and I want absolute silence, or I'll stop. Do you understand?'

'What? Honestly, Marc – I'm not sure I can.'

'Put this in your mouth.' He holds the cane length ways in front of my mouth. 'Do as you're told. Open your mouth.'

I do, and he puts the cane between my teeth.

'Good girl. Now bite down. I like you this way.' He takes out his iPhone and snaps three pictures: one from behind and one from each side.

'Open your legs up for teacher, there's a good girl.' He doesn't wait for me to move my feet this time, he just forces my legs apart with his hands and pushes himself between my thighs. 'Oh God, do you know how hard it is to be controlled around you?'

I feel hardness pushing against me and I want to moan, but I bite the cane instead.

'Knowing you were in here, ready and waiting for me. I nearly ripped open the door and fucked you with everyone listening,' says Marc. 'I thought I could control myself, but it's dangerous with you. You're testing my limits.'

He pushes himself a little inside me.

Oh god. It feels so good.

I want to moan. I want to cry out. But I can't.

His hand slides around the front of me as he pushes himself further and further.

He's so big that everything feels tight, full. He inches in further, and I'm almost too full, but it feels good too. He keeps me just on the threshold of pain. Bearable.

The further he gets inside, the more difficult it is to stay silent. I notice his hand rubbing too, and warmth builds.

I bite into the cane.

When he begins to move back and forth, pushing himself further inside with every stroke, I know I'm leaving teeth marks on the wood.

Oh. Oh.

Back and forth he moves, further and further inside. I feel him almost in my stomach at times, but the fullness is unbelievably good. His rhythm gets faster, and I feel his hard breathing on my neck.

I move forwards to stop him going in too far and causing me pain, but he responds by grabbing my buttocks and pulling himself completely inside of me.

Pleasure and pain mix together, and I feel an orgasm overtake me.

Marc pulls me too him, completely filling me up.

I fall into the ropes, breathing hard, feeling pleasure all over.

Marc pulls out, takes me carefully in his arms and unties the ropes, then helps me into my clothing.

I glance down and see he's wearing a green condom that seems stretched to bursting point.

Wow. That thing was inside of me? Amazing. I'd never have thought it could fit.

Then something else occurs to me.

'Didn't you come?' I ask.

He shakes his head.

'Why not?' *Didn't you want to? Was I too disappointing?*

'I like to stay in charge,' he says. 'It wouldn't do to lose control in front of you. I'm teaching you about pleasure. I'll take my own later.'

'How?' I ask, thinking about the woman he spoke of in the hospital. 'With another woman?' I cringe as I say the words. *Another woman. It's not like you're his girlfriend ...*

Marc smiles. 'Would it bother you if it was?'

'Yes.' I look at my fingernails. They've always been bitten, but they're so much worse since this weekend. I realise how stupid I'm being. I've been swept along by this man, but everything is on his terms. 'Yes. It bothers me. And it bothers me you didn't come.'

'Why?' Marc asks.

'I suppose it's the control thing. You can control me. How I'm feeling. But you're not allowing me to have an effect on you.'

'Oh believe me,' says Marc, taking off his suit jacket and throwing it on the desk. 'You're having an effect on me.'

'But you're not letting me in,' I say. 'You're not letting me close to you.'

Marc stares at the plays lined up along the shelves. 'I've let you closer than anyone has ever been.'

Chapter 41

'Really?' I ask.

Marc nods. He looks at his knuckles, and I see they're criss-crossed with scars. I guess he must have got them from the boxing movies he starred in. Just like his martial arts, I heard Marc did serious boxing training for his movies, and even fought a few competitive fights off set.

'It doesn't feel like you're letting me close at all.'

'I am. For me I am.'

'What does that mean?'

'Everyone else, I've just had fun with, in my own fucked up way. But with you ... it's something more. That first time I saw you perform ... bringing light to a character that was so dark. That night, I couldn't sleep. It was like you'd got inside me.'

'Got inside you?'

Marc nods. 'When I was ten, I caught pneumonia. My father wouldn't let me tell anyone I had it, because it would have meant not acting, and I needed to earn money for him and my sister. So for a week, I worked on this movie about a runaway kid in London. But I was delirious half the time.

'Coughing up blood, not able to focus. I couldn't for the life of me remember the script, and I *always* remember the script. It was like something had gotten into my brain and shut it down, and all I was left with were feelings. And you know what? I gave the performance of my life. People still talk about that movie.'

'What are you saying?' I ask.

'I'm saying that you've got inside me, and I'm not myself. I can't concentrate.'

'Thanks for the pneumonia analogy.'

Marc smiles. 'You've got closer to me than anyone. Your pleasure is so much more important to me than my own.'

I breathe out, wishing I had the courage to ask him again about other women. But something inside tells me I won't like the answer.

Marc puts his hands on either side of my face, and brings me closer. Our eyes meet, and my stomach flips over. I can't breathe. I see his long, handsome nose and the points of his red lips, and I know he's taking in every aspect of my face too. This man – this handsome Hollywood star – says I've got inside of him.

'I'm looking forward to our next lesson,' he whispers. 'You've had a lesson in inhibition. And self discipline. Now I think it's time to stretch your boundaries. To have you try things you'd never dream of.'

I stare at him. 'You think I've dreamed of being tied up in a stationery cupboard?'

He nods. 'If you'd used your imagination, I'm sure you could have dreamed it up, in the right circumstances. Some nice student boyfriend. A few drinks. He finds a bit of rope and wants to play around.'

'So what wouldn't I dream of doing?'

'That's what we're going to find out,' says Marc. 'But not on campus.'

'Where?' I ask.

'My townhouse. Tonight. We'll have dinner. And we'll get to know each other a lot better.'

And here I was thinking we knew each other pretty well.

'Your town house? Are you sure?' Going to his home for dinner – it sounds almost too normal.

Marc nods. 'There are no lectures tomorrow. It's a study day. So you'll have plenty of time to recover.'

'What time tonight?' I ask, knowing I sound breathless. 'And – how am I going to get there without anyone seeing me. The press ...'

Marc checks his watch. 'I'll let you know. In the meantime, don't study too hard.'

'I have a class with Denise Crompton now,' I say. 'Singing. It's a nice class. She doesn't work us half as hard as you do.' I raise an eyebrow at him and smile.

He smiles back, and my insides melt.

'I love hearing you sing,' says Marc.

'What? When have you heard me sing?'

'In the woods.'

'The woods?' I go red. 'You were listening to me?'

'Go to your class.'

'How did you -'

'Go to your class, Sophia.'

Chapter 42

As usual, the class with Denise is great fun, but I can tell she has her eye on me. When the class finishes, she pulls me aside.

'Everything okay, my love?'

My expression tells her all she needs to know.

'It's a little stuffy in here, isn't it?' she announces. 'Let's go for a walk.'

We head out of the classroom, and towards the woodlands.

'I love it back here,' I say.

'I know you do,' says Denise. 'Marc tells me you come here every morning.'

'He told you that? How does he ... how does he even know that?'

'Oh, he likes to keep an eye on his students.' Denise takes a step back as a wood pigeon flaps up from a trail of ivy. 'Some of them more than others.'

'He's spoken to you about me?'

Denise nods. 'Often. More than he realises. Enough to tell me he's feeling something he doesn't quite know how to deal with. And perhaps you for him, if my intuition is on the money.'

I don't know what to say. Once again, I'm astonished by how perceptive Denise is.

'You're surprised I have you so figured out?' Denise raises one of her very thin, pencilled eyebrows. Her skin is soft and buttery in the afternoon sunshine. 'Don't be. If we all listened to our intuition more, we'd understand the world a lot better.'

'I wish I could understand Marc,' I say. 'I'm surprised he's spoken about me. Truly. I find him very, very ... complicated.'

'Oh, he's that alright,' says Denise. 'It's what makes him such a truly amazing actor. But he's been through some hardships to get there, just like your hardships make you a great actor, too.'

'I don't see myself as a great actor,' I say. 'I'm not of Marc's calibre.'

'Maybe not at twenty two, but by the time you're twenty seven I see no reason why not. You're better than Marc was at your age, and he started younger than you. He was bullied into it. Acting. Did he tell you that?'

'He told me a little about his father, earlier,' I say. 'But not much.'

Denise nods, and takes a sip of tea. 'Poor little lamb.'

I nearly choke on my tea. How could anyone think of Marc Blackwell that way? Commanding, intense, angry Marc Blackwell, a poor little lamb? Really? But then ... I think of how his voice grows soft sometimes, when he's expressing his concern for me. And the story he told me about pneumonia.

'It's strange to think of him that way,' I say, twiddling my hair. I shiver a little in my jumper and jeans – it's cold out here without a coat.

Denise nods. 'When I met him, he was so vulnerable. A little man, of course. All the way. Taking charge of his family. Earning money for them. Trying to shelter his sister from the worst of his father. But vulnerable.'

I think of the movie I saw when Marc was younger. He had looked more open, then. Less guarded. Perhaps more willing to let people in.

'His father was a monster,' Denise continues. 'An absolute monster. A failed actor, of course. Performed in all sorts of bad films and TV dramas, and insisted Marc perform from a young age. Too young an age.

'When I first met them, I was performing on Broadway. I know, I know. Broadway. You wouldn't think it now, but years ago I was quite something. Anyway. Marc was playing Oliver Twist and I was Nancy. He was such a dear little lad, but so serious. So afraid of his father. A boy that age should never have had such responsibility put on his shoulders.

'When his mother died, I took him under my wing. I loved having him as my surrogate son, and I gave his father a piece of my mind more than once. His father hit him. If he didn't win a part or perform perfectly. Horrible man. Repressed. Taking his rage out on his boy.

'When Marc was twelve, his father went to Egypt on a business venture and I offered to put Marc up for a few weeks. Those few weeks turned into months, and Marc and I had a wonderful time. I made sure he went to school every day, and insisted his evenings and weekends were free to do whatever he wanted.

'Often, he wanted to perform in plays. Well, that was fine. As long as it was his choice. Then his father came back and all hell broke loose. He said I'd been holding his boy back. Stopping him from fulfilling his ambition.

'I was offered a part back in London, and I asked if Marc wanted to come live with me in England. He did, but his father wouldn't allow it. Said LA was the place. So he kept Marc there, and at sixteen Marc left home and pursued his dream alone.

'By then, Marc was already well known for being an amazing young talent with the worst mood swings in the business.

'We still kept in touch. He'd ring me every Sunday, and tell me about the parts he was playing and the wonderful locations he was being flown to.

'Then he had this college built to help young talent, and to my amazement he offered me a lecturer's position. I love having him back in England. It's where he belongs. He grew up in England, you know. In London.

'When he came back here, he fell in love with it all over again. I think London reminds him of his mother. He buys property left, right and centre here – I think to feel grounded. To try and establish roots. That's why he bought this college at first, you know. Developers were going to tear it down, and he couldn't bear the thought of something that had been in one spot for so long being destroyed.'

'The more I learn about Marc,' I say, 'the more I realise what a hard life he's had.'

'But so have you,' says Denise.

'Not compared to ... no, I don't think I have. Not really.'

'Well.' Denise folds her fingers together. 'If my feelings are right, and you and Marc are growing closer. I don't condone it, but I don't disapprove either. Marc's a decent man. Responsible. You're both consenting adults. What I will say is, are you happy having a relationship that, right now, is kept hidden? Do you really want that for yourself?'

I shake my head, and feel tears sliding down my face. 'No,' I whisper. 'But it doesn't seem as though I have any other choice. I don't want Marc to stop being a teacher here. He offered, but I couldn't live with myself if the whole class lost him because of me.

'No one would plan a relationship like this. In fact, I wouldn't even call it a relationship. I don't know what it is. But I'm in the middle of it, and there's no turning back. Not without venturing further in. Without getting myself completely caught up in him, and then probably completely hurt.'

'It sounds like you're already completely caught up with him,' says Denise.

'Yes,' I say. 'I am.'

'You've got some difficult choices to make,' says Denise, getting up and putting her arms around me. She smells of soap and camomile tea. 'You're a grown woman, so it's up to you to decide. But just so you know, I'll always be here if you need me.'

'Thank you,' I say, smiling through tears. 'Thank you so much.'

Chapter 43

When I leave Denise's classroom, I feel happier. Lighter. But I'm also thinking very hard about what she said, particularly the part about keeping things hidden.

As I head outside, into the grounds, I find Tom and Tanya waiting for me.

'Are you okay, Soph?' Tom asks. 'We were worried you were in trouble with the teacher.' His wheelchair is balanced half on the path and half on a grassy verge, so I move him in case he tips over.

'No, it was fine,' I say. 'Honestly.'

'Jolly good. Well then. Are you all set for the theatre trip tomorrow?'

'The what?' I ask.

'To the Globe. College outing.'

'Really? A class trip so soon?'

'It was in our introductory paperwork,' says Tom, pulling a diary from his rucksack and thumbing through. 'Let me just double check. Ah! No, not tomorrow. The day after. In the afternoon. We're meeting on campus, and being driven there in the college minibus.'

'I've always wanted to see the Globe,' I say. 'That sounds great.' *But in the meantime, I have dinner with Marc Blackwell to contend with.*

'So what did you and Denise talk about?' Tanya asks.

I look from Tanya to Tom. They're both such good people. I hate lying to them. I think of what

Denise said about keeping secrets and not wanting that for myself.

'She wanted to talk about ... someone I'm seeing.'

'Someone you're seeing?' Tom takes a bag of Wotsits from his rucksack and rips them open. 'Cheesy crisp?'

'No thank you,' I say.

'You're seeing someone?' Tanya says. 'Who?'

'Just ... someone I shouldn't. Someone a little older than me.'

'An older man? Since when? I want to hear EVERYTHING!'

'What's he like in bed?' asks Tom, with a mischievous raise of his eyebrow.

I laugh. 'Honestly, I'm not all that sure. At least, about the bed part. I've only been in bed with him once.'

'Only once?' says Tom. 'What kind of sex are you having?'

'Tom!' Tanya glares at him. 'Just because you're obsessed, doesn't mean we all are. She may not even be having sex with him.' Tanya turns to me. 'Are you?'

'I don't know if you could call it sex. I mean, at least not in the usual way.'

Tom's eyes light up. 'Ho, ho! Sounds exciting. Tell us more.'

'It's ... unusual,' I admit. 'Weird kind of sex. Super hot, but weird sex. He takes charge of everything. So I haven't really got to touch him or do anything without his say so.'

'He sounds like a total sexist pig,' says Tanya.

'Each to their own, Tans,' says Tom. 'If Soph is up for it, who are we to judge?'

'I've never known anything like this before,' I say. 'I've never felt this way about anyone. But ... part of me thinks I should run away. It doesn't feel healthy.'

'Who is he?' asks Tanya. 'Do we know him?'

I pull in my bottom lip. 'It's ... I can't tell you who he is.'

'Why not? Is he married or something?' Tanya asks.

'Something like that. Let's just say it's sort of forbidden, us being together. We can't tell anyone what's happening.'

'I bet that makes everything all the more exciting, eh?' says Tom, leaning forward to slap my thigh.

I blush. 'Yes. It makes it super hot, actually. But ... it also means it's not a relationship. In a real relationship, you don't have to sneak around. And things are more equal. But with him, he's very firmly in charge. I know I should probably walk away, but it hurts to think of ending what we have. You know? I'm really falling for him.'

'Ditch him,' says Tanya, grabbing a handful of Tom's crisps. 'No man should be in control of you. The sooner you do it, the easier it'll be.'

'But I think, maybe if I could just get closer to him, get him to open up ...'

'They'll be other men,' says Tanya.

'Not like him,' I say. 'I've never met anyone like him before.' I feel so empty at the thought of ending things with Marc, I just can't bear it.

'I don't think I can walk away,' I whisper. 'I want more. And until I have it, I'll always be wondering.'

'That's how men like that operate,' says Tanya. 'He'll always leave you wanting more. Always. Walk away before it gets even harder.'

I nod, but Tom touches my arm lightly.

'Soph, love. Do you want the wheelchair guy's opinion?'

'Yes please,' I say.

'Do you know how many girlfriends I've had?' Tom asks.

I shake my head.

'None,' he says. 'I talk to girls online, and I visit disabled websites and have virtual relationships, but I've never had a real relationship. Not ever. And do you know what? I probably never will have.'

'Oh Tom,' I say. 'I'm so sorry. It's so tactless of -'

'No, no, no.' Tom waves my comment away. 'Don't give me the sympathy card. That's not what I'm asking for. What I'm saying is, I'd give anything in the world to be in your position. To be on the edge of love or lust or whatever it is you're feeling, and dive right in, no matter how hard I fall and how much it hurts. To have the opportunity to get my fingers burned. That's what I'd give anything for. Getting your fingers burned is what life is all about. So take every opportunity. Because one day, you might not have that chance. When you're old and ugly, who's going to want to sleep with you?'

'Thanks a lot,' I say, playfully slapping his leg.

'Ouch!' He mock winces. 'The nerve endings still work, you know. Anyway, that's my two-pennyworth. Throw yourself in at the deep end. I'm sure you won't actually drown. And even if it all goes horribly wrong, you'll come out stronger. Just whatever you do, don't get pregnant.'

I smile, and for the first time in days I feel my teeth showing when I do. I give him a big hug, squashing his Wotsits against his chest and knocking his hat to the floor.

'I guess that's the advice she was looking for,' says Tanya with a smile, picking up his hat.

Chapter 44

Dinner with Marc Blackwell. Dinner with Marc Blackwell. I pace back and forth in front of my huge wardrobe, feeling like I don't have a thing to wear.

I've pulled out dress after dress and laid it on my bed. Thank goodness I went shopping with Jen when I got my scholarship. She forced me to buy going-out clothes, and gave me her mum's advice: buy it and the occasion will come. Well, the occasion has come. And now nothing seems good enough.

I analyse every outfit, from the message it sends out (Confident? Desperate? Prudish?), to how flattering it is, what shoes go with it ... I'm driving myself mad.

I get Jen on Skype and hold up different outfits. She laughs when I hold the camera to the wardrobe, and she sees there are hardly any clothes left on their hangers.

'It looks like you've emptied your whole wardrobe onto the floor,' she says.

'It's not funny,' I say, although I can't help but smile. 'Help me, please.'

'Maybe this is too big a job for either of us,' says Jen. 'I mean, *Marc Blackwell*, Sophia. This is all a bit crazy, don't you think? I've thought about it, and ... I don't know. He's never publically had a girlfriend, and to make the moves on one of his younger pupils ...'

'He's only a few years older than me,' I point out.

'But still ... okay. Look, usually I'd try and talk you out of something like this. You know what a pushover you are.'

We both laugh. I'm not a pushover when it counts, actually, but Jen can call me whatever she likes. I know what she means. Easy going. I don't like arguments.

'Anyway,' Jen continues, 'I can tell just by the way you're talking that you've got it bad. And I can't say I blame you. So. I'm going to help you be sexy and confident and in control.'

'Fat chance with Marc around,' I say.

'Well, let's try,' says Jen. 'That red dress, hold it up.'

'This one?' I hold up a thigh-length red dress. Half the side has silk flowing down it like a waterfall, and there's a red silk rose at the bust. It's extremely fitted, in an expensive, crumpled sort of way, and strapless. 'It's a bit too red carpet.'

'Exactly,' says Jen. 'Confident. Sexy. He won't know what hit him. But tone it down a bit with the shoes. Those boots are perfect. And wear some sort of big necklace so you don't look naked around the shoulders. That silver coin one.'

'Okay,' I say, picking up a necklace from the wardrobe shelf. I put everything on and look in the mirror.

'Wow,' says Jen, when I stand in front of the camera. 'If he won't make you his girlfriend, then I will.'

I laugh. 'Spoken like a true friend.'

'Where is his house, anyway?' Jen asks.

'I have no idea,' I say.

'So how are you getting there?'

'I have no idea about that either,' I say. 'Marc texted me earlier. He told me to walk to the campus's car park entrance and wait there.'

'What a gentleman,' says Jen. 'He'd better take care of you, or he'll have me to answer to.'

Chapter 45

In the end, I choose the clothes I feel most comfortable in – grey jeans, an oversized black sweater and silver jewellery. I put two glittering bird studs in my ears and hang a rose quartz on a silver chain around my neck.

It's cold outside the campus car park gates, as I watch cars zooming past. I'm early as usual, and shiver in my sweater. I wish I'd brought a coat along, but when Jen and I went shopping they didn't have the winter ranges in yet, and I don't want to wear my old rain coat.

Like the main entrance gates, the car park gates are wrought iron, gothic and beautiful. If I wasn't so nervous I'd be captivated by them. But I am nervous.

I check my watch again.

On the road I see a long, black limousine. Its indicator comes on as it approaches the college, and it begins to slow down.

Is that for me?

I watch in amazement as the limousine stops outside the college gates.

The back window rolls down, and Marc's face appears.

'Sophia.' He opens the car door. 'Get in.'

I duck my head and climb into the limo, closing the door behind me.

Marc sits on a leather couch inside, his legs crossed, watching me. He's wearing a plain black t-shirt, black jeans and slightly scuffed biker boots.

One of the boots is propped over his thigh. His lips aren't smiling, but his eyes are.

I take a seat on the leather couch opposite, putting my hands on my knees. I notice a drinks cabinet, lit with yellow lights, and a flat screen TV. It's dark in the car and smells like leather.

Marc's hands move to the drinks cabinet. He clicks open a can of tonic, then pours it into a glass with ice and lemon.

'Here,' he says, passing me the drink. 'It's too early for champagne.'

I look at the drink fizzing away, and think: *is it?* 'I think I can manage some gin in this,' I say, and to my surprise, Marc finds a bottle of Gordons in the cabinet and pours a small measure into my glass. I take a large gulp.

'Aren't you drinking?' I ask.

Marc throws me one of his smouldering, intense looks and I grip the glass tighter, feeling its chill against my fingers. 'Not yet.'

The car pulls out, and I see the college become smaller through the tinted windows.

'How did you like singing class?' Marc asks.

'I liked it very much,' I say. 'I liked Denise. She spoke with me. About you.'

'Really?' Marc raises an eyebrow. 'Nothing gets past her.' He looks out of the window. 'I remember, when I was a teenager, being amazed by the things she knew about me.'

'Oh really?' I raise a playful eyebrow. 'What sort of things?'

Marc smiles, and his cheekbones look sharp and lethal. 'All sorts of things. I wasn't the most wholesome of teenagers.'

'How did I guess?' I say, grinning now. 'She told me lots of things I didn't know about you. About how you grew up.'

Marc's smile disappears. 'It wasn't the best of upbringings. If it weren't for Denise, I could have gone in a very different direction. One of the reasons I love London so much is because she's here.'

The car drives west along Oxford Street, and I see crowds of shoppers trying to peer into the windows when we stop at traffic lights.

'Can they see us?' I ask.

Marc shakes his head. 'They can't see a thing. The windows are specially designed.' He leans closer. 'I'm glad you're getting on with Denise. It seems I'm not the only teacher you've been pleasing. Should I be jealous?' He smiles again, and my insides melt.

'Maybe,' I say. 'Denise is much more open than you've been.'

'Ah.' Marc leans back into the leather, and it squeaks under his body. 'Openness. I've had bad experiences with openness.'

'I'm sorry to hear that.'

Marc takes the rose quartz that's around my neck in his fingers. 'I like this. It brings out the colours in your eyes.'

'It's a rose quartz,' I say. 'The stone of love. I keep it close to me when I want to feel safe and protected.'

'And you don't feel safe and protected around me?'

'Yes. I do. But you make me nervous, too.'

Marc takes my gin and tonic, and places it on the walnut counter.

Then he takes my hands. 'You shouldn't feel nervous.'

'Sometimes I feel I should be protected *from* you,' I admit. 'This is all so ... intense.'

I like the way his hands feel on mine.

'But you trust me?'

'I trust you.'

'And yet, you're inhibited around me.'

I nod. 'Yes. I feel so many things when I'm with you. It's hard to relax and completely be myself.'

Marc sets my hands in my lap. He looks out the window. 'Being in this car is a good opportunity to learn something about inhibitions and trust, don't you think?'

'Is it?' I reach for my gin and tonic, and take a nervous sip. 'Why?'

'All these people, peering into the limo windows. It feels like they can see us, doesn't it?'

I nod. 'You're sure they can't?'

'Sophia. Do you think I'd own a limo that people could see in to? And take you across London in it? When you're with me you'll be safe, and that means your reputation too. No one will know you're spending extra time after class with me. Not unless you want them to.'

'Right now, I don't want them to,' I say. 'I want you to stay at the university. I don't want the other pupils to miss out on your teaching.'

'Just so you know,' says Marc. 'If it starts to bother you, doing things in this clandestine fashion, I'll stop teaching any time you ask me to.'

'And like I said. I can't do that to the other pupils.'

'Take your clothes off,' says Marc.

My hands fly to my chest. 'Are you being serious?'

'Deadly serious. I gave you an instruction. Take your clothes off.'

'You really are being serious, aren't you?' I say. 'You want me to take my clothes off right here, in the back of this car?'

'All of your clothes. Right here, right now.'

'But I feel like people can see me.'

'That's exactly right,' says Marc. 'And that's what I mean by teaching you to lose your inhibitions. I take your tuition very seriously. Now do as you're told before I tie you up and cane you again.'

Just hearing him say those words makes me feel hot, and I'm not sure I like it. I always thought of myself as a normal sort of girl with normal sorts of needs. But being with Marc has opened up a whole new world of feelings that I'm not sure I'm comfortable with.

'Now,' says Marc.

Chapter 46

I slide my arms out of my sweater, taking my time, hoping he might change his mind.

'Faster, Sophia. I mean it. If you don't hurry up, I've got a slipper waiting for you at my town house.'

I wriggle out of the jumper, and take off my shoes and socks. Then slowly, I slide down my jeans and take off my vest.

I see the faces of shoppers and tourists lining Oxford Street as we judder slowly in tight traffic, and for a moment I want to fling my clothes back on again. But I trust Marc when he tells me they can't see.

'Your underwear too,' he says, resting back on the couch and pouring himself a whisky and soda from the drinks cabinet. The glass is cut crystal and shines under the yellow lights.

I unclip my bra, and slide off my panties. I do it quickly, like jumping into a cold swimming pool. I think the quicker I do it, the less painful it will be. But as I sit here, completely naked, with cool leather under me, I feel more exposed than ever before.

The limo stops at another traffic light and more faces peer into the car. Teenage boys, tourists, couples – it feels like people from all walks of life are looking at me with no clothes on.

'I feel like they can all see me,' I whisper, my arms wrapping themselves around my ribs.

'Maybe they can,' says Marc, setting his drink down. 'Do you trust me, Sophia? When I say they can't see you, do you trust what I'm saying?'

I nod. 'I do. But it just feels like ... it feels like they can.'

'When a director asks you to do something, it may go against all your instincts,' Marc says. 'But you have to trust what they're saying. More importantly, this is a little lesson in showing yourself in front of lots of people. This is what you're going to have to do, Sophia, if you want to make it as an actress.'

'Not all actresses take their clothes off.'

'It's not about nudity,' says Marc. 'It's about baring your soul. Showing everything in here.' He puts a fist to his chest. 'A good actor is always perfectly in control, but totally exposed. That's what makes it such a difficult profession. To show your soul to millions of people, without losing yourself in the process. You're an amazing actress, but you're inhibited. I'm going to help you break through that last boundary, so you can show the world what you're capable of.'

I watch the pedestrians, and with every minute that passes, my nakedness seems less.

'Now,' says Marc. 'Turn around and face the window.'

I turn around, knowing my rear end is now facing him. I look out of the window, watching shops go slowly past. The traffic has showed no signs of easing off and we're stopping and starting, stopping and starting.

'I want you to press your breasts against the window,' says Marc.

'What?'

'Do as you're told, Sophia.'

'But everyone will see -'

'No one can see a thing. It just feels that way.'

Reluctantly, I lean forwards and press my chest against the cold glass. It's freezing, and goose bumps instantly cover my breasts and arms.

I feel Marc part my legs, and see a condom packet fall onto the couch.

'What are you doing?' I whisper.

I hear him unfasten his trousers, and feel his long fingers on the insides of my thighs, pushing my legs even further apart.

'Not here in the car,' I murmur. 'Please.'

Marc runs a finger up to my mouth and presses it against my lips. 'Let me teach you. Let me help you be better.'

He edges forward, and I feel him against me.

'Marc -'

He slides a little inside of me, and I moan as I feel his fullness.

A little at a time he inches in, until I'm trapped by him, squashed firmly against the glass.

'Keep watching the street, Sophia. All these people are going to see you come.'

'Marc, no. You said -'

He begins to move back and forth, and my words fall dead.

'I know what I said, but what if they could see you? How would you feel about that?'

'I'd hate it,' I moan, syncing my hips to his rhythm. 'I wouldn't want them to see.'

'So you want me to stop?'

'Don't stop,' I hear myself say, and his strokes go further and further inside

'Relax,' Marc whispers, moving back and forth. He reaches around and begins to stroke, slow at first, and then faster.

'Oh,' I moan, as the car reaches the end of Oxford Street.

'They can all see you, Sophia. They'll all see you as you come. Do you want me to stop?'

'No,' I say.

'Do you want me to fuck you harder, then?'

'Yes,' I say.

'Yes sir.'

He moves harder against me, pressing me up against the cold glass. He's merciless, holding me tight, thrusting deeper and deeper until I'm only dimly aware of all the shoppers outside the car window.

'I don't care,' I hear myself say. 'I don't care if they can see me. Don't stop. Please don't stop.'

Marc wraps his arm around my stomach and pulls himself further inside.

I cry out with pleasure, and come just as we drive past Marble Arch. Waves of pleasure run all over me, and over where Marc is inside of me, still hard. He pulls himself free, and I collapse onto the leather sofa.

Marc pulls his trousers back on, then rubs at my cold breasts until the circulation comes back. He helps me into my clothes.

When I'm fully dressed, I sit on the couch, looking out of the window. Eventually, I say, 'You lied to me.'

Marc shakes his head. 'I didn't lie to you.'

'You did. You told me no one could see. Then you made me feel like they could. Stop the car. I want to get out.'

'If you want to get out, at least let me drive you back to the college. But listen to me. No one could see you, Sophia.'

'You made me feel like maybe they could.'

'It was for your own good. Trust me. I have your best interests at heart. That little experience helped you. Believe me. Imagine how you'll feel about playing a seductive role now.'

I think about it. Compared to thinking the whole of Oxford Street could see me just now, playing someone like Jennifer feels like far less of a problem.

'I still didn't like you doing that,' I say. 'I felt tricked. You manipulated me. Telling me that when I was so vulnerable.'

'Vulnerable?' Marc raises an eyebrow. 'Is that what you call it?'

'When I couldn't say no.'

'You could have said no,' says Marc. 'At any time. But you didn't want to. If you don't have any self control, perhaps we need another lesson in that area.'

I think of the ropes and the stationery cupboard, and shiver. At the time, it was torturous, but now every time I think about it, I feel hot and cold all over.

I wish he would put his arm around me or hold my hand. Or kiss me. I want to sit beside him, but some instinct tells me not to. I take a long drink of gin and tonic.

'I'm going to have a lot of fun with you at my townhouse,' says Marc, stretching out his long arms along the leather couch. 'So many things to teach you, so little time.'

Chapter 47

'Maybe I don't want to learn anything more today,' I say, still angry with him for humiliating me.

'Oh, I think you do.'

I shake my head. 'I think I've learned plenty.'

'Fine,' says Marc. 'Say the word, and I'll turn the car around and take you back to the college. Or if you'd prefer, I'll have a taxi called out for you. Whatever you want.'

'You hurt me,' I say, feeling tears under my eyes.

Lines of concern appear above Marc's nose. He leans forward. 'I hurt you just then? In a way you didn't like?'

I think about it. 'I feel humiliated,' I say. 'So, on an emotional level, yes. You did hurt me.'

'Embarrassment isn't the same as hurt,' says Marc, and his voice is almost gentle. 'Embarrassment is a block. It stops you from truly letting go. I'm helping you work through it. Look. We'll have dinner. That's all, okay? Until you're ready for more. I give you my word, that's all we'll do tonight.'

I think about that for a moment. 'Okay.' I can manage dinner, although I'm still feeling vulnerable and raw.

'Will you hurt me, though?' I ask, looking right at him. 'Eventually?'

'No,' says Marc.

'I think you might,' I say, looking out of the window.

'Oh, Sophia, how wrong you are,' says Marc. 'It's me who'll get hurt. I've known that all along.'

We sit in silence as the limo drives down long, wide streets of three-storey town houses. There are large oak trees lining the pavements.

'Do you know where we are?' Marc asks.

I shake my head.

'Richmond,' he says. 'My favourite part of London.'

I see the steel gates on one of the houses swing open, and the limo drives down a slope and into a huge garage under the house.

I hear the scuffle of feet on concrete, and then the driver opens the door nearest me.

'After you,' says Marc, helping me out of the limo.

I can't bear to look at the driver. Does he know what just happened in the back of the car? I don't even want to think about it.

Fortunately, the driver doesn't hang around. He says a quick word to Marc about coming back later, then disappears through a back door.

Marc leads me past five extremely shiny cars, all of them probably very expensive. I know nothing about cars, but I notice one is wasp yellow and open-topped, with square corners that look like they could cut someone. The car doesn't suit Marc at all, and I wonder if it belongs to him.

'Is that car yours?' I ask.

Marc stops walking and looks at me. 'No,' he says slowly. 'Why do you ask?'

'It doesn't feel like you,' I say.

'Feel like me?'

'Yes,' I nod. 'That car over there -' I point to a beige Rolls Royce. 'That feels like you. So does that one.' I point to a black Jaguar. 'So who does this yellow car belong to?'

'It was my father's,' says Marc, mounting a set of stone steps and opening a creaking wooden door.

'Your father's? I thought ... I thought you and your father didn't get along.'

'We don't.'

'So why -'

'Keep your enemies close, isn't that what they say?' Marc doesn't look at me when he says that, and I get the feeling there's more to that car than he's letting on. 'Follow me.'

I follow him, and find myself in the entrance hall of his town house. The floor is white marble, and the staircase is fitted with deep, red carpet.

It's grand, but it feels a little empty. There are no plants. I always think plants bring a place to life. Along the wall are pictures of historic London buildings – Big Ben, the Houses of Parliament, St Paul's Cathedral and of course, Ivy College.

'You like London,' I say.

'I love London,' he replies. 'I feel at home here. The buildings, the history. It's astonishing to me, after spending so much time in LA, that buildings can stay in one place for hundreds of years. I love to look at them.' He pauses by the picture of Ivy College. 'Rooted to the spot. For so long. I imagine that's why you like plants so much.'

I smile. 'I like plants because they're alive, and they respond to you. You can care for them, nurture them. How often do you stay here?'

'Whenever I'm in London,' says Marc.

'It's beautiful, but it doesn't feel lived in,' I say. 'I guess you must be out a lot.'

'Actually, since I formed the college, I'd say quite the contrary,' says Marc. 'Especially this year.' He looks at me. 'I've had a lot to think about, and I'd rather do that alone.'

'Mr Blackwell, is that you?' I hear footsteps on marble. A slim man in a pink jumper, white trousers and flowery apron comes into the entrance hall. He has short red hair and is my father's age.

'Ah. Rodney. Please meet my guest, Miss Rose. Miss Rose, this is Rodney, my house manager.'

'I heard the car,' says Rodney. 'I've got your meal all laid out on the roof terrace. You go on up.' He looks at me. 'Don't worry.' He winks. 'His bark's worse than his bite. He scared the life out of me when I first started working for him, but he's a big softy at heart.'

To my amazement, he gives Marc an affectionate slap on the shoulder.

'I'll be back tomorrow to clean everything up. You two have a nice evening.'

Rodney disappears through the huge front door, which takes him some effort to open and close.

'We'll take the elevator,' says Marc, leading me to a set of gold doors by the staircase.

'But I'd like to see your house,' I say.

'Maybe another time,' says Marc. 'Right now, dinner.'

We take the elevator up four floors, and it opens right out on the roof terrace.

'Wow,' I say, seeing the bright lights of London spread below us. There are so many pretty slate roof tops and chimneys, I feel like I'm in *Mary Poppins*.

The view is amazing, but the roof terrace has no plants or life, only a smoky grey floor and gold railings. There's a sheltered area with a sink, fridge and barbeque. I see lobster smoking on the grill.

There is a large wooden table laid with white plates and gleaming gold cutlery. The chairs are wooden too, but topped with plump red cushions. Champagne sits in a gold ice bucket on the table. Two tall, red candles flicker in the breeze.

'Everything's gold and red,' I say.

'I like red,' says Marc, leading me to the table. 'It's strong. Gold – that was my house manager's idea. Apparently it goes with red. Personally, I like black better. Take a seat.'

I sit down and look over the rooftops. It's chilly, and I shiver.

'I thought you might be cold up here,' says Marc. 'So I asked Rodney to buy you a coat. I never noticed you wearing one on campus.'

'I haven't had a chance to buy a winter coat yet,' I admit.

'Well, maybe you'll like this one,' says Marc, going to the sheltered area, and retrieving a large square parcel wrapped in tissue paper and pink ribbon.

'I ... thank you,' I say. 'That's very kind of you. Aren't you cold?' I look at his bare, muscular arms in his black t-shirt. They're pale in the crisp autumn air.

'I don't feel the cold.'

I carefully tear open the tissue, and find a black, cashmere coat inside. I don't recognise where it's from. I hold it up. It's fitted at the waist, with slim, yet structured, shoulders that I know will fit me perfectly. It flares out a little at the bottom.

'I love it,' I say, truthfully. 'It's beautiful.'

I think I see the flicker of a smile on Marc's face, although I can't be sure.

I slip on the coat, and Marc pops the champagne and pours me a glass.

'It's beautiful up here,' I say.

'To you, everything is beautiful,' says Marc, filling his own champagne glass.

I smile.

Marc goes to the sheltered area and opens the fridge. 'Foie gras to start,' he says, bringing two dishes to the table and placing one in front of me.

It's full of ice chips, and at its centre sits a glass bowl of liver-coloured paste. On the other dish sits thin crisps of toast and what looks like little pancakes.

'Blinis,' say Marc. 'Russian pancakes. Delicious with foie gras.'

I stare at the foie gras. I know how it's made – they force feed ducks to make their livers extra fat, and then tie ropes around their necks to stop them vomiting.

Marc pauses, about to serve me blinis. 'Sophia, what's wrong?' His voice is anxious.

I shake my head. 'I can't eat that. And you shouldn't either.' I rarely get angry, but the thought of what they do to those ducks makes me feel sick. 'Get rid of it,' I say. 'The foie gras. Get rid of it. Don't you know how it's made?'

Lines appear around Marc's mouth as he fights back a smile. 'I'm aware of how foie gras is made.'

I fight to slow my breathing. 'I don't even want it on the same table as me.'

'Sophia.' Marc takes my hand. 'This isn't French foie gras. The ducks haven't been force fed.'

My breathing slows, and I look at him. His eyes are bright with amusement.

'I still don't like it,' I say. 'Even the idea of it. What it represents.'

Marc scoops up the dish, heads to the barbeque area and drops the whole thing into a bin, dusting his hands. 'There. Better?'

I nod. 'Thank you.'

'Three hundred pounds worth of cruelty free foie gras, in the trash, at your command Miss Rose.'

'I'm sorry,' I mumble. 'I just hate the idea of it.'

'You don't need to be sorry.' Marc crouches down to the fridge, his long legs jutting up towards his chin. 'Now. I have some caviar in here. Would that work for you? Any objections to fish produce?'

I give a little laugh. 'No. That sounds nice.'

Marc returns to the table, and spoons caviar onto my plate. I wait for him to sit down and serve his own caviar. Then I spoon caviar onto a little pancake.

I take a bite. It's delicious. 'I didn't expect caviar to taste this way,' I say.

The next course is grilled lobster with champagne sauce, and it's equally delicious. Dessert is a thin slice of dark chocolate torte with a drizzle of vanilla cream on top.

'So you like architecture?' I ask, taking a bite of chocolate torte, and looking out over the rooftops.

'I love anything that stays in one place for a long time,' says Marc. 'Trees, mountains, lakes. I had a lot of inconsistency growing up. Wherever my father could find work for me, we went.'

'How did you manage with school?' I ask.

'I didn't go. Except when I was with Denise.'

'Really? But you're so ... educated. At least you seem that way.'

'Self educated.' Marc follows my gaze over the rooftops. 'I read a lot as a boy. The classics, mainly. Dickens, Thomas Hardy, Hemingway. Dickens especially.'

'It sounds like you had a rough upbringing,' I venture.

'No rougher than many,' says Marc, but his eyes cloud over. I sense he wants to change the subject.

We eat and talk about plays and movies we've seen, what we think about London, my life at college ... normal things. And for a moment, it feels like we're just two people, enjoying a dinner date, getting to know each other.

Marc, unsurprisingly, likes darker movies than I do. Apocalypse Now, the Godfather and Citizen Kane. I admit my guilty pleasure of Disney, and he rolls his eyes, and tells me he might have guessed, but he's smiling as he says it.

I tell him about my family, and how I feel guilty for not seeing them last weekend. I explain how my dad and Genoveva need my help, with housework and Samuel.

After dessert, my second glass of champagne makes me bold. 'Tell me about your father,' I say. 'Why do you still keep his car?'

Marc's jaw ripples. 'I don't *keep* it. It was given to me when he passed away, and I haven't got round to selling it yet.'

'He passed away? I'm so sorry.'

Marc nods. 'Four years ago. I didn't go to the funeral.'

'You didn't?' Part of me feels like I'm entering dangerous territory, but I can't help pressing on. 'Why not?'

Marc stands up, taking his glass of champagne. He downs it in one gulp. 'I saw no reason to. Funerals are about saying goodbye to loved ones. He wasn't a loved one.'

I nod. 'I heard you didn't have the best of relationships.'

Marc puts down his glass and hooks both thumbs into his jean pockets. 'I hated him,' he says simply.

Chapter 49

'Oh.' I don't know what to say.

'He was a tyrant and a bully and I'm not sorry he's gone. Have I opened up enough for you?'

'It's okay,' I say, standing and putting my arms around him. 'You don't have to tell me anything. I was just asking. I wanted to be closer to you.'

He looks down at me, confused. Then he puts his arms around me. 'Why did you have to be my pupil? Why did it have to happen that way?'

'I don't know,' I say, 'and I don't know about completely accepting everything on your terms.'

Marc pulls me tighter into him, and I feel his heart beat. 'You should walk away from me, Sophia. If you've got any sense, you'd run. I shouldn't have started anything with you, but ... there's something about you that's irresistible. Completely irresistible.'

'Is it because I'm your pupil?' I ask, wincing inside. 'A sort of sex thing? Because you like being in charge?' I'm not sure I want to know the answer.

'No,' says Marc. 'It was in spite of you being my pupil. I wish you weren't. In fact, I fell for you before you became my pupil. At your audition. If it was down to me, I wouldn't have chosen you for the course. Too dangerous. But I do like being in charge, and I can't pretend the dynamic doesn't work for me. Do you like me being in charge?'

I nod.

'But ... I don't feel like I should like it.'

'I would never do anything you didn't truly like.'

'But in the limo ...'

'You didn't like it?'

'I liked it, but I was humiliated. You took away control from me. You brought me to a place where I couldn't say no, and then you told me something that made me vulnerable.'

'But you were never truly vulnerable,' says Marc. 'And you could have said no at any time.'

'But you made me *feel* vulnerable,' I say.

'Sophia,' says Marc. 'I'm teaching you how to open yourself up. To show yourself to hundreds, thousands of people. Because I truly believe you have the potential to reach millions of people.'

'You do?'

'Yes,' says Marc.

The moon is high and silver over London, and I think for the first time what an amazing thing it is to have all this architecture and all these people in one place.

'But Marc, how can you talk about me being open, when you're not open yourself?'

'As an actor, I'm open,' he says simply. 'Even if in my personal life, I find it difficult, I'm open when I perform.'

'But ... I saw a movie of you when you were younger,' I say. 'There was something in your eyes, in your expression, that was much more vulnerable. It drew me in, more so than in your darker movies.'

Marc frowns. 'That was before. When someone else was in charge of me. Now I'm in charge of my own life, and so shoot me if the darkest depths of my soul aren't on screen for all to see. I give enough. I give plenty. I have the awards to show for it.'

Suddenly, there's a flash of something white, like lightning, but there's no rain or thunder. The sky is clear.

Marc pulls me away from the railing. He throws the cashmere coat over my head and hauls me towards the elevator.

Chapter 50

'Paparazzi,' he says, bundling me through the gold doors. 'They were on the ground. Which means they didn't get anything. But it also means they're outside.'

He jabs the lift button and the doors slide closed. As the elevator descends, he paces back and forth. 'Christ, those parasites. Always at the worst moments.'

The lift opens on the floor below, and I see soft red carpet and a hallway of closed doors.

'In here,' he barks, opening one of the doors. There's a giant four poster bed inside, made of dark wood. The bed is so high that there are wooden steps leading up to it.

Stretching along one of the walls is a bookcase made of rosewood, filled with books. A complete collection of Dickens novels run along one of the shelves, but to my surprise, the books look brand new. Untouched.

'The windows in this room are one way,' Marc explains. 'No one can see in.' He runs a hand through his hair. 'I can't stay with you in here. Not after what I promised you in the limo. I won't be able to stop myself, Sophia, if we share a bed.'

'Maybe it's you who needs a lesson in self control,' I say, with a smile.

'There's no maybe with you around,' says Marc, lifting me onto the bed. He runs a hand languidly down my body. 'Tell me you don't want me to do anything. Tell me to leave. Tell me to stop.'

I shake my head. 'I don't want you to stop.'

'In the limo you said you didn't want anything to happen tonight.'

'Maybe I've changed my mind.'

He shakes his head. 'That's not acceptable. Wait there.'

I pull myself further up the bed, and rest on the over-sized cream pillows.

'Is this your bedroom?' I ask.

'Sometimes,' he says, going to a wooden wardrobe that stretches from floor to ceiling. He opens the door and reaches up to a high shelf inside.

'Do you bring girls up here often?' I ask, forcing a smile.

He pauses, mid-stretch. 'Sometimes,' he says, and I feel deflated.

'How many times?' I ask.

'A few,' he answers, taking down a pair of leather slippers.

'What are they?' I ask.

'Turn over. I'm going to slipper you.'

I stare at him in disbelief. First the cane, now the slipper. 'You're really taking this teacher thing seriously,' I say.

'Don't talk back,' says Marc, climbing the steps onto the bed and flipping me over. He undoes my jeans and pulls them down.

Once again, I feel fresh air on my buttocks, but I can't see where Marc is, which is pleasantly torturous. I hear whooshing sounds as he takes off his t-shirt and jeans.

'Marc?'

I feel myself sliding over the bed as he pulls me towards him. My legs bump over his naked thighs, and suddenly I'm bent over his bare knee. I can felt the heat of his torso against my side, and the tension of his skin.

'Marc, what are you -'

He smacks me hard with the soul of the slipper.

I'm stunned. It feels good in a 'pain is pleasure' sort of way, and when he hits me a second time I cry out.

'I won't fuck you,' Marc whispers. 'I made a promise.' He lifts me onto the bed, resting me stomach down on the duvet. 'Are you going to do as you're told from now on?'

'Yes,' I stammer.

'Say yes sir,' he barks.

'Yes sir.'

I moan again as he smacks me with the slipper.

'Turn around,' he orders. I do, and find myself face to face with Marc's bare chest. There are scars on it – little ones, like the ones on his knuckles.

'Give me your hand,' he says. 'Now undo my trousers.'

Finally. I get to touch him. I unbutton and unzip him. Then I lean down and take him into my mouth.

I expect him to try and stop me, but instead he lets out a little moan.

I keep going, up, down, up, down, and I can feel the tension building in him. He moans again, and I move faster, bringing my hand around him and tightening it.

He grips my wrist. 'Stop,' he pants. 'Too close.' He lifts my chin away, and sits back on the bed, getting his breath back.

'What was too close?' I ask.

'Me. To you. A few more seconds and I would have come.'

'What's so bad about that?' I ask. 'I want you to. I want to share with you -'

Marc shakes his head. 'What you want from me, I can never give you.'

'What are you saying? That you'll never come with me?' I ask. 'I don't understand. Why not?'

Marc pushes himself back in his trousers. 'I don't want to lose control in that way. Not ever.'

'But you were saying acting is all about being vulnerable. And you're the most amazing actor.'

'Acting is *all* about being in control,' says Marc, climbing down from the bed. 'Every performance, I show my soul, but I'm in perfect control. You – stay in here tonight. There's an en suite, towels, whatever you need. I'll make sure it's safe before you leave tomorrow. I'll be leaving first thing. Have Rodney bring you whatever you need.'

'Aren't you staying in here with me?'

Marc shakes his head. 'It'll be safer if I stay in the next room.'

He leaves the room and closes the door.

I lie on the huge Alice in Wonderland bed, the feather duvet folding me in softness, and think about what just happened.

Part of me feels good that I can have an effect on Marc. Part of me feels sad that I can't be as close to him as I want. To make him feel as good as he makes me feel.

I watch the silver moon outside the tinted window. It must be gone midnight. Thoughts turn around my mind, some good, some bad.

I get up, drink water from the bathroom tap and splash some on my face. The en suite is just as grand as the bedroom, with a huge, round swimming-tub bath and two different sinks to choose from.

I think about Marc in the next room. It's a little chilly in my underwear, so I put on my jumper and creep to the bedroom door. It opens with a loud creaking sound, and I stop dead, listening. Then I poke my head out into the hallway.

The door next to my bedroom is slightly ajar, and I guess this must be where Marc is sleeping.

I creep towards the door, pushing it open little by little. Inside I see another giant bed. It's not as high as the one in my room and it's not a four poster, but it's still pretty big.

There's a sleeping figure on top of the duvet. I see Marc's beautiful profile. He's fully clothed in his black t-shirt and jeans, and lying on his back, his chest barely moving. His brown hair falls softly back onto the pillow, and there's the tiniest of frown lines either side of his nose.

I creep closer, my heart pounding at the sight of him.

Marc's chest moves more quickly as I approach, and I can smell him and see the pores on his skin. It's amazing to be this close. To be allowed to look at the details of his handsome face in the flesh, see light brown stubble growing through his cheeks.

He's all straight lines, I realise. Straight nose, straight jaw, straight teeth. The only curves are the quirks of his lips and eye lids, the curved lines either side of his mouth, and the round hollows of his cheeks. His lips are parted, just slightly, and I'm desperate to lean down and kiss them.

I crawl onto the bed, listening to his breathing. I'm tempted just to rest beside him and put one of his arms around me, but that would be too easy.

Instead, I gently climb over his body and sit with my legs either side of him.

We're both still clothed, but I begin to move back and forth.

I feel him hardening beneath me, and my heart beats faster. Should I be doing this? I know the answer. I have a reality check, all of a sudden, and realise I have crept into Marc Blackwell's bedroom and am now sitting on top of him. But his growing hardness keeps me moving.

Marc begins to moan in his sleep, and I feel myself smile.

What if he says someone else's name? I think suddenly. But it feels so good, moving on top of him like this, and watching his eyelids flicker with pleasure.

I move faster and faster, and Marc moans louder.

I see his eyelids flutter and suddenly I'm staring into his blue eyes, still moving back and forth.

'Oh god,' he shouts, 'Oh Sophia. Oh god. Don't.'

'I don't want to stop,' I say. 'All I want is to make you feel the way you make me feel.'

'No.' Marc shakes his head and grits his teeth. He throws me onto the bed, and for a moment I think he's really mad at me. But suddenly he's reaching into my panties and thrusting his fingers back and forth inside.

'You started this,' he says. 'Now I'll finish it.' He pulls a condom from the bedside draw and struggles out of his trousers. Then he puts the condom on, and pulls off my underwear.

He gets on his knees between my legs and slides himself inside me. It's a tight fit, and he only gets around halfway in. I feel the fullness, and as he moves back and forth he touches all the right places.

'Oh, Marc,' I moan.

'Have I been a good teacher?' Marc whispers.

'Yes sir,' I breathe.

He moves further and further inside, and I stuff a knuckle into my mouth to stop myself crying out.

'You like me being inside you?'

'Yes sir.' I watch him. 'You won't pull out?'

He shakes his head. 'Right now, I couldn't if I wanted to.'

He keeps going and going until my world explodes into stars, and I feel like I've been dipped into a warm bath.

Marc moans and keeps moving.

'Please Marc, stop,' I say. But he won't.

At first, the feeling is too intense. Having him push against me after I've just come – I'm too tender and soft. But then the pleasure begins to build again and I hear myself crying out.

I see sweat on Marc's forehead, and feel his hand gripping and squeezing my buttocks. I come again, and as I do I feel Marc push right into me, going deeper than I ever thought possible.

'Oh God, Sophia,' he shouts. I feel the base of him beating against me, and then he wraps his body around mine, strong limbs holding me tightly.

Did he just come? No. He's still hard.

I lie under him, feeling safe and warm and protected, and wonder what just happened. Because something changed in him – I know it.

Marc rolls me against him so we're side to side, him still inside me, hard and throbbing. He's breathing heavily as he slides himself out of me. Then he pulls the cover over us, wraps his arms around me, and I fall into a deep sleep.

Chapter 51

When I wake up the next morning, Marc is watching me, elbow propped on the pillow.

'Morning,' I mutter sleepily, feeling shy. He doesn't look angry. I wonder how well he remembers last night.

'Morning,' he says quietly, not taking his eyes off me.

'I thought you had to leave early,' I say.

'I do,' he says, climbing out of the bed. He leaves the room and returns fully dressed – black suit, black shirt and a black suit jacket over his arm.

'Rodney will bring you breakfast.' He throws on his suit jacket and heads for the door.

'Marc, about last night -'

'Things got out of hand,' says Marc, his hand on the door. With that, he leaves the room.

What's going on? I pull the thick, feathery duvet over myself, feeling tired and hurt, and longing for him to come back.

When I hear the front door click and his car drive away, I rub my eyes and climb out of bed. In the corner of the room, I notice two cardboard boxes, stacked up.

They look out of place in Marc's bare home, and I find myself heading towards them. I want to find out more about this man I'm caught up with, and since he's not telling me much ...

The first box is full of books – but not stiff and new like the ones in the Alice in Wonderland bedroom. These are old, scuffed up and clearly very well read. I see Oliver Twist and Far From the Madding Crowd, amid a pile of other classics. Unlike the hardback covers on the shelf next door, these books are paperback and have colourful illustrations on the front.

There's a small copy of Romeo and Juliet, with a green cover, and well worn pages. I flick it open, and see hundreds of spiky biro marks scrawled in the margins.

Marc. I run my fingers over the biro indents, feeling him through his writing. Don't ask me why, but I know the handwriting is his. It's so angular and hard, but with the occasional artistic flourish. The notes are all about the play – his interpretations.

I read, '*He loves her in this scene, but doesn't know it.*' I put the book to my chest for a moment. Then I realise where I am, and that Rodney could walk in at any moment.

I return the book to the box. Then, gingerly, I lift the first box up and look in the one underneath.

Inside are framed photographs of a woman.

I gasp, and nearly drop the first box. Gently, I put it down and peer closer at the photographs. The woman is brown-haired and very pretty, and as I look closer, I see she has Marc's nose and high forehead.

In one picture, she's in a squalid looking house with beer cans propped on sofa arms and window ledges, smiling as she holds a brown-haired baby in her arms. It's an English house – I can tell from the fireplace. Small. Probably terraced. A normal family home.

At the bottom of the box are unframed photos. One is of the same brown-haired woman, smiling, but with a sad look in her eyes. She has a blonde baby in her arms, and wears a pink dress. She stands beside a tall, angry looking man, and a brown-haired toddler sits at their feet.

It's a family photo, but what a family – no one looks happy. There's a tension to the scene that's obvious to anyone with feelings.

I turn the picture over and see, in faded biro: *The Blackwell Family, Joan, Mike, Marc and Emily*.

The brown-haired woman is Marc's mother. But why are her pictures shut away like this, in a box? Marc said he was at this townhouse a lot. Why aren't the pictures of his mother up on the walls?

Carefully, I put everything back in place, my mind in a whirl. I dress and head to the kitchen, smelling coffee and fresh pastries.

Rodney is in the kitchen, wiping the marble surfaces with a look of deadly determination on his face. He looks up when I come in.

'Oh! Sophia.' He throws the cloth in the sink and washes his hands. 'Let me fix you breakfast.'

'You don't have to,' I say. 'Honestly.'

'No, Marc gave me strict orders.' He brings a bowl of Bircher porridge, topped with fresh pomegranate seeds and toasted granola. 'There are pastries too,' he says, opening the oven and bringing out a tray of maple pin wheels. 'And coffee.'

He pours me a cup. I'd prefer hot chocolate, but this coffee smells delicious.

'Thank you,' I say, taking a seat at the breakfast bar. 'This looks great.'

Rodney beams. 'It's nice having guests -' He stops himself. Does that mean Marc often brings women back here? I don't like that thought at all.

'Is Marc a nice person to work for?' I ask.

'The best employer I've ever had,' says Rodney. 'The kindest and most generous. And he's never, ever made me feel like his inferior. We're equals. You'd have to go a long way in London to find someone like that. I guess it's because he grew up without all this.' He waves his hand around.

'Did he?' I ask, taking a sip of coffee, and thinking about the photos. 'The way he is, I thought there might be money somewhere in the family.'

'Not at all,' says Rodney. 'All his money, he earned himself. He grew up in a normal terraced house in London.'

'Oh?' I put my elbows on the breakfast bar, intrigued.

Rodney nods. 'His mother died when he was very young, poor thing. He idolises her. And then when she passed away, his father took him and his sister to America. He'd already seen Marc's talent for acting, and thought he could make him a superstar.'

'Poor Marc.' I shake my head. 'My mother died when I was young, too.' I wonder, for a moment, if that's why Marc feels a connection to me. 'May I ask ... how did she die?'

Rodney picks up a tea towel and swipes at a cobweb on the window. 'If you ever find out, let me know. Marc's lips are sealed on that subject. I wouldn't bring it up, if I were you.'

'Right.' I take another sip of coffee.

'I'm sorry to hear about *your* mother,' says Rodney. 'It must have been hard for you too.'

'At times,' I admit. 'You envy the other children, growing up. There's always a part of you that feels missing. And for me, I had to look after my father too – he went through some dark times after Mum died.'

Rodney nods, hanging the tea towel and pouring himself a cup of coffee. 'Sounds tough.'

'In a way,' I say. 'But really, I feel tremendously lucky. I have a father who loves me and made it through a really bad depression. He's got a new girlfriend now and he's happy. I have a best friend who's like a sister to me, and her mum was always taking care of me when I was younger, giving me good advice, buying me girly stuff.'

'How do you get on with your dad's new girl-friend?' Rodney asks.

I think about that. 'I don't think she likes me being around much, except to clean and look after the new baby.'

'New baby?'

'My dad and his new girlfriend had a baby. Samuel. He's gorgeous. Six months old.'

Rodney smiles. 'Mine are all grown up now, but I remember that age. They're lovely, aren't they?'

I nod and take out my phone. 'Here he is.' I show him the hundreds of pictures I have of Samuel, smiling, looking serious, chewing things.

'How did you meet Marc?' Rodney asks.

'I ... I'm on his course at Ivy College.'

'You're his student?'

I nod, looking at my coffee.

Rodney doesn't say anything, but his silence speaks volumes. Eventually he says, 'Well, I'd better go start on the bathrooms.'

In the silence of the kitchen, I sip coffee and think. Rodney clearly loves Marc, but his reaction to me being Marc's pupil was perfectly normal. In fact, he's probably more understanding than most, given that he seems to love Marc so much. What chance do we have? Even if Marc does soften – even if I manage to soften him – everyone will judge us, and for good reason. It's not a normal way to start a relationship.

I look out at Marc's garden through the patio doors. It's overgrown, covered in ivy. I smile. It's been left to go wild, and needs to be arranged better. I'm itching to go outside and start tending to it, but when I try the patio door it's locked.

Suddenly I feel out of place. A stranger in this huge house. But I don't know how I'm supposed to leave without the paparazzi seeing me.

'Rodney,' I call up the stairs. 'How should I leave?'

He comes to the top of the sweeping staircase. 'The press have all gone now,' he says. 'They never stay outside if Marc has just left. They know he won't be back all day.'

'So I just walk out the front door?' I ask.

'No,' he says. 'Marc left his driver for you. He's waiting in the garage. He'll take you wherever you want to go. Marc had an idea you might want to see your family today.'

'He did?'

Rodney nods. 'Do you know your way to the garage?'

'Yes,' I say, heading around the staircase. 'Thank you.'

Chapter 52

In the garage, the limo is waiting. I knock on the driver's window, and see a cheerful-looking grey-haired man in a peaked cap.

He rolls down the window, and I hear Radio 2 announcing the traffic news. 'Sophia?'

I smile. 'Yes. And you are?'

'Keith. Where would you like to go today?'

'Home,' I say. 'Back to my village. I'd like to see my dad and baby brother.'

'And where's home?'

'Halstead. Essex.'

'Not too far then. Hop in. Let's get going.' He gets out of the car and opens the back door.

'Do you mind if I sit in the front with you?' I ask. 'I'll feel lost in the back on my own.'

'Yeah, of course,' he says, smile lines appearing around his eyes. 'I'd love a bit of company. Nice to meet any friend of Marc's.' He runs around to the passenger side and opens the door for me. 'Hop in.'

The drive home is quicker than I expect, and mostly made up of motorways and electricity pylons, with a brief drive through the Dartford tunnel.

Keith and I talk the whole way. He's been employed by Marc for nearly ten years.

Marc's a very loyal employer, apparently. He likes to have the same people around him. Keith has watched Marc go from teen heartthrob to Oscar-winning movie star.

I ask about Marc's girlfriends, and Keith gives a knowing smile. 'Oh, you want to know about his love life, do you?'

I blush. 'Yes. If you want to put it that way.'

'Well, there's never been anyone serious,' says Keith. 'Not in the time I've known him. He has flings, but no one stays the night. You're the first.' He gives me a sideways glance and a smile.

'I am?' My heart glows. It's not much, but it's something. Something to lift my mood after Marc's sudden, cold exit this morning.

'Yes,' says Keith, pulling onto a country road that leads to my village. As usual, there's a tractor bumping along and we get stuck behind it, moving at ten miles an hour.

Keith honks his horn, and the tractor pulls over and lets us past.

We drive onto the village high street, and down the back roads that lead to my family home. Everyone turns to stare at the car – it's a very unusual sight in this part of the world.

I ring Jen to see if she can get free from work for an hour and come over to my dad's place, but she can't. I tell her it's fine, and that I'll try and give more notice next time.

When we arrive outside Dad's cottage, it feels extremely strange to be pulling up in such a fancy car.

My dad's girlfriend, Genoveva, comes to the door with Samuel in her arms. She looks exhausted, and Samuel is crying, but she's not so tired that her eyes don't widen when she sees the car.

When I step out, I think her eyes are going to pop out of her head.

'Sophia!' she says. 'What on earth is going on?'

'I came to see you and Dad, and Sam,' I say, going to Samuel and kissing his head. Sam reaches out for a cuddle.

Keith calls out, 'I'll come pick you up in a few hours and take you back to your college. Until then, I'll make myself scarce.'

'Do you want to come in for a cup of tea?' I ask.

'No, no. You've got a family reunion. I wouldn't want to interfere.' He drives away.

Genoveva holds Samuel close and I can see he's grown, even in the short time I've been away.

'Well I must admit, we've missed you around here,' says Genoveva. 'Your father has been talking about you non-stop. I'm utterly exhausted. I was expecting you back last weekend. I had a hair appointment booked. I had to cancel it.'

'I'm sorry,' I say. 'I wanted to come back, but Dad insisted I stay put, and I was glad to, really. There was a lot of settling in to do.'

'So I see,' she says, watching the retreating limo.

'I'll try to come back at least every other weekend,' I say. 'I miss you all. Can I hold Samuel?'

Genoveva holds out the baby, and I take him and kiss him all over his blonde head.

'Sams! You got big, didn't you? You've grown.'

He clings to me.

'Will you help me do his washing?' says Genoveva, running a hand through her long caramel-coloured hair. 'He's got nothing left to wear. I don't know where to start. It's all built up since you left. And we're nearly out of milk. Your dad tries but ...'

'I know.' I smile. 'He's a domestic nightmare. Don't let him near anything, he'll make twice as much work for you. I figured that out years ago.'

I walk into the house, bobbing Samuel on my hip. It's an absolute bombsite inside. A tower of washing up in the sink, piles of laundry on and around the washing machine, Samuel's toys all over the floor. A fly buzzes around the dishes, and three tied-up rubbish bags sit by the bin. I can tell by the smell that at least one of them is full of Samuel's nappies.

'Here.' I pass Samuel to Genoveva and he gives a little whimper. I pick up the rubbish and run it outside to the wheelie bin. Then I start putting away plates from the draining board, but half of them are covered in dried food. They'll have to be washed again.

I take all the washing out of the machine, frowning as I see some of it has shrunk or been damaged. The washing smells of mould, so I put it straight back in again with a mould removing tablet and set about doing the washing up.

Samuel crawls up to me and tugs at my leg. Genoveva collapses on the sofa, complaining of a headache. It's like I never left, and in a weird way, I'm glad I'm still needed.

An hour later, I've done all the washing up, made Genoveva a cup of tea and started tidying the living room, when Dad walks in.

'Love! This is a nice surprise. Don't you have classes?'

'It's a study day,' I say.

'Sit down, sit down, don't feel you have to tidy the place when you're here.'

'Oh, it's no bother,' I say.

'Look at you! Got this amazing scholarship in London, and the first thing you do is come back and start tidying. Sit down, I'll make you a cup of tea.'

Dad can't make a cup of tea to save his life. In fact, I'm fairly certain I once caught mild food poisoning from a cup of tea he made for me.

'It's fine,' I say with a smile. 'Sit down, I'll do it.'

'Always running round after other people,' says Dad, ruffling my hair. 'I don't know what I'd do without you. You've been missed around here.'

On the sofa, I see Genoveva's lips go thin. 'You know how hard things are for me with my headaches.'

'I know,' says Dad. 'It's just nice to have her back, that's all.'

We sit down in the living area, and I pull Samuel onto my lap and sing him a song.

'So, tell us about college,' says Dad.

'It's ... very different,' I say.

'Made any friends yet?'

'A few,' I say. 'There are all sorts of different people there.'

'What are your teachers like?'

I hesitate. 'Good.' I say. 'The lady who teaches us singing is a really lovely woman.'

'What about *Marc* Blackwell?' says Genoveva, leaning forward.

'Yes, what's he like?' Dad asks.

'He's an amazing actor,' I say. 'And ... a very interesting person. I'm still not sure what to make of him. The jury's out.'

'Right, of course,' says Dad. 'He seems a bit on the stuck up side when you read about him, but is he better in person?'

'Yes,' I say. 'Definitely.'

I bounce Samuel on my lap, and Dad and I drink tea and catch up. One of the village bus services has stopped, apparently, which is bad news for local teenagers. And the post office got raided a couple of days ago.

After an hour or so, a car horn sounds outside and I realise Keith is waiting on the driveway.

'I should get going,' I say. 'I need to get back to campus.'

Chapter 53

On the drive back, I check my mobile incessantly for messages from Marc. There are none. I think about the coldness of his exit this morning, and feel an aching in my heart. What if it's all over? What if I really crossed the line, and will never see him again?

When I get back to my bedroom, I toy with the idea of texting him.

Don't be stupid, a voice says. *You'll only make a bad situation worse. If he's being cold with you because you got too close, the last thing you should do is push things.*

But the waiting is just agony. I can't help myself. I type out a few words:

Thanks for last night, hope to see you soon.

Delete, delete, delete. Too desperate. I try:

Had a great time last night. Thanks for the view of the city.

No. Too nicey nicey, and it doesn't have anything in it that might make him reply. Oh. This is so difficult. I write:

Will I see you again soon?

And before I can think too much about it, I press send. Then I spend the next hour in agony, waiting for a reply. When there's none, I spend another hour in agony, re-reading the message I sent and analysing how he could have taken it.

I ring Jen, and we hash out the whole scenario together. I leave out a few key details, like his fondness for corporal punishment, but I tell her we had sex last night, and that he left first thing this morning.

'It sounds like you got too close,' she says. 'Probably not a good idea to send a text message. If a man doesn't reply within an hour, then he'd better have a pretty good reason. Otherwise, get rid of him, whoever he is. I don't care if he's some big film star.'

'Nor do I,' I say. 'I couldn't care less about anything like that. It's who he is that matters to me, and that's what I've fallen in love with.'

'Soph – have you?' Jen sounds worried.

'I think so,' I admit. 'The way I feel is like nothing I've ever felt before. When we're together ... it's hard to describe, but it's like we just ... fit.'

'Wow. You really do fancy him.'

'It's more than that,' I say. 'I feel taken care of. And ... he's good for me. He tests me, makes me stronger and better.'

Jen snorts. 'Are you sure you're not just madly in lust with an extremely hot film star?'

'It's not just sex,' I say. 'At least, I don't think it is. He's teaching me about myself -'

'I bet he is.'

'No, I mean he's helping me come out of myself more. To be a better actress. A more confident person. To believe in myself.'

'Well that can't be a bad thing,' Jen admits. 'When will you see him again?'

'We have a class tomorrow morning. This is torture. Why did I send him that stupid text message? He must be running a mile right now.'

'You had to send it,' says Jen. 'You'd be torturing yourself even worse if you didn't. At least now you know. Or probably know. He's freaked out. Leave him to it. He might come back, he might not. Go out and have fun in the meantime. I wish I was there with you. I could come down -'

'You have work,' I interrupt. 'Don't worry. I'll be fine.'

Even though it's only mid-afternoon, I crawl under my duvet, feeling lonelier and emptier than I ever have in my life. Life without Marc – there's no magic to it. No excitement. I can't stand this. I just can't stand it.

I stare at my phone, willing it to ring, willing the message alert to beep. But it doesn't.

I have a singing class with Denise this afternoon, but I just can't manage it. I'm too tired after last night, and emotionally exhausted after today. I stuff my phone under my pillow and lie looking at the ceiling, thinking, thinking, thinking.

I watch movies on my new laptop, trying to take my mind off Marc, but in everything I choose there's something that reminds me of him. In Love Actually, the hidden romance between the Prime Minister and his assistant ... in Pretty Woman, the dynamic of a rich older man with a young girl ... I see Marc everywhere.

As evening falls, I know I can't face dinner with Tom and Tanya. They'll know straight away that something's wrong, and I don't have the energy to lie to them. All I can think about is seeing Marc tomorrow.

I feel torn in two directions. Part of me is desperate to see him. Another part of me is afraid. What if it's over?

At 10pm, I pull the duvet over my head and drift into a troubled sleep.

Chapter 54

The next morning, I consider skipping class. But I know there would be so many questions from Tom and Tanya, so I get dressed and wait outside the lecture theatre, my stomach hollow from yet another 'too nervous to eat breakfast' morning. I haven't eaten since yesterday lunchtime, and I feel weak and scared.

Every click of a shoe makes me jump.

'Hey.' I feel a hand at my elbow. It's Tom.

'Hey, Tom.'

'You look exhausted, my love. Late night?' He raises a mischievous eyebrow. He's wearing a black cowboy hat today, and a pink cowboy shirt with embroidery around the shoulders.

'No.' I smile. 'I wish.'

'Looking forward to our lecture this morning? It's great to have the man himself back, is it not?'

I'm about to reply when I hear hard footsteps clicking down the corridor. I turn and see Marc, striding towards the lecture theatre.

My heart jumps into my mouth and I clutch my books tighter. It feels strange not to say hello to him after being so close, but it doesn't feel appropriate somehow. Or welcome.

'Good morning, Mr Blackwell,' Tom says, in his cheerful, booming voice. 'How are you today?'

'Fine, thank you.' Marc glides past him and into the lecture theatre, without even looking at me. This again. The silent treatment. I know I'm about to cry, and although part of me wants Marc to see how upset I am, another part of me can't bear him to see my tears if this is the end of things.

'I'll see you later,' I say to Tom, running down the corridor.

'Are you okay?' he calls after me.

'Fine.'

I hurry out into the grounds, running over the grass, into the woodlands. When I'm surrounded by trees, I throw my books onto the cool, damp earth, and feel sobbing take over me. Then I sit on the soil and breathe in and out. The natural sights and smells calm me and help me feel myself again.

Through the trees, I see a tall figure striding towards the woodlands over the dewy grass. I quickly wipe the tears away and stand up.

It's Marc. He sees me and walks faster.

I pick up my books and stumble away from him, heading towards the accommodation block.

'Sophia,' Marc calls.

I start to run, clutching my books tightly to my chest.

'Wait.' He's right behind me now, and grabs my elbow. 'Sophia, wait. I need to talk to you.'

I shake my arm away. 'There's nothing to talk about. I got too close and you didn't like it.'

'Come back to class. We can talk at the end of the lesson. I don't like you being out here on your own.'

'There's nothing in the trees that can hurt me,' I say. 'It's the person in the classroom I should be scared of.'

Marc drops his head. 'You're scared of me?'

'Of course I am.' I wipe tears from my cheeks. 'I'm scared you'll hurt me. *Have* hurt me.'

He puts both hands on my shoulders. 'I'm sorry.'

I feel tears welling up again. 'Don't,' I say, shuffling away. 'Not here.'

'Come back to class,' says Marc. 'We'll talk afterwards.'

'Fine. I'll sit in class, take notes and pretend nothing has happened. That I don't feel anything for you.' I turn and head towards the lecture theatre.

'I'm sorry,' says Marc, walking beside me. 'I never meant to hurt you, but this is new territory for me. I haven't worked out how best to handle it yet.'

'It's okay,' I say, feeling empty and defeated. 'I knew this couldn't last. We both did. I knew it had to end and I knew I'd get hurt.'

'It doesn't have to end.'

'Oh? You've made your feelings pretty clear. Let's get real Marc. Like you said, you can't offer me what I want.' I walk faster.

Chapter 55

Back at the lecture theatre, everyone stares as I squeeze into my seat. They must guess I'm upset by my red eyes, and maybe a few students realise I'm upset over Mr Blackwell. They probably think I have a crush, and he's just told me to forget it.

Marc goes to the front of the theatre and begins his lecture, which is about body language. He's so strong and in control. I got to him last night, but now the barriers are up again.

I try to listen to the lecture, try to see Marc as the intelligent, controlled teacher he's portraying. But now I see something more – a vulnerability behind his upright posture and intense stare. A tender part of him that has been trampled down, and is too frightened to come out.

I realise I truly am in love with him – all of him. The amazing, charismatic, intelligent actor that everyone sees, and the vulnerable boy he's trying to keep hidden. It hurts so badly that we can't be together. But I always knew it would end this way.

When the class files out, I head out too. I have no desire to hear Marc's goodbye speech, and I'd rather just let things end with dignity. But I feel a hand on my elbow as I'm leaving, and turn to see Marc, his eyes cloudy, two vertical frown lines above his nose.

'Sophia, may I talk with you?' His words are soft, and lack their usual fierceness. I feel a pain in my chest.

The class files out and it's just me and him. Alone.

'Look, I don't need the *Dear John* letter,' I tell him. 'I get it. You don't want what I want. So ... let's go our separate ways.'

'No.' Marc shakes his head.

'I think we should end this before I get more hurt than I already am.'

'You really want to end things?' Marc's thick eyebrows pull together.

'Yes,' I say, although it's not true. I'm trying to be strong, but under Marc's gaze I have precious little strength left.

'Then tell me again,' says Marc, moving closer to me. 'Tell me we should end this, and I'll never bother you again.'

'I think we should.' I whisper.

'We should what?' he asks softly, bringing his face closer to mine.

I look away.

Marc moves my chin so I'm facing him. 'You think we should what?'

End it, I think. But the words melt in my mouth, and the next moment he's kissing me and I'm lost in the clean, sharp smell of his skin, the strength of his hands on my arms. His eyes, closed and slightly pained looking, with those long eyelashes fluttering as his mouth moves on mine.

He lifts me up and puts me on the desk.

'Tell me you don't want me,' Marc whispers into my neck. 'And I'll never touch you again.' He pulls me closer. 'Tell me we can't be together.'

I try to say the words, but my mouth just opens and closes.

He pushes my skirt up over my thighs. 'I can't be without you right now.' Marc pulls aside my underwear. I see the silver of a condom packet, and feel the foil scratch my thigh. 'Something about you ... it's changed me. And I don't seem to be able to change back again.'

I let myself mesh with his body. The protestations in my head are partly drowned out by the tugging that pulls me to him. But some doubts still break through. 'You were so cold when you left,' I stammer.

Marc slides inside me, and my protestations fall silent.

'*Oh,*' I moan as he moves gently back and forth.

'We're meant to be together,' he says. 'I can't think of anything else but you.'

'Don't ... stop,' I hear myself say, as pleasure builds in my abdomen.

Marc moves faster and harder. He grabs my buttocks and pulls me into him, and I moan louder.

'I've wanted to have you on this desk since you walked into the class this morning. Did you know that? Do you know how hard it was to keep my eyes off you?'

I can't answer him. I'm too lost in what I'm feeling. He carries on moving, sliding himself further and further inside.

'I thought I couldn't handle it,' he whispers. 'After last night. I thought I couldn't handle it. But then, the thought of losing you ... when you ran out this morning, I realised losing you is what I'm really afraid of.'

His words have little impact on me right now. The sensations are building up. I'm completely filled up by him, in every way. The harder he moves, the better it feels.

I come, and fall against him. We stay like that, wrapped in each other's arms for a moment, until I realise where we are.

'Someone might come in,' I say.

He slides himself out of me, and I see him take off the condom and tie it. He pushes himself back inside his trousers, and I see his bulk pressing against trouser fabric.

'How can you stand not to come?' I ask. 'I don't get it. I want you to feel what I'm feeling.'

'I need to stay in control,' says Marc, walking back and forth. 'But I'll be the first to admit it's getting difficult.'

'Then let yourself go,' I say.

Marc shakes his head. 'It wouldn't be right. Especially while I'm still your teacher. Now. You've got another class to go to in ...' he checks his watch, 'about ten minutes, am I right? Singing, with the wonderful Denise.'

'Yes,' I say, wanting his arms back around me. To spend every moment I have with him.

'Then you should go,' Marc says. He runs a hand over my hair. 'I'll see you on the trip to the Globe this afternoon.'

I nod. I'd forgotten about that trip. 'I didn't realise you were going,' I say.

'I organise the class trips every term,' he says. 'And as usual, I'm going on all of them. I need to make sure my students get the most out of the experience.'

'Okay,' I say, 'but ... when will I see you again? Properly?'

He smiles. 'Soon.'

Chapter 56

Denise's class is fun, and I think she can tell I'm happy. She gives me the occasional smile, now and again, and it feels good to know she cares.

After Denise's class, and lunch, we're on our way to the Globe Theatre, courtesy of the college minibus.

The theatre is on the bank of the Thames, and the weather is windy and rainy. I stand with the other Ivy College students, shivering, waiting for our guide. The minibus dropped us off a little early, and we have a ten minute wait.

Marc arrived separately, we're told, and is inside the theatre, trying to hurry the tour. Tanya also thinks he's inside to avoid being mobbed by adoring fans, who are waiting on the banks of the Thames. They've closed the Globe especially for our trip, and word has got around that Marc Blackwell is inside.

The theatre is huge, round and beautiful. Its walls are white and smooth, with dark wooden beams running around them, and there's a straw roof on top. I stare up at this famous building, thinking what it must have been like for people to visit the actors here in Shakespeare's time. It's not the original theatre, but it's a very good likeness, and enough to set my imagination racing.

A woman in a green anorak approaches, her hood pulled up.

'Good afternoon, Ivy College.' There are wiry glasses on her nose and coral pink lipstick stains her mouth and teeth. 'It's a pleasure to have you here. I'm your guide to the Globe. Come on inside.'

We follow her to the main doors, which she unlocks, and we find Marc waiting for us in the reception area. He looks as handsome as ever, wearing jeans and a t-shirt. How is he not feeling the cold?

His lips tip up a little when he sees me, and he holds my gaze. I look away, fighting back a smile.

'Mr Blackwell!' says the guide, breathlessly. 'A pleasure, an absolute pleasure.' She does an odd sort of curtsy. 'So good of you to come with your class.'

'A pleasure to be here,' says Marc, shaking her hand.

'I'll lead you straight through to the theatre itself,' says the guide, her hand to her cheek. 'And then we'll walk through the museum, and you can learn more about this fabulous building.'

She leads us out into a huge, round, open-air space, which has a gritty floor with wooden seating and banisters curving around us. There are three tiers of seating, and I can see part of the straw roof sheltering the seats from the elements.

A light spray of rain is whirling around the open-air part, and the guide leads us to the sheltered seats.

Tanya, Tom and I wait until last, so we can carry Tom up the steps and place him at the end of an aisle. Marc comes forward to help, checking that Tom's brakes are in place.

'I remember these things,' says Marc. 'I forgot the brakes a few times when I was acting in one, and nearly broke my neck.'

Tom nods and smiles. 'Fancy Shakespeare not catering for disability. What a bastard.'

Tanya and I stand either side of Tom, but to my surprise, Marc doesn't move. Instead, he stands behind me.

The guide looks sorry that Marc isn't by her side any more, but quickly recovers and starts telling us how the theatre was lovingly recreated from historical pictures and documents. She tells us about the stage itself, and points out the wooden balcony above it.

'Modern actors have played Juliet on that balcony,' she says, 'calling to her Romeo. But in Shakespeare's day, the balcony was used to seat important guests, such as members of the royal family. In those days, it was less about what you saw than what you heard. So the best seats in the house couldn't see the actors all that well.'

I feel Marc's breath on my neck as the guide tells us about the history of the theatre. I try to listen to the guide, but my entire body is tense. All I can think about is Marc being so close to me. I can feel the heat from his body.

As the guide tells us how the new theatre was built, I feel a palm on my behind.

I give Marc a poisonous *not here* glare, but he gives me that quirky smile, then squeezes my buttocks under his fingers. I have to turn my lips inward so I don't make a sound.

I turn again and sneak a glance at him. There's the tiniest of smiles on his face as he catches me looking at him, but in the main he looks completely impassive, one hand rested nonchalantly on a wooden beam, the other working my backside.

I smile and shake my head at him. His jaw ripples as he stares straight ahead.

Having his hand there, kneading and pushing, I can hardly stand still. It's a relief when the guide finally stops her talk and announces it's time to see the museum.

The class files down the steps, and Marc's hand drops away. Now it's gone, I miss its heat. Marc lifts Tom down from the steps, and Tanya and I wait for them. Then we all walk towards the museum, but as I reach the doorway, Marc catches my hand.

I stop, looking stupidly at Tom and Tanya's retreating backs.

'Come with me,' he says.

'What were you playing at, back there?' I snap. 'Someone could have seen.'

'Just helping you with your acting,' says Marc, with that teasing smile of his. 'Come on.'

'Where?' I ask, watching the door to the museum swing closed.

'Up here.' He squeezes my hand and leads me up the wooden steps onto the Globe's stage.

'Are we allowed up here?'

'I am,' says Marc. 'I'm a patron of this theatre.' He leads me through one of the rounded doorways, and up some creaky wooden stairs. Suddenly we're on the balcony above the stage, looking out at the Globe Theatre.

'This is amazing,' I say, looking out at the empty seats. 'Imagine this place full of people.'

'Amazing building,' Marc says. 'A perfect recreation – as perfect as possible.' He tilts my chin up. His eyes dart back and forth. 'Go to the balcony rail.'

I do, holding the smooth wood and looking out over the theatre. It truly is amazing. I could stay here all day.

Marc strokes the hair from one side of my neck to the other, and goose bumps run down my arms. Then he sucks hard on my neck, and I give a little gasp.

'Marc, what are you doing? Don't you know where we are?' I grip the balcony.

'I'm well aware of where we are, Miss Rose. The perfect place for your continued education.' In one smooth movement, he lifts my dress and slides my bra upwards so my breasts are exposed. Then he covers my breasts with his hands and presses himself against me.

'I'm planning to test your boundaries today.'

Chapter 57

I look out at the empty theatre. 'I think my boundaries are pretty much tested.'

'Oh, I don't think they are.' Marc uses one hand to pull down my panties and free himself from his trousers. Then he slides a finger between my buttocks.

'Has anyone else ever had you in there?' he asks, sliding his finger further inside until my buttocks clench.

'Oh my god,' I say, as his hand tightens on my breast. 'No. Never. I've never done anything like that. Marc -'

I turn to see what he's doing, but he forces me back around to face the front.

'Marc, I don't think – oh!'

He slides himself between my buttocks and I feel he's hard, but much more slippery than usual.

'What are you doing?'

'Something you need to try,' Marc replies. 'Don't worry. I have a special condom. No chance of breaking.'

'Marc, I'm really not ready for this. Please. This isn't the place.'

'It's exactly the place.' He slides himself further and further between my buttocks.

'I don't see how -'

'Then let me show you.' With one swift movement, he pushes himself inside me – a different me. A me no one has ever been in before.

I grip the rail.

'I'll go slow,' he whispers. 'Trust me, Sophia. I know exactly how far to go with you. This is the right test for you today.'

'It's too much,' I murmur, feeling the tightness.

He inches further in. 'Not yet it isn't. You can take it. Trust me.' I start to feel sore, and hear a gasp – my own.

'I promise this will feel good. Just relax.' He slides one hand between my legs and moves it back and forth, all the time inching further and further in.

He's so hard, everything feels too tight and suddenly he begins to move slowly back and forth.

Oh. *Oh.*

At first it feels far too strange, and I almost ask him to stop, but as he slides his hand back and forth, it starts to feel good.

I moan as he pushes himself deeper and deeper. I grip the rail, and everything turns blurry. All I can think about is Marc and what he's doing to me. It feels so good.

'You like it?' Marc asks, moving faster. 'I knew you would.' His hand slides back and forth, faster and faster. I hear him moan then, and that feels better than anything.

'Oh god,' he says, pushing further inside me with every stroke. 'You're a very accommodating student. Very, very accommodating.'

I can feel he's nearly all the way inside, and I come, feeling my knees go weak, and hearing myself calling his name.

As waves of pleasure ripple through me, I feel him slide all the way inside me until his body presses against my buttocks.

'Oh god, oh Sophia.'

I feel the beat of him against me.

He collapses against my shoulders, grasping my breasts and pulling me into him. He holds me tight for a long time. Then he slides himself free.

I see he's still hard, and feel disappointed. He didn't come.

He puts the condom into a plastic bag, and it's then I realise he must have been planning this all along.

'You planned this,' I say.

Marc nods. 'Call it lesson preparation.'

'I don't know how I feel about what just happened,' I say, pulling my dress down. 'Or where.'

He wraps his arms around me. 'You think too much. It was good for you. I promise. You'd better get back to your trip. Catch up with the class.'

'What about you?'

'I don't want anyone to get suspicious about where you've been. I still have your reputation to think of. I'll leave by the fire exit and meet you later on.'

'Okay.' I swallow, not sure how I'm going to make it down those creaky wooden steps. My knees are still so weak. 'Where?'

'I have something planned for us,' he says. 'A little extra-curricular trip all of our own. I'll have a car come pick you up from the campus gates in two hours. Bring your passport. Now go.' He gestures to the staircase. 'They'll be getting suspicious.'

My passport?

'Okay.' I head towards the staircase, then take careful steps until I reach the bottom. I cross the stage, and turn back to see Marc on the balcony. He's staring at me, deep in thought. When he notices I'm looking up, a fondness passes over his face that makes my heart melt.

'It's going to be hard to wait,' he says.

'I know,' I say. 'What are we going to do, Marc?'

He runs a hand through his hair. 'That's what I'm trying to figure out.'

Chapter 58

After the museum tour, Tom, Tanya and I have coffee in the Globe restaurant. It looks out over the Thames, and we watch the grey waters churn under rain and wind.

'I'm loving this place,' says Tom. 'Wheelchair ramps aside, what a great day out. And apparently, it's educational! Shame you dawdled, Soph. The museum was by far the highlight.'

'I thought it was pretty boring,' says Tanya. 'Soph had the right idea – hang around and get a better look at the theatre itself. What an amazing building.'

'It was,' I agree.

'Did you like the stage?' Tanya asks. 'You know Marc performed on that stage, don't you?'

'Yes,' I say quietly. 'I loved the stage.' *And Marc performed again on that stage this afternoon.*

'Well,' says Tom, taking a sip of cappuccino. 'A little London tour awaits, do we think? Shall we walk and wheel ourselves back to the college, and take in the sights on the way?'

'You do know how far it is to the college, don't you?' says Tanya.

'Of course I do. I grew up in London. Are you saying because I'm in a wheelchair, I can't go very far?'

'No,' says Tanya. 'I'm saying because you're incredibly lazy, you can't go very far. You moan about going over the grass on campus, and that's just a few metres.

Which means either Sophia or I will end up pushing you most of the journey.'

'I understand,' says Tom. 'The two of you will squabble about who gets to push the famous Tom Davenport. Well, squabble not ladies. You can take it in turns. I like to be fair.'

We all laugh.

'I don't mind pushing you,' I say.

'Nor do I, really,' says Tanya.

'Then what are we waiting for? We've got no lectures this afternoon, correct? So we've got all the time in the world.'

'Actually, I have to be back on campus in an hour,' I say, checking my watch.

'Really?' Tom raises an eyebrow. 'A hot date with your older man?'

'Something like that,' I admit.

'Sophia, be careful with him,' says Tanya. 'He's older than you, and ... well, you know my thoughts. Exactly how much older is he?'

'Five years,' I say.

'Hardly an age difference,' says Tom. 'I'm dating a thirty five year old divorcee online.'

'Yes, but this is different,' says Tanya. 'This is real life. I don't want you being taken advantage of, that's all. Has he met any of your friends yet?'

'In a way.'

Tom's eyebrows shoot up. 'In a *way*? Intriguing.' He's silent for a moment, and I can almost see the cogs working. 'Mr Blackwell disappeared very quickly this afternoon, didn't he?'

'Did he?' I scratch the back of my neck. 'I didn't notice.'

'And you vanished suddenly too ...'

Tom stares out at churning waters. 'Older man. In control. Five year age difference ...'

I look at Tom, my eyes begging him not to think too much about this. But I'm too late.

'*Mr* Blackwell.'

Tanya stares at Tom. 'What are you talking about?' Then her eyes cloud over as she does some thinking of her own. '*Oh*. No. It can't be. Can it? Soph?'

I look into my hot chocolate.'

'*Soph*?' says Tanya.

Tom clears his throat and puts a hand on Tanya's shoulder, shaking his head. Then he turns to me. 'It's okay, my dear. Your secret's safe with us.'

'Please don't tell anyone,' I whisper. 'It's all so ... confusing right now.'

Tom and Tanya nod solemnly.

'But it's true. Mr Blackwell and I are ... more than just teacher and pupil.'

'Shut UP,' says Tanya, slapping Tom's arm.

'Keep your voice down, Tanya, before the whole bloody restaurant hears,' Tom whispers.

'Sorry.' Tanya's hand flies to her mouth. 'Sophia, you have my word. I won't tell anyone. I promise.'

'Nor will I,' says Tom. 'But you have to tell us what he's like in bed, our Mr Hollywood hot shot. Does that white skin go all the way down?'

I laugh. 'From what I've seen. Which actually isn't a lot.'

'Intriguing,' says Tom.

I nod into my drink. 'As far as Marc's concerned, nothing is normal or straight forward. Some days I feel like I'm getting closer to him. Other times, it's just ... I don't know. Weird. I mean the whole thing is weird.'

'You got that right,' says Tanya. 'Weird and wrong. He shouldn't be messing around with a student.'

'I know,' I say. 'But sometimes ... haven't you ever been attracted to the wrong person?'

'Never,' says Tanya, shaking her head. 'I wouldn't let myself. It's not in my mental wiring.'

'Well, sometimes people fall for someone they shouldn't,' I say. 'And if that happens, what can you do?'

'You do whatever you like, and worry about the consequences when it all goes wrong,' says Tom.

'You control yourself and stop yourself getting involved,' says Tanya.

I feel somewhere between their two answers lies the right advice. I'm just not exactly sure what that advice is.

Chapter 59

At six o'clock, I find myself at the campus gates again, only this time I'm not shivering. I'm wrapped in the cashmere coat Marc bought me, and watching a robin hop along the wrought iron gate.

A black car pulls up, but it's not a limo this time. It's a sleek Mercedes with tinted windows.

Keith jumps out of the driver's seat and opens the passenger door for me.

'Thanks,' I say, climbing in. 'How have you been?'

'Not bad,' says Keith, adjusting the mirror. 'How are you, young lady? Is Master Blackwell treating you alright? I hope so. I've never known him behave this way over a woman.'

'I wouldn't know how he usually behaves with women,' I say, staring out the window. 'But to me, nothing that's happened with Marc tells me I'm anything special.'

'You'd be surprised.' I see Keith smile.

As the car pulls into Marc's garage, I see Rodney waiting by the beige Rolls Royce.

He opens the car door for me. 'Mr Blackwell has asked me to escort you up to the den,' he says, opening the door to the house and walking up steps.

'Thank you,' I say, following him. 'Bye, Keith.'

Keith waves as I enter the dragon's cave. The entrance hall smells of polish and lemon juice, and the framed pictures of London sparkle.

'The den's on the first floor,' Rodney explains, leading me up the huge flight of stairs. 'I tried to get Mr Blackwell to put up posters of his movies on these walls. Or perhaps his award certificates. Or *something*, just to say who he is, what he's done. He should be proud of his career. But he's not into showing off, our Mr Blackwell. Everything low key. All those black clothes.'

He takes me to a closed door.

'He's in there,' he says, knocking on the door 'Mr Blackwell! Your guest is here.'

I open the door, and see a room of leather sofas, red carpets and glass coffee tables.

Marc is sitting on a sofa, one leg sprawled along its length. As usual, he's wearing all black – black t-shirt, black jeans and black socks. He's holding the green copy of *Romeo and Juliet* I saw in his room, and closes it carefully when he sees me.

'Good evening, Sophia.'

'Good evening.'

'Have you eaten yet?'

I notice a selection of food on the small glass table. Balls of mozzarella with fresh basil, rustic breadsticks wrapped in ham, cherry tomatoes on skewers, shavings of parmesan cheese. Behind the food are two bottles of red wine, and champagne sits chilling in a glass ice bucket.

I shake my head. 'No. Not yet. I had a lot to think about today. I didn't feel much like eating.'

'I had a few things I thought you might like brought up for you.'

'You thought I might like Italian food?' I notice the parmesan looks very fresh, and the mozzarella is the delicious gooey kind you only usually find in Italy.

'It's the best food in the world,' he says.

'My mother was from Italy,' I say. 'I go back there sometimes. It's true. The food there is amazing.'

Marc's mouth hints at a smile. 'You're half Italian?'

I nod.

'I should have guessed. Take a seat.'

'Thank you.' I sit on the sofa, feeling the familiar effect Marc has on me. Knee trembles, a slight sickness and an overwhelming sense of excitement.

'You look nervous,' says Marc, placing the book on a huge glass coffee table at the centre of the room. 'Don't be. I'll go easy on you after today, okay?' The table is empty, except for a gold bottle opener, a remote control and a bottle of Peroni. 'Wine?'

'I *am* nervous,' I admit. 'And I'll take beer if you have it.'

Marc grins at me, and my insides go soft. 'Beer? Not such a delicate thing after all.' He opens the arm of the sofa, and I see six beers inside. He opens one and passes it over. I feel his fingers against mine and shiver. The beer is cold, so I guess the hole under the sofa arm must be a fridge.

'Thanks,' I say, taking a long sip.

'So.' Marc sits up. 'You must be wondering what I have planned for you this evening?'

I nod. 'Yes. Wondering, nervously.'

'Come sit next to me, Sophia.' I do. The leather sofa creaks as I sit down, and our eyes meet. Marc breathes deeply and closes his eyes. I feel like he's inhaling me. His eyes flicker open.

'God, you're beautiful,' he says. 'Just so, so beautiful. Inside and out.'

'Thank you,' I mutter. 'I never ... I mean I don't feel that way about myself.'

'You should.'

I take another sip of beer. There's a tension in the room. I know we both feel it. I'm aching for him to touch me, but as usual this is all at his pace. I'm pretty sure if I try to touch him, he'll stop me.

Marc turns to the television and picks up the remote. 'So. I've been teaching you about losing your inhibitions,' he says. 'Showing you how to let go. Tonight, I thought we'd take the other perspective.'

'Marc, all this teacher stuff. Can't we just be normal? For tonight at least? While we're still ... figuring things out?'

Marc considers this for a moment. Then he reaches out and stokes my hair. 'I'd like you to try this for me, Sophia. I think it would be good for you.'

'What do you mean by, the other perspective?' I ask.

'I'd like you to watch movies of other people letting go,' Marc says, simply.

'What?' I feel scared. What does he mean? I have an uneasy feeling that he's going to show me films of other women he's been with. 'I'm not sure I'm up to what you're suggesting,' I say, swallowing more beer. 'If you want me to watch your other women -'

'I don't.' Marc holds up a hand.

'So what is it you want me to watch?'

'Something that I hope will open you up even more.'

I clutch my beer like a life support.

'I thought we were getting closer,' I say. 'In a good way. A ... couple way. Marc, will it always be about this for you? About you taking charge of me, sexually? I need more than that.'

'And you'll have it,' Marc whispers, wrapping my hair around his fingers. 'I promise. I'm working hard on making that happen. But for now, let me do things my way.'

He presses the remote control and a classroom fills the screen. There's a man standing by a blackboard, a mortar cap on his head, and a swooping black cape around his shoulders. He's dressed as an old-fashioned teacher stereotype, but he's young, handsome and tanned.

A woman walks into the room, dressed in a Britney Spears style school uniform, sucking a lollipop. She has bleached blonde hair, and huge breasts squeezed against a white blouse. She's clearly no teenage school girl, and I'm guessing she is, in fact, a few years older than me.

The camera moves very close to her mouth, filming her sucking at the lollipop. She moves her tongue around it, and pouts at the teacher.

Oh my god.

'You want me to watch porn with you?' I ask, my heart beating hard. My palms are slippery, and my stomach feels like it's been sprinkled with salt. I don't like this. I don't like this at all.

'Don't be afraid,' says Marc. 'Watching can't hurt you, I promise. You've never watched pornography before?'

I shake my head. 'Not really. At least, not ... seriously.'

'Not even with boyfriends? What about magazines – have you never had a boyfriend who read porn magazines?'

'Probably,' I say. 'But they never showed me them.'

'Sit here.' He lifts me onto his thigh. I feel the firmness of his leg muscle between my own legs. He puts his hands on my waist. 'It's okay,' he whispers. 'If you really don't like it, just say the word and I'll turn it off.'

The schoolgirl sits on a desk in front of the teacher. Her pleated micro-mini skirt rides up to show stockings and suspenders.

'Do you want to fuck me, sir?' she asks, batting her huge false eyelashes. She lifts up her skirt, showing crotch-less panties and bare, shaved skin.

I swallow and take another sip of beer. I'm so embarrassed watching this, and Marc must know it. But at the same time, I feel myself growing warmer and Marc's thigh between my legs is ever present.

The teacher paces back and forth, then takes a paddle from the rim of the blackboard. 'How dare you behave this way in front of your teacher?' he barks, his cape flying. 'You deserve to be spanked.'

The girl squeals as he picks her up and puts her over his knee. He lifts her skirt and smacks her hard on the behind. 'You bad, bad girl.'

'How does it make you feel, watching this?' Marc asks.

'I don't know,' I say. 'Confused. A bit sick.'

'It doesn't turn you on at all?'

I blush. 'Yes. A little. Do you watch this sort of thing often?'

'No. I bought this just for you.'

Now I feel even more embarrassed. 'For me? You think I'd like this?'

'The teacher student thing was my little private joke. But yes – I thought it would be good for you to see people who are uninhibited in their sexuality.'

'I guess you don't need to watch anything like this yourself,' I say. 'There are plenty of women who would do anything you want in real life.'

Marc gives a little smile. 'True. But that doesn't mean I always take them up on it. Life can get very boring when you can have anything you like, believe me.'

On the screen, the teacher flips the schoolgirl onto her back. 'Please sir, please no. I'm a virgin.'

'You should have thought of that before you acted like such a slut.'

The teacher has sex with the woman on the desk, and even though she cries, 'no, sir, no,' when the camera films her face she starts to moan with pleasure.

I feel even more embarrassed, and don't know where to look, but I have to be honest – watching the video really is turning me on. I wish I wasn't here, being scrutinised by Marc. I don't know what he wants from me. Is he doing this to humiliate me?

I feel his hands tighten around my waist, and he begins to slide me back and forth along his thigh.

Chapter 60

I try to look away from the film, but Marc turns my head back. The school girl is on her knees now, and the teacher is forcing her head into his crotch. He undoes her shirt, and her breasts are naked underneath.

I hate that Marc is watching this naked woman. It feels like an intrusion. But the friction between my legs is making me hotter and hotter. I feel like I'm burning.

'Stop,' I say, climbing off him. 'I can't watch any more of this. It's ... it doesn't feel right.'

'Why not?' Marc asks, turning off the TV. 'Is it the teacher pupil thing?'

'No.' I shake my head.

'I know that little scenario turned you on,' says Marc. 'I could feel your breathing getting quicker –'

'I didn't like watching it with you. I don't like you seeing another woman naked.'

Marc laughs. 'That's what it is? Jealousy?'

I smile, realising he's right. 'Okay, I admit it. How do you feel about me watching another man like that?'

Marc shrugs. 'It doesn't bother me. All I care about is whether you're turned on or not.' He slips a hand down the back of my jeans. 'And from what I can feel, you are.'

I squirm away from him. 'So what if I was *with* another man. Would that bother you?'

Marc's expression darkens, and the red colour leaves his lips. 'I'd hate it.'

I feel warmth in my chest. 'You would?'

Marc nods.

'I'm happy about that,' I say.

Marc picks up the remote control. 'Ready to watch some more?'

'Maybe this is a step too far for me, today.'

'Mmm.' Marc downs his beer. 'Then I'm doing my job well. You need to be shaken out of your comfort zone. Or you'll never grow. Wait there.'

He leaves the room, and I take hurried sips of beer. I'm feeling so self-conscious now, and so tiny in this huge place.

When he returns, he has a school uniform hanging from his fingers. 'Put this on,' he says.

'You have to be kidding me.' I shake my head.

'A good actress will try on many different costumes in her life,' says Marc, lifting me from the sofa by my hands. 'And I know you're a good actress. Put it on. See how you feel.'

I hesitate. What is it about Marc that makes me do things I'd never ordinarily do? I feel safe with him, I have to admit. Even though he's testing my boundaries, I feel as though he'd never hurt me.

'Right here?'

Marc nods slowly. 'Right here.'

I slip off my shoes and tight jeans, feeling his eyes on me the whole time. The room is nice and warm, but I still shiver. I take off my jumper and vest, leaving on my underwear.

I wrap my arms around my torso, waiting for Marc to hand me the uniform.

'Don't cover yourself. I want to see it all.'

I let my arms fall to my sides.

'Take off your underwear.' His voice is stern now. 'I won't tell you again.'

I peel off my bra and panties and let them fall to the floor.

He holds out the school uniform, and I put on the navy blue pleated skirt, short-sleeved blouse and grey and red-striped tie.

Marc watches me for a moment without saying a word.

'How do you feel?' he asks.

I look down at myself. It's been a long time since I wore a school uniform, and it's straining in all the right places. Under the blouse, I see the shadows and fullness of my naked breasts, and my hips and rear end are tight in the skirt.

'Good,' I say.

'How would you feel if I told you that, wearing that, every man in the country would want you?'

I shrug my shoulders. 'I feel good and bad about that.'

'And what if you were asked to play the part in a movie?'

'What do you mean, a sexy schoolgirl part?'

'Exactly.'

'I'd feel ... nervous. That maybe it was a step too far for me.'

'Okay. Then take it off.'

I'm surprised. I thought he was going to have sex with me in the uniform, and I was kind of looking forward to it.

'You're not going to ... do anything to me?' I ask.

'Do you want me to?'

I nod.

Marc shakes his head. 'Not today. After this afternoon ... I don't think I could control myself.'

'But I don't want you to -'

'But I do,' Marc snaps. 'And while I'm still your teacher, I will. We can't get too close this evening, but ... here.' He pulls a drawer at the bottom of his leather sofa, and inside I see a huge black vibrator and what I can only guess are other sex toys. There are soft pink objects, and black spiked things and strings of beads.

Marc hands me the vibrator.

'What should I do with it?' I ask, feeling self-conscious.

'I want you to put it inside you and pretend it's me,' says Marc. 'And I'm going to watch. But from a distance.'

He clears the bottle opener and remote control from the giant glass coffee table.

'Get up on this table.'

'On the glass table? It'll break.'

'No it won't.' Marc shakes his head. 'It's specially made.'

He puts two cushions on the table, and lifts me onto it. I kneel on the cushions and take the vibrator, feeling how heavy it is. It looks and feels sort of sinister, and even holding it feels alien and strange.

Marc takes something else from the drawer, then slides under the table effortlessly, in a way that tells me he's done this dozens of times before. I don't like that thought at all, but seeing him beneath the glass, those dark blue eyes staring up at me, I can think of nothing but him.

I want to touch him, and put a hand to the glass. It's cold.

'Slide the vibrator inside yourself,' says Marc pushing his palm to meet mine against the glass. 'I'll watch you, but from where I can't touch.'

I slide the vibrator into myself. It's cold and thick, and feels nothing like Marc.

As he watches, his eyes darken. Then he snaps something in his palm and the vibrator begins to buzz.

'Oh!' It takes me by surprise. 'How did you do that?'

'I have a remote control,' says Marc. 'Push it further inside yourself.'

I do, and he clicks his palm again. The buzzing grows more intense, and the vibrator begins to revolve.

'Oh,' I say again. 'Oh god.' It moves around and around and it feels so good. I look into Marc's eyes and feel like I'm falling into them.

He clicks his palm again and the vibrator spins faster.

I nearly fall forwards, but catch myself. I come straight away, moving back and forth against the vibrator.

Marc slides out from under the table. He wraps me in a red blanket and lifts me into his arms. Then he carries me upstairs to the second floor, and into the bedroom where we slept last time.

'Is this your bedroom?' I murmur.

He nods.

'You're putting me into your bed.'

He nods again.

'Will you get in with me?'

'I'll watch you until you fall asleep.' He slides me under the silk-covered duvet, and slips under the covers with me.

My head finds a soft silk pillow, and I remember Marc's head laying on it before, his beautiful face calm in sleep.

'How many other girls have you done that with?' I ask.

'Done what with?' Marc whispers.

'With the coffee table.'

'One,' he says, and my heart sinks.

'What about the school uniform?'

'I bought that just for you. Again. A little private joke. But I thought it might be good for you.'

I don't know if that makes me feel better or worse. I close my eyes, feeling his arms around my shoulders. 'Tell me about how you met Denise,' I say. 'She's so fond of you.'

There's silence, and for a moment I think Marc won't answer. But then he says, 'And I'm fond of her. I'd be a very different person if it weren't for her. She took in a young, difficult boy when no one else wanted him. She was like a second mother to me.'

'My mother passed away when I was young, just like yours,' I say.

I hear Marc inhale, and feel his chest heave into my back. He lets out a long, slow breath.

'I know. Actually, I guessed. From reading about your family set-up on your entry form, and the way you are. Independent, but fragile.'

'I felt really fragile today,' I admit. 'I feel like maybe I'm in too deep. Way over my head. You're so experienced. And the way you have to be in control.'

Marc laughs. 'I'm not so unusual, believe me.' He strokes my hair. 'And you liked it. I knew you'd like it or I wouldn't have tried it.'

'Maybe,' I murmur, feeling sleep take over me. I fight it. I don't want to lose a moment with Marc, and this is one of the nicest moments we've had. I feel the bare skin of his arms against mine, and his stubble against my shoulder as he talks. 'How did you lose your mother?'

'Car accident,' says Marc, but the unusual tone to his voice tells me that maybe he's not being completely truthful.

I remember his words from the hospital and parrot him: 'I'm an actor too, you know. I know when someone's lying.'

Marc laughs. 'Okay. It wasn't a car accident. It was a brain tumour. Long and slow and painful. I watched her turn from my mother into a grey, shadow of a woman, and my father turn from a proud, controlling man into a tyrant.'

I'm wide awake suddenly. 'That's terrible,' I say, turning to face him. He won't meet my eye.

'I always felt, as a young boy, that I could have saved her,' he continues. 'But ... I've had a lot of therapy. There was nothing I could have done. At least, that's the logic.'

'Your father must have taken it very badly,' I say. 'I know my dad was a mess after it all happened. He couldn't eat. He couldn't sleep. I had to make sure there was food in the house, and that all our clothes were washed.'

'Little Cinderella,' says Marc, stroking my hair.

'I was happy to do it,' I say. 'It helped me cope.'

'I can understand that,' says Marc.

'What about your dad?' I ask. 'How did he take it?'

'By bullying and controlling my sister and I,' says Marc. He wraps the duvet around me.

'Marc?'

'Yes?'

I peer into the corner of the room, and see the boxes. 'I have a confession.'

'Oh yes?'

'I looked in your boxes.'

There's a long silence, and for a moment I regret owning up.

'I just wanted to know more about you. Are you angry?'

Marc lets out a long breath. 'No. I'm not angry. I'm ... disappointed that you needed to do that. That I can't open up to you in the way you want. Yet.'

'I saw the pictures of your mother,' I venture, and suddenly the whole room goes still. His breathing has stopped.

'Why don't you put them on the wall?' I ask.

'Go to sleep. We've got a big day tomorrow.'

'A big day? Marc -'

'Go to sleep.'

Chapter 61

When I wake up the next morning, Marc is sitting on the end of the bed watching the sun rise out of the window.

He sees me stir, and turns around. 'I wanted to make sure you didn't sleep in. We have to leave soon.'

'I hardly ever sleep in,' I say, stretching my arms. 'I love mornings.'

'Rodney has bought some clothes for you. They're laid out at the end of the bed. Get dressed, then come down to the garage. Breakfast will be in the limo, on the way to the airport.'

'Airport? But what about college?'

'Didn't you read your introductory paperwork? Today and tomorrow are for performance practise, and believe me – you'll be practising. Don't ask too many questions.' He kisses me quickly on the head, then leaves the room. 'Dress. Meet me downstairs. No arguments. Shower. Wear what I've given you.' He slams the door behind him.

I look at the end of the bed, and see a light, white summer dress lying on the duvet, with a pair of strappy cork wedges underneath them. There's a silk strapless bra with a lace-up back and a matching g-string and navy blue cardigan.

But it's autumn, I think, examining the skimpy clothing. The dress and cardigan are by Prada, and the shoes are Kurt Geiger. The underwear is Agent Provocateur.

I shower, towel myself dry and slip on the underwear, which feels amazing. The bra seems to structure my whole body as I pull the laces tight, and the g-string disappears under the dress, making it look like I'm wearing nothing at all underneath.

I don't usually wear heels, and teeter a little as I try to walk. By the time I reach the garage, I've got the hang of them, and see the limo's lights are on.

I jump in the back of the car, and find Marc lounging in the leather interior, wearing loose, grey cargo trousers and his usual short-sleeved black t-shirt.

The car interior is warm. Tropical, even. It smells of fresh coffee and pastries, and I see a silver cafetiere steaming above the drinks cabinet. Next to it is a basket of fresh croissants.

Marc pours me a coffee. 'You look absolutely beautiful.'

'Thank you,' I say, taking the cup. 'Now will you tell me where we're going? I think I'm going to freeze to death in this dress.'

'You think I'd let you get cold?' Marc asks.

'No,' I say. 'I don't think that. I just wish I knew where you were taking me that doesn't require warm clothing, and isn't somewhere people are going to film and photograph us. Well. You. With me.'

'All in good time.'

Chapter 62

We arrive at city airport, and check-in at a private desk. Then the limo drives right up to a private jet, which sits smartly on the runway.

'What about photographers?' I ask.

Marc shakes his head. 'There won't be any here. I only use companies and locations that are discreet.'

A thought occurs to me. 'Is that why the press always say you never have girlfriends? Because you're so discreet?'

Keith opens the car door and helps me out. Marc follows.

'The press are right,' he says, as we reach the aircraft steps. 'I never do have girlfriends. You're the closet thing I've had to one in a long time.'

The closest thing? What does that mean? I'm not sure whether to feel happy or offended.

I'm a little shaky in my high shoes, and Marc takes my hand.

'Here,' he says. 'Let me help you.'

My insides do somersaults at the gesture, and I feel giddy as I take the steps up to the plane.

Inside, the plane is all beige leather. Two frozen margaritas wait for us, decorated with lime and salt, by the luxuriously large seats.

'It's a little early for drinks,' says Marc, with a frown.

'I don't know about that,' I say, as Marc leads me to a seat. 'I think I might need one.' I take a sip of the tart drink, feeling the alcohol rush into my veins.

Marc takes the drink from my hands. 'I told you,' he said. 'Too early.' He checks his watch. 'You can drink it in an hour. I'll have Merile make you another one.'

'Who's Merile?'

'She'll be taking care of us while we're on board. Serving our refreshments.'

The plane door closes and the engines start up. 'Now will you tell me where we're going?' I ask. 'And if we're going a long way away, how am I going to survive with just one outfit?' *And one set of underwear.*

'I had Rodney buy a whole new wardrobe for you,' says Marc. 'A summer wardrobe. You'll have plenty to choose from.'

'You didn't have to do that,' I say.

'While you're with me, I'll take care of you,' says Marc. 'It's as simple as that.'

The plane jolts, and I feel it begin its drive along the runway.

'I'm a little scared of flying,' I admit. 'I've only ever been on one plane before.'

'Don't worry,' says Marc, leaning forward to do up my seat buckle. 'It's safer than driving.'

He pushes a button, and a flat screen and keyboard unfold in front of his seat, from some mysterious place in the beige leather. 'I need to schedule some repairs for the college, while we're flying. The entire east wing is weather damaged, and then there's the roof. The college is listed, so it's a complicated business, but it can't wait. Don't worry –Merile will look after you.'

'Okay,' I say, watching him tip tap on his computer. His brow is furrowed, and soon he's deep in concentration.

So much for finding out more about him on this trip. Still, I have him close to me in a confined space for at least a few hours. I consider attempting to distract him, but his expression screams: *leave me alone.* And I'm buckled in. I don't think he'd be too happy about me un-strapping myself.

Chapter 63

Half an hour after the plane takes off, I'm flicking through the film choices on my own flat screen computer, when a beautiful Asian lady appears from the front of the plane. She has long, black hair wound into a tight bun, and she's dressed in a blouse and pencil skirt.

She bows and offers me a steaming towel that smells of lemon. When I reach forward, she uses the towel to massage my hands.

'Relax,' she says. 'Please. Lean back.' I do, and she lays the towel over my face, then places each hand carefully on my lap. 'Mr Blackwell asked me to manicure your hands and feet. But first, would you like some refreshment? Something to eat or drink?'

I pause, throwing a sideways glance at Marc. 'Do you have Coca Cola?' I ask, feeling like he'd disapprove.

Merile bows and disappears, returning with an ice-cold bottle of coke, and a glass of ice and lemon. She pours the drink and sets it on the table next to me.

'I'll manicure your fingernails now.' She pulls a black box from an overhead locker and opens it up, revealing Neal's Yard pampering products and twenty colours of nail polish.

'Thanks so much,' I say. 'I've never had a manicure before.' I look at my shabby, half bitten nails. 'But you can probably guess that.'

Merile smiles, and begins rubbing my hands, cuticles and nails with various oils and lotions. They smell divine, and soon she's pushing my cuticles back and snipping and filing my nails. She buffs each nail, then holds out three shades of polish – navy, dark green and silver.

'I think these will suit you best,' she says.

'I like the dark green,' I say, thinking of the ivy in Marc's garden.

She flicks two coats over each nail, then bows at my feet and carefully takes off my new shoes. She massages each foot, then fetches a bath of steaming water and places my feet carefully in the lavender-scented liquid.

I turn and notice Marc watching me, a half smile on his face. 'Ask Merile for whatever you need,' he says. 'I'll be done by the time we land.'

'How long until we get there?' I ask.

'Maybe another eight hours,' he says. 'The pilot will get us there as fast as he can, but ... we'll see.'

After my nails are done, Merile fetches me a lunch of crab salad, followed by the lightest and most delicious lemon soufflé I've ever eaten.

I eat, dose a little, watch movies and – more often than is decent – watch Marc. We pass through night time, and then the sun comes up again, and I watch the horizon, fascinated. I've never seen the sun rise twice in one day before.

I have thin slices of melt-in-the-mouth steak for dinner, and poached pear for dessert.

Then the plane begins to descend, and it sudden-ly hits me that I'm thousands of miles away from home and have no idea where I'm going. This should be a terrible idea, and yet ... I trust Marc.

Completely. Despite his need to be in control, I know he'd never let anything happen to me.

The plane begins to bump around. Turbulence, I guess.

Now I feel nervous and sick. My breathing gets quicker and quicker, until I feel like I can't breathe.

Marc flashes me a look. 'Sophia. Are you okay?'

I nod. 'Just a little ... scared. And ... sick.' I put a hand to my mouth and look out of the window. Marc unclasps himself and kneels beside me. He takes my hand.

'Sophia – look at me.'

I do, and my breathing gets faster. Each breath doesn't feel like enough. I have to have more air, and I begin to gasp.

'Take deep breaths,' Marc says. 'Merile!'

Merile rushes out from the front of the plane. 'Mr Blackwell. You should be buckled in.'

'Bring the medical kit,' says Marc, 'then strap yourself in.'

She nods and rushes away, returning with a white box. 'Mr Blackwell. Allow me.'

Marc shakes his head. 'You go strap yourself in.'

Merile looks reluctant, but I guess if she's worked with Marc before, she knows not to argue with him. She returns to the front of the plane.

'It's okay, Sophia,' says Marc, opening the kit. 'You're just having a little panic attack. There's oxygen in here if you need it, but I don't think you will. Breathe. Breathe. Nice and slowly.'

I take longer breaths and Marc holds on tight to my hand. The plane bumps, and he staggers back on his haunches, then catches himself.

'Sit down,' I say between breaths. 'You should be strapped in.'

'Just keep breathing,' he says.

I feel calmer with him holding my hand, even though the plane is both descending and bumping around. I see the sun high in the sky, and shimmering sea and white sands below.

After what feels like an eternity, the plane bumps onto a runway and I hear a rush of air as we pull to a stop.

Marc has held my hand the whole time.

'Thank you,' I whisper, as the plane door rolls open. 'You really didn't need to do that. I was having a silly panic attack.'

'Sophia, I brought you here,' says Marc. 'I gave you my word I'd take care of you.'

Warm air rushes into the plane, and I stand up shakily.

'Where are we?'

'See for yourself.' Marc walks me to the plane steps, and I look out past the concrete runway and flight tower, and see green trees, sand and ocean. The sky is bright blue, and the air feels like a warm bath. Birds twitter in the trees, and in the distance I see an oval-shaped building made of glass.

'It's beautiful,' I say, breathing in the sweet scent of flowers.

'We're in the Caribbean,' says Marc. 'This place is totally secluded. No press. Nothing but us.'

'Nothing but us,' I breathe, feeling warm air on my skin. 'But I still don't know where we are.'

'We're on my own private island,' says Marc.

Chapter 64

I remember reading that Marc had his own island. It was in some magazine article about celebrities who were mega-millionaires. I remember some other famous person, I forget who, had a collection of jet packs. But Marc has an island. A whole island.

'Your own island,' I breathe, walking down the plane steps. 'Look at the trees. They're amazing.'

Marc smiles. 'There are all sorts of plants here. More than just ivy.'

I smile. 'I'd love to go walking in that forest,' I say, pointing to the canopy of green.

'Later,' says Marc. 'First, we need to go through passport control. Then I'll take you to my place.'

A huge Rolls Royce drives us from the airport, down secluded dirt roads to the glass oval building I saw from the plane.

We walk through a glass door, up glass steps and onto a glass balcony that looks out over the sea. Because most of the whole building is one big window, it feels like we're floating in the forest and above the beach, part of nature.

The house is decorated with fur rugs and leather sofas, but I get that sense again that the decoration needs more personal touches. There are lots of flat screen televisions, remote controls and gadgets around, and – just like in Marc's townhouse – a bookshelf stuffed with classics of literature, their spines crisp and un-cracked.

'How do you like it?' Marc asks, strolling to the window that looks over the sea.

'It's beautiful,' I say, 'but it reminds me of your house in London. It needs some warmth to it.'

Marc turns to me, and his lips tilt upwards. 'Warmth?'

'Things that make it feel like a home. Plants, maybe.'

'You'll have to enlighten me about that one.'

'And these books – you can't have read any of them. They're too new looking.'

Marc's face breaks into a broad grin. 'Are you implying, Miss Rose, that I haven't read Dickens?'

'I'm not implying that at all,' I say, remembering the well-read paperbacks in Marc's bedroom. 'I'm just saying that *these* books look unread. It's like you have them here, just for show.'

'It makes me feel secure to have them around,' says Marc, wandering to the book case and running his hand along the covers. 'You're right – I don't read these particular versions.' His eyebrows pull together in realisation, and he turns to me. 'I guess you've seen the versions I read. The paperbacks.'

He catches my eye, and I feel embarrassed. 'Yes.'

'You could say that what's in those boxes is the real me. And what I put on display is ... what I feel comfortable showing.'

'I'm sorry for prying.'

Marc shakes his head. 'It's okay. I'm testing your boundaries. It's only fair that you test mine.'

'Have you ever brought girls ... a woman, here before?' I ask, thinking perhaps I don't want to know the answer to that question.

'Once,' says Marc, looking out over the water. 'Years ago.'

'One of the girlfriends you don't really have?' I ask, with a smile.

'She wasn't my girlfriend,' says Marc, not smiling back. 'She was a friend's girlfriend, and it was a mistake to bring her here.'

'Why?'

'She had a certain fantasy she wanted fulfilling that involved both me and my friend.'

I swallow. 'Meaning?'

'Meaning she wanted to have two guys at once, and I was the lucky other guy. But my friend wasn't all that happy about it, and I've never seen them since.'

'Oh.' I stand awkwardly, wishing I'd never started the conversation. I feel sick, actually.

Marc turns to me and smiles. 'You didn't like that answer, did you?'

'No.'

'You've heard about Pandora's box?'

I nod.

'Sometimes, it's best not to know too much. You might not like what you find out if you ask too many questions. I'm not what you call wholesome. I have a past. Not a great past.'

He goes to the open plan kitchen and opens a silver Smeg fridge. Its door is full of champagne, and he takes out a bottle and pops the cork.

'I think we should drink to celebrate your arrival here.' He takes down two glasses and pours the champagne.

I take a glass. 'This house is yours and yours alone?' I ask.

Marc nods.

'It doesn't feel lived in,' I say. 'Nor did the town-house. It feels ... a little empty.'

'Well, maybe I'm empty,' says Marc, taking a sip of champagne. 'I'm certainly morally empty, if you look at my choice of companion on this trip.'

'I don't think you are,' I say. 'You didn't want any of this. You would have walked away right at the start, but I didn't let you.'

'I'm five years older than you, Sophia,' says Marc. 'I should have been able to say no, regardless of my feelings for you. A good man doesn't fuck his students. No matter how hard he falls -'

He stops himself, taking a sharp sip of champagne, and looks out at the beach. 'Look. What I mean to say is, this isn't a habit for me, okay? I never, ever thought something like this would happen. I've never done anything with any of my pupils before, and after you I never will again. But that doesn't make me morally decent. I should have said no.'

'You're talking like I had no say in the matter,' I say. 'It was my choice as much as yours. More so. You tried to walk away. I didn't want you to. And you're not morally empty. But this place ...' I gesture with my hand. 'There's no love in it. Only things.'

'It wasn't built for love,' Marc snaps. 'All your fantasies can come true here. I can make anything you want, happen.'

'I want you to lose *your* inhibitions.'

'Sexually, I don't have any inhibitions,' says Marc. 'I've fucked women in every way there is to. Nothing is off limits for me.'

'But have you ever come with a woman?'

'A few times. When I was younger.'

That answer knocks me sideways. I don't know what I was expecting. It hurts me to think he's shared things with other women he's never shared with me. 'But with me you never ...'

'I learned very quickly to stay in control. That intimacy leads to all sorts of places I don't want to be. *Didn't* want to be. But with you ...' He looks at me so tenderly, then, that I want to run into his arms.

'Do you want to be closer to me?' I ask.

'I've been closer to you than I've ever been to anyone in my life,' says Marc. 'That's what you don't seem to understand.'

'Even though you've never come with me?'

'The way I feel for you ... it's different. But what if this is as close as we can get? What if I can't give you any more?'

I think about that. If I believed this was the most Marc could ever offer me – the occasional show of closeness, followed by a coolness that freezes me to my core – then I would walk away. But I don't believe it. I know deep down he wants to let himself go, but he can't. He's too scared.

Marc sips his champagne and sets down the glass. He walks over to me and takes my hands. 'I didn't bring you here to talk. You do know that, don't you?'

A warm feeling runs through my stomach, and I feel my thighs pull together.

'I guessed as much,' I say.

Chapter 65

Marc leads me towards one of the rooms. 'I'm going to totally dominate you here. I knew as soon as I had you in the stationery cupboard, you wanted more. You want to be totally taken charge of.'

'I'm not so sure about that.'

'Oh, *I* am,' Marc whispers, opening a door. Inside I see a round bed right in the centre of the room. It has no headboard, just white sheets, but I notice hoops screwed at even points around the base of the bed.

A length of rope lies on the sheets. There's a paddle next to the rope, and Marc slaps it against his palm.

'You couldn't take your eyes off this, when we were watching that movie,' he says. 'Don't think I didn't notice. But I have lots more. Paddles. Studded paddles. Floggers.'

'You do?' Oh my god. Just when I thought things were getting normal. 'Marc, can't we just -'

'Be quiet,' Marc orders, throwing down the paddle. 'Take off your clothes and get on the bed.'

His voice, so deep I practically feel it in my feet, does things to me as usual.

I take my clothes off and climb onto the bed, seeing birds fly over the ocean, through the panoramic window.

'Turn over,' he says, coming behind me and tying my wrists to the hoops on the floor.

Marc pulls his t-shirt over his head and throws it down. I see the soft hair under his arms and scattered over his taut chest. I love his chest. He paces back and forth, hands on hips, surveying me.

Now I'm trapped. Vulnerable. He can do whatever he wants to me.

I crane my neck, seeing him prowl around the bed. He picks up the paddle again.

'Would you like to feel this against your backside?'

My arms are held tight. 'You're going to hit me with that?'

'Hit you, beat you, call it what you like.'

'Will it hurt?'

He runs a thumb over the paddle. 'Yes. A little. What would be the fun if it didn't?'

I swallow, and he presses the edge of the paddle into my buttocks. 'You want to try it?' he whispers.

'Yes,' I say.

'Yes, what?'

'Yes, sir.'

He brings the paddle down hard on my buttocks, twice.

'Ouch.'

'Good ouch?'

'Yes,' I admit.

'You're turning a very nice colour,' he observes, spanking me again. I cry out. 'You'll stay here until I'm finished with you.'

I see his taut backside saunter in trousers out of the bedroom, and hear champagne being poured. He comes back with a full glass and the champagne bottle, and rests the bottle on the bedside table.

'Spread your legs for me,' he says, resting his champagne glass on my buttocks. 'Now.'

'What are you going to do?'

'Do it.'

Reluctantly, I spread my legs.

He picks up the champagne bottle, setting the glass down in its place. Then he pushes the cold glass of the champagne bottle between my thighs.

I gasp.

'Does it feel good?'

'Cold,' I stammer.

'Wider,' he says.

I spread my legs as wide as I can, feeling hot and breathless.

He slips the top of the champagne bottle inside me, and turns the cool glass.

'Ooh,' I moan, as he pushes it deeper.

Then he tosses the champagne bottle to one side, and goes to the cabinet. He pulls out a thin, silver vibrator.

'I'm going to slip this inside your backside, and if you make the tiniest noise I'm going to spank you again.'

'I can't do that,' I murmur, squirming a little at the thought. 'I can't keep quiet.'

'Try.'

He comes behind me and lays a hand on my buttocks, whilst he works the vibrator inside me.

I bite my lip, trying to keep quiet, but when he turns on the vibrations I start to moan.

He picks up the paddle and spanks me five times, and I moan even louder.

'Please Marc,' I say, as the vibrations make me feel fuller and fuller.

Marc spanks me again, harder this time, and I feel so desperate for him that I don't think I can take it. 'Please fuck me,' I beg, as spanking sounds ring out around the room.

Marc walks around to the front of the bed, and I see he's slipped himself free of his trousers. His huge erection is in front of my face. He stalks behind me, and I turn my head again, desperate to see where he's gone.

I feel him climb on top of me and slide between my legs.

'Oh god, Marc. Please. This is too much. I can't take it.'

The vibrator goes further up my backside as Marc moves back and forth.

He moves harder against me, going further and further inside. A warm feeling is building up, and I'm so desperate to touch myself that I struggle against the ropes.

Suddenly Marc lies right on top of me, pressing me into the bed, rubbing me against the sheets as he moves.

Warmth envelopes me and I feel sensations everywhere – Marc's lips and tongue at my neck, his hands on my hair and buttocks. The vibrator inside me and Marc filling me up. He rubs me back and forth, back and forth, with such skill, keeping me just on the brink of unbearable, pulling back just as he gets too far inside. It's like my body has become part of him, and he knows just what to do.

As the good feelings build to a climax, Marc slides his hand further into my hair, and winds it tenderly through his fingers. He moves his lips up to my ear and whispers, 'You're mine, now. All mine.'

Colour flashes before my eyes, and I feel pleasure shooting all over my body. I moan and push back into him, feeling the ropes bite at my wrists.

'Marc,' I call, as I come, and I feel his arms wrap around me.

I breathe heavily into the bed, not sure if I'll ever get my breath back. I feel the warmth of him against my back, and don't want this feeling to ever end.

Marc softly unties the ropes and flips me over, passing my legs over his chest. His hand feels between my buttocks and pulls out the vibrator, but the whole time he stays inside me. When I'm facing him, he moves slowly, staring right into my eyes.

'I want to come in you,' he says. 'But I can't. I just can't lose control again. Not yet.'

I nod, moving stray hair from his eyes.

He falls forward, pulling me into his arms. We lay like that until morning.

Chapter 66

I wake in the morning, and find the space beside me empty. Sitting up, I look through the panoramic window at the tropical paradise outside. It's beautiful. I can feel the warmth of the sun through the windows, even though the air-conditioning has chilled the air.

I dress and go downstairs, finding Marc in the gym room, pounding a punch bag. He looks so lethal as he punches – very able to do some damage – and I'd feel sorry for anyone who took the place of that punch bag.

He never wavers, never stops to lean against the bag and get his breath back. He just punches and punches, his back straight and face determined. His grey t-shirt and sweatpants are drenched in sweat.

Eventually he stops, and grabs the bag to stop it swinging. Throwing off his boxing gloves, he wipes his face with a towel, then notices me in the doorway.

'You're up early,' he says, his usual cool, unflappable self.

'I told you,' I say with a smile. 'I always am. And I could say the same thing about you.'

Marc flings the towel around his shoulders. 'Yes, you could. And you'd be right. I have a trip planned for you today.' He throws off his t-shirt. I notice his arms are bulking up again, and guess he must have another action movie planned. He's so disciplined. To be able to transform his body back and forth like that.

'What sort of trip?' I ask.

'A shopping trip,' he says. 'Merile will take you by boat to a nearby island, where the stores are. There's one I have in mind – a very famous lingerie store. Ayten Gasson. I know the owner. She's ready to fit you out in whatever you'd like.'

Wow. 'Aren't you coming along?' I ask.

Marc shakes his head. 'I need to train. And I don't want to risk you being photographed with me. I'd never forgive myself if you were hounded by the press.'

'I know, I know.' I feel sadness creeping into my chest. 'My reputation and all of that. But maybe ... Marc, maybe as long as you stay at the college and keep teaching the other pupils, I don't care. Just like you don't care. Maybe all I want is you.'

'You don't know what you're saying,' he says. 'It's hard enough being part of my world, but considering the way we met ... the press would never leave you alone.'

'I can handle it,' I say.

'I don't want you to handle it,' says Marc. 'I want you to be happy.'

'I'm happy when I'm with you,' I say. 'I'm not happy sneaking around. Not knowing when I'm going to see you next.'

Two lines appear above Marc's nose. He spreads out his broad palms, and his blue eyes look lost. 'I don't know a way to solve that right now. Don't be sad. Come here.'

I do, and he puts his arms around me, pulling me into the hot, dampness of his chest. He smells so good. I press my cheek to his body and let out a deep sigh. I don't know how we're going to do this, either. So I may as well just enjoy it while it lasts.

The lingerie store is low lit, with purple velvet couches and flickering candles everywhere. It smells like a spa. When I explain that Marc Blackwell sent me, a lady in a purple dress escorts me to a couch and gives me a crushed cherry and brandy cocktail.

'We've found a model who's similar to your size and build,' she explains, pointing towards a series of crushed velvet curtains. 'She'll be modelling our latest range for you, and you just choose what you like.'

Now I'm glad Marc isn't with me. I don't like the idea of him watching a model dressed up in different ranges of underwear.

The model appears from behind a curtain. She's beautiful, with a slender waist and long, willowy legs and arms.

'She's my build and size?' I say. 'Are you sure?'

'Absolutely sure,' says the purple dress lady. 'You're very similar shapes.'

The first set of underwear is white silk, sewn with dozens of glittering black stones. It's beautiful, but not quite me. Then comes a dazzling parade of fairy-tale style green and blue pieces sewn with fairy-wing mesh and embroidered with gothic, black trees.

'I love those,' I say, and the purple dress lady signals for a set to be bagged.

I see a dozen other styles and designs, including stockings and suspenders, and choose a navy blue set with frills and net, a pack of panties with frills on the rear and a black suspender belt with little crosses sewn all over it.

When I arrive back at the glass house, Marc inspects my purchases. He chooses the fairytale set and tells me to put them on right now. Then he hands me a script.

'You're going to perform this scene in your underwear,' he says.

I look at the script. It's for a play called *The Sex Diaries* – a play infamous for its nudity, and the fact it follows married couples on their sexual adventures around London.

'You know I'd never audition for a play like this,' I say. 'Not yet.'

'Exactly,' says Marc. 'But I'm hoping together we might fix that little failing. I'd like you to perform the scene starting on page 52. You're Georgia. I'll play Harry.'

I might have guessed. The simulated sex scene in which Georgia, a middle-aged married woman, seduces Harry, her friend's husband, in the upstairs bedroom at a party. In the play, she ends up completely nude on stage.

I take a deep breath, shake my arms and try to get into character. I try to feel Georgia in my body. Her confidence and exhibitionism.

What would she be doing right now? Smiling. I smile at Marc. 'You know,' I say, my voice becoming louder and more refined, 'if you want to have sex with me, you only have to ask.'

Marc raises an eyebrow. I can tell by his expression that he's still Marc. 'I'll bear that in mind. And may I just add, if I wanted to have sex with you, I'd be much more direct. I want you to rehearse this scene for good reason. It's to help develop you as an actress.'

'Oh.'

'And since you're in your underwear already, I thought this was a good part to stretch your boundaries and lose some of your inhibitions.'

'What's left of them,' I say.

Marc laughs, and moves me to the window by my hips. 'Here. You're looking out of the window.' He hands me the script and turns to page 50. 'Start with this line.'

I cough, and read the line. 'Darling, I'm just getting dressed. You don't mind do you?' I try to loosen my body even more.

'Why should I mind?' Marc reads Harry's line with smarmy confidence, transforming into the married stockbroker whom Georgia has an affair with. It's amazing. His face changes. His posture changes. He becomes a different person.

'We're all naked under our clothes at the end of the day,' I say.

'That we are,' says Marc.

I check the script. 'Would you help me with this?' The stage direction says: *Georgia holds the bra strap behind her back. Harry undoes it for her. She turns around, removing her bra entirely and showing her naked breasts to Harry.* Ordinarily, I'd falter at that. But having had so many experiences with Marc now, it feels tame.

I feel Marc behind me, unhooking my bra. But he doesn't do it in a Marc-like way. His movements are quicker and slightly fumbled. I feel like I'm in the presence of someone who doesn't have my best intentions at heart, and it's a little unnerving.

I wonder if I'll ever be able to do a scene like this in public. I grasp hold of the bra, then slip it down and turn around.

Chapter 67

'I expect your wife's breasts used to look like these,' I say, trying to bring into myself the confidence and swagger of a femme fatale. 'They're pretty, aren't they?'

'Very pretty,' says Marc, coming forward and taking me in his arms. Again, it's not Marc who's here with me, but Harry. He carries me to the sofa and throws me onto it, and the face I look up at is greedy and grasping.

I check the script. It says: *Harry picks up Georgia and puts her on the bed. They have sex, moving in time to the music. The curtain closes.*

Marc moves between my legs, back and forth in a gentle rhythm. I move with him, but I can tell he's working hard not to become aroused. He's acting, and he's professional as ever.

'Very good,' Marc whispers.

'Thank you,' I say.

'You'd better get dressed,' he says. 'Because you're playing that part for real this evening, in the theatre on the main island. So you'll need to start learning your lines.'

'You're kidding me.'

'No, I'm not kidding you. I happen to be guest-starring as Harry in this play tonight, and I'd like you to be my Georgia. She's only a small part. I told you I'd stretch your boundaries. Challenge you. Break you out of your comfort zone and make you a better actress. Well. That's exactly what I'm doing.'

'But I can't play that part.' I'm on the verge of tears. 'Not in public. Topless on stage. In front of a live audience -'

'Some parts call for nudity,' says Marc. 'When I played King Lear, I was fully nude. And a theatre is nothing compared to a movie, where a film camera closes in on your naked body, then projects it on a giant screen for millions of people to see.'

'Maybe public nudity is a barrier I just can't break down.'

'You don't understand,' says Marc, shaking his head. 'It's not about the nudity. It's about the openness. Exposing yourself totally. Your soul. For everyone to see. Nudity is just one tenant of that openness. If you're not open to playing a part properly, everything closes down. Your body is the vehicle for your expression. If you're too self-conscious to show your body, you can't express yourself fully.'

'You're one to talk about openness.'

'We've had this discussion before -'

'I can't do it, Marc.'

He tips my chin up with his fingers. 'You can do it. Now get dressed and learn your lines. At five, a boat will take you to the main island, then a car will drive you to the theatre. I'll be there already. I'll meet you onstage.' He kisses my nose and pulls me into his arms. 'I believe in you.'

Chapter 68

In the car on the way to the theatre, I'm a bundle of nerves. I want to run, I want to hide, I want to scream at Marc, that he's making me do something way beyond my capabilities. But deep down, I know he's right. I do need to practise these sorts of roles. Even if I never perform nude ever again, it will stretch me and help me grow as an actress.

The car pulls up behind a modern theatre – a square, grey block of concrete with queues of people outside. I think how lucky we are in London to have such elegant, beautiful historic buildings.

I'm led to a dressing area, where a tiny, blonde actress helps me into Georgia's lingerie, red dress, wig and make-up.

Then I'm led to the side of the stage, where I see the play has already begun. I flick hurriedly through my script, trying to find out how far into the play we've got. Page 49. I swallow three times to stop myself being sick, and watch Marc strolling back and forth on the stage, wearing a pin-striped suit.

He really is an amazing actor. I don't see Marc at all, but Harry.

The lines race along, and I put my script down by the curtains and see a stage hand running towards me.

'I thought you were still in the dressing room,' he whispers. 'Final call. You're on in less than a minute.'

'Right.' I wait for my entry line: *I'll see if I can find her.*

Sweat prickles my forehead, and my palms feel slippery.

'I'll see if I can find her,' says Marc.

And boom. I walk on stage, seeing hundreds of shadowy people in the audience, their faces watching me expectantly. I'm wearing nothing but underwear, and soon I'll be wearing even less.

God I'm nervous. But I've done this. Lots of times. Fully clothed, granted, but Marc's right – it shouldn't matter. *Just become the part,* I think. *As long as you're playing the part, you're safe.*

I clear my throat, but the script goes right out of my head. I look at Marc, and start to panic. I'd be so humiliated if someone had to shout out my line.

Marc waits for me, calmly and with a look in his eyes that tells me he knows I can do it. I decide to ad lib.

'What's a nice man like you doing in a place like this?' I say, my lips extending into a pout, hands falling onto my hips.

'Looking for a not very nice girl,' says Marc.

I laugh, throwing my head back. 'I think you've found her. Darling, I'm just getting dressed. You don't mind do you?' The script starts coming back to me.

'Why should I mind?'

'We're all naked under our clothes at the end of the day.' My hands begin to tremble at the thought of what's coming next.

'That we are,' says Marc.

'Would you help me with this?' I say, turning around and holding the back of my bra strap. The words sound confident, which surprises me. The way I'm feeling inside, I expected them to come out all of a wobble.

Marc unhooks my bra, and the audience falls completely silent. They know what's coming. Anyone who reads the newspaper knows what happens in this scene. I take a deep breath, and turn around, removing my bra and throwing it to the floor.

Hundreds of faces stare at me. I can't see their expressions. I look over their heads.

'I expect your wife's breasts used to look like these,' I say. 'They're pretty, aren't they?'

'Very pretty,' says Marc, lifting me into his arms. He places me on a prop bed, with a thin mattress that would leave me black and blue if I ever slept on it.

I throw my arms behind my head, and Marc stands between my legs.

Music starts, and I feel Marc begin to move. Unlike the last time we performed the scene, I feel him growing hard. As soon as the curtain falls, he stands back and pulls in deep breaths.

'Okay?' I ask.

'You were excellent,' he says, pacing back and forth. 'I'm very proud of what you achieved today. But. This was a bad idea. I wanted to test myself, too. To prove I could control myself around you. If I'm ever going to let go, I need to know I can get the control back. I thought maybe I could. But ...' He marches off the stage.

I walk after him, following him down to the star dressing room, which is all thick red carpet, silver paint and white roses.

'Wait,' I say, and Marc turns at the dressing room door. 'Is it such a bad thing?'

'We shouldn't talk out here.' He pulls me into the dressing room, slamming the door behind us.

'I said, is it such a bad thing?' I repeat. 'I mean, we all lose control sometimes.'

'Not me,' says Marc. 'Not on stage. Not in real life. Not ever. Not any more.' He looks at me, and his eyes are lost. 'I don't know what's happening. How can I look after you if I'm not in control?'

'You can,' I say, sitting on his lap. His arms come around me. 'Because you're even closer to me that way.'

There's a knock on the dressing room door, and we spring apart.

'Mr Blackwell,' says the stagehand. 'On stage in five.'

'You should go back to the house,' says Marc, pulling me onto his lap and burying his head in my hair. 'I'll see you there.'

'Okay.'

Back at the glass house, Marc seems younger, somehow, and a little lost. He brings Thai food from the big island, and we eat on the glass balcony, overlooking the sea. Marc holds my hand under the table, and talks and talks.

He tells me about his sister, and how he supports her and her fiancé. He tells me he doesn't like his sister's fiancé, but until his sister works out for herself what's right for her, there's nothing he can do. I don't ask him about the drug dealing, and he doesn't tell me. It's not the right time. He's revealing nice things about himself, not wounds, and I'm fine with that.

He tells me about his mother, what he remembers of her. In his head, she was a beautiful, brown-haired angel who sang to him and put magic dust on his cuts and bruises. She'd been an amateur actress herself, and won him a junior role in one of her plays. It had led to a chocolate bar commercial, and from there his father took over, honing him for fame and fortune.

I tell him about my baby brother and my step-mother – how I feel they can't survive without me. How Genoveva can't really cope, and how my father is muddling through. He listens intently, his knuckles bent under his chin. When I tell him about my mother – how much I love her and still miss her – he squeezes my hand tightly.

'It's Saturday, tomorrow. You'll want to see your family.'

'Yes,' I say. 'I should.'

'Then we'll fly back.'

When the sun goes down, we go down to the dark beach and watch the silver ocean lap back and forth.

Marc tells me about the first time he saw the ocean. It was in California, and the sand was so hot it hurt his bare feet. He discovered that no matter how long he stayed in the sun, he never tanned. Apparently, whenever he needs to be tanned in films, it's all done by a makeup artist.

We talk about tomorrow, and the fact we'll be heading back to London. Neither of us have any answers. All we know is, we don't have much time left.

We sit on the sand, right by the warm ocean, letting the waves lap at our feet. The moon is round and silver above us.

I turn to Marc, and see his eyes are glistening, but his expression is pained.

'What?' I ask. 'What is it? What's wrong?'

'I love you,' says Marc simply, staring at the ocean. 'But this isn't a movie. I don't know how this will end.'

When we get back to the house, Marc sleeps beside me in the round bed.

Chapter 69

In the morning, the sun is brighter than I've ever seen it. I see Marc asleep next to me, and watch his beautiful, peaceful face. His nose, straight and handsome, and the gentle curves either side of his mouth, look so familiar now. One large hand rests on his toned chest, and the other lays out, open, long fingers outstretched.

His eyelids aren't flickering. Everything about him is still, except for his gentle breathing.

I stroke his face, and his eyes open immediately.

When he recognises me, his face relaxes. 'Sophia,' he whispers.

'We have to go back today,' I say. 'But I want to be with you. Properly. A proper couple. I don't care who knows. I don't care about my reputation. Just as long as you keep teaching the other students. I don't want them losing out because of me.'

'Sophia, you don't know what you're saying,' says Marc. 'You don't know what you'd be giving up to become part of my world. Your freedom – gone. Just like that. They'd trawl through your past, bother your family ... I won't let you go through it. Not for me.'

'What if it wasn't your choice?' I say. 'What if when we go back to London, I tell the press myself?'

Marc stares at me. 'I'd forbid you from doing that.'

'You'd *forbid* me?' I laugh. 'What if I didn't listen?'

'You'd really go and do something like that? Without my permission?'

'If it means being with you, out in the open, then yes.'

Marc sits up. 'It means that much to you, having a relationship with me? That you'd give up your privacy. Your freedom ...'

'Yes.'

Marc rubs his eyes, and stares at the sun rising above the sea. 'No one has ever thought what I offered was worth giving anything up for. I never expected ... I don't know how I've got you into this situation. Christ.' He puts his hands to his forehead. 'I'm always so careful. So controlled. I plan everything. How could I let this happen?'

'Feelings aren't something you can plan,' I say.

He looks at me, then. A long, steady look. 'Don't I know it. If you were determined to bring us out in the open, then I'd get my PR people to manage a campaign around you to mediate the damage. Make sure you were set up as the good girl. Make sure I took all the blame.'

He gets up and begins dressing. 'I'm going to strike a deal with you.'

'A deal?'

Marc nods, sliding on his boxer shorts. 'Wait until we've got back to London, then go back to your family. Talk to your father. Don't make the decision straight away. And if, after all that, you still decide you want us to come out in the open, I'll support your decision. I'll come meet your father and explain myself.'

'You would?'

The hollows in Marc's cheeks grow tight and shadowy. 'Yes,' he says eventually. 'I'd support you. I'd support us. But if you make that decision, you have to be prepared for a lot of negative attention. I can only protect you so much.'

'I think I can handle it,' I say. 'If it means being with you.'

The flight back is smooth and calm, but I'm too anxious to relax. The thought of telling my father about Marc is overwhelming, and Marc's warnings haven't fallen on deaf ears. I know there might be a hate campaign against me. I know I might be painted as the slutty student who seduced Marc Blackwell. Or the naive student who's fallen for a wicked older man.

When we land, Marc arranges for Keith to take me straight to my dad's house.

Chapter 70

I knock on the door tentatively, knowing Dad isn't expecting me.

Dad opens the door with strawberry jam on his forehead and pastry in his hair.

'Love!' He throws his arms around me. 'This is a nice surprise.' Sam is in the background in his highchair, also covered in jam.

'Good to see you too.'

'Come in, come in.' Dad opens the door. 'Sam and I were just making jam tarts.'

'Where's Genoveva?'

'Having a facial. She's needs to relax. This is all very hard on her, parenthood late in life.'

The house is a bombsite, made worse by Dad's baking attempts. Sam bangs the highchair table when he sees me, his hands and face covered in pastry and jam.

I pick him up, and put the kettle on.

'I'm glad Genoveva isn't here,' I say. 'There's something I need to talk to you about alone.'

'Oh? Nothing serious is it, love? You're not ill, are you?'

'No.' I shake my head. 'Nothing like that.' I make two teas and set them on the dining table.

'So, what then?'

This is so much harder than I'd imagined. And imagining it was pretty difficult.

'It's about a man I'm seeing.'

'Are you ... in trouble or something?'

'No, no.' I shake my head, taking a seat and putting Sam on my lap. Dad comes to sit down too.

'Because you know I'll support you one hundred percent, whatever you want to do. Your mum had you very young, and I've never regretted -'

'Dad, will you just listen? I'm not pregnant. But ... I'm seeing someone at university.'

'Well, you're twenty two,' says Dad. 'Nothing wrong with that. I'm glad you're seeing someone. Is he a nice chap? I'd like to meet him.'

A nice chap. Those aren't the first words I'd use to describe Marc. And yet, truly he is.

'He's ... a lecturer,' I say. Sam grabs at my watch. I carefully unpeel his fingers.

'Oh.' Dad takes a sip of tea and looks thoughtful. 'Right. I suppose that's a little different. For a start, he must be a lot older than you.'

'Not really,' I say. 'Only five years.'

Dad considers this. 'It's not very ethical, for a lecturer to be having a relationship with a pupil. I can't say I respect the man's morals all that much.'

'I understand that,' I say. 'But neither of us planned this. He was absolutely dead against anything happening between us. It was me who made the decision. If it had been left up to Marc, he would have quit the university for us to be together, or never seen me again.'

'Marc?' says Dad. 'As in Marc Blackwell? Is that the man you're seeing?'

I nod.

'Who does he think he is? Just because he's famous, doesn't mean he can take advantage of -'

'It's not like that,' I say. 'We really feel something for each other.'

'I haven't heard good things about him at all,' says Dad. 'He seems like a very cold, snooty sort of man. Not the sort of character most men would be happy about their daughter seeing.'

'Yes,' I agree. 'He does come across that way. But he's a very good person. I promise.'

Dad nods. 'I suppose I can't imagine you choosing someone who wasn't.'

I smile at him.

'Would your mum have approved of this man?'

I think about that. 'Yes,' I say. 'I think she would.'

'Well.' Dad rests his elbows on the table. 'I suppose I'd like to meet him.'

'I'd like that,' I say. 'And so would he. You can meet him today, if you'd like.'

Dad nods. 'Yes. We can make some lunch. I won't put that on Genoveva at short notice, we'll order something in.'

I smile. 'I can cook, if you'd like.'

'Would you love? That would be wonderful.'

Chapter 71

I ring Marc, and he picks up straight away.

'Sophia. How are you?'

'Okay,' I say. 'It wasn't as tough as I'd thought. Dad wants to meet you. Would you like to come over for lunch today?'

'I can't think of anything I'd rather do.'

He hangs up, and I set to work making lunch. There isn't much in the house, but there's flour and potatoes in the cupboard and I find some frozen beef and peas in the freezer, so I make a steak pie with mashed potato and gravy. It's getting colder outside – good weather for comfort food.

Genoveva comes back from her appointment, and squeezes her lips together when she sees me in the kitchen.

Dad tells her about Marc coming over for lunch, and she hurries upstairs to get ready. An hour later, she comes down plastered in makeup, her black, bobbed hair shiny and styled. She's wearing a white linen suit, gold jewellery and heavy rose-scented perfume.

'She never makes the effort for me,' Dad whispers, with a conspiratorial wink. 'Looks like she's a bit star struck.'

Just as I take the pie out of the oven, there's a knock at the door.

I open it and see the surreal sight of Marc Blackwell on my doorstep, his arms full of red roses, wine and a small, wrapped gift.

He's back in his black suit and shirt, freshly shaven, and hair combed back. He looks and smells expensive, and I love the way he can go from being causally handsome in a t-shirt to oh-so refined.

'Hello,' I say, trying to hide my smile.

'Hello.' Marc smiles at me, that subtle, quirky smile. 'It's good to be here.'

I wonder what he'll make of our little house, with its open plan living area and rustic, country charm.

Genoveva comes rushing over and curtsies before him. 'Mr Blackwell. I've heard so much about you. Welcome to my home.'

'The pleasure is all mine,' says Marc. 'You must be Genoveva. I bought these for you.' He hands her the roses.

'Oh!' she gushes, smelling them. 'They're beautiful. Please. Follow me to our dining area.'

She leads him to the dining table, where my dad is sat, drinking a coffee. Dad stands as Marc approaches.

'A pleasure to meet you, sir,' says Marc. 'You must be Sophia's father.'

'Yes,' says Dad, looking him over. He looks small next to Marc, but he's holding himself with a quiet dignity.

Marc puts the gift and wine on the table, and shakes his hand. 'I hope you don't mind. I bought a little something for Samuel.'

'He's sleeping right now,' says Genoveva, picking up the gift. 'May I?'

'Of course,' says Marc.

Genoveva tears open the paper, and inside is the simplest of gifts: a set of plastic, stacking cups. They must have cost all of three pounds, and I can see Genoveva looking them over, confused. Here is a man who can buy anything he wants, and he's bought the most inexpensive present for her son.

'Thank you,' she says, eyeing the cups uncertainly.

'My sister has a son a little older than Samuel,' Marc says. 'He loves these things. Can't leave them alone. I've given him all sorts of toys – a mini motorbike, a jungle gym, a train set, but he likes these best.'

I smile. 'They're perfect,' I say.

'Would you like to take a seat?' Dad asks.

'Thank you.' Marc sits beside my father. 'I'd just like to say it's a pleasure to be in your home. And you must be very proud of your daughter. She's a remarkable person.'

'Yes,' says Dad.

'We ... I never planned for the way things have turned out,' says Marc. 'It was never my intention to have a relationship with a student. I planned to leave the university, in fact, when I realised I was falling for Sophia. This must be so difficult for you. If I were in your position, I wouldn't respect a man like me. I wouldn't think a man like me would be good enough for my daughter. I'm hoping to prove that I am. For Sophia's sake as much as anyone's.' He gives a sweet, humble smile that I've never seen before. 'For some reason, she thinks I make her happy.'

Dad gives an approving cough. 'Yes. Well. Early days.'

'Let's have lunch,' I say.

Chapter 72

Predictably, the men at the table eat hearty portions of the pie, while Genoveva picks at her piece and I only have a small slice. I'm too nervous to be hungry.

I love watching Marc eat. There's something about the measured, controlled way he uses his knife and fork that does things to me.

'You made this?' Marc whispers, on his second slice. 'I can't believe you've never cooked for me before.' He gives me that playful half smile and slips his hand into mine.

We drink wine, eat and Dad cross-examines Marc about everything, from his acting pedigree to why he formed the college.

'I wanted to send the elevator down,' says Marc, simply. 'I wanted other young actors to have the chances I've had. Acting is my life. It's what keeps me sane. And I know that's true for a lot of young people, but many of them won't ever have an acting career, no matter how talented they are. My goal is to help them into the profession.'

'Very admirable,' says Dad, taking a swig of wine.

'And I had to save that building,' Marc adds, glancing at me and smiling. 'All that beautiful greenery in the middle of London. I couldn't let it be destroyed.'

By the end of the meal, I feel Dad has – if not thawed completely – grown a little warmer towards Marc.

'Sophia, I have to leave,' says Marc. 'I have a meeting booked with my PR team.'

I feel my stomach tighten. 'Okay.'

'Would you like me to take you back to college?' Marc asks. 'Or would you like more time with your family?'

'I should head back,' I say. 'I have a singing class this afternoon, and I'd rather not miss it.' I turn to Dad. 'I'll come back next weekend, okay?'

I hurry upstairs to kiss a sleeping Samuel, and when I come back down, Marc and my dad are shaking hands again.

'Perhaps you can come again sometime,' Dad is saying. 'And we'll have a proper drink. None of this wine nonsense.'

'I'd be delighted to,' says Marc.

We head outside, into the chilly autumn afternoon. There are orange and brown leaves all around.

Marc sees the photographer before I do. I only see a bright white flash, and Marc pull me to him. He bundles me into the car, and I watch through the tinted window as Marc sprints down the country lane after a man in a denim jacket. Marc is fast, but the photographer has a head start, and I imagine terror must be putting a spring in his step.

I hear the roar of a motorbike, and see Marc turn and bolt back towards the car. He's barely out of breath as he leaps in the back.

'Are you okay?' he asks me.

'I'm fine.'

'I don't want to chase him in the car. It's too dangerous.' He rolls his knuckles down the window. 'Parasites. To come to your family home.

They must have followed me here. I thought we were careful, but ... I'm so sorry.'

'It's okay. It was bound to happen sooner or later.'

'They've got nothing,' says Marc. 'They don't know anything about why I was visiting. But it forces our arm a little. It's started. They're not going to back off. Once they have an idea for a story, they won't give up.' He turns to me. 'I'll call you after my PR meeting, and we'll figure out what's going to happen. One thing's for certain. Things can't carry on as they are. We have to decide whether to jump or not. And soon.'

'Right.' I swallow. I feel scared. Uncertain.

'Sophia, are you sure you really want to do this?' Marc asks. 'Your life will change forever. And you won't be able to go back. There's still time to change your mind.'

I nod. 'I feel like I'm about to leap off a cliff without a rope. But not to jump ... that doesn't feel right either.'

Marc takes my hand. 'I'll take care of you,' he says. 'I have things in place that can protect you. I'll make it as easy as can be, but there will still be problems. Issues. If you're ready for that, then we can do this. You should take some time to think.'

'Okay.'

'I'll take you back to college. Go ahead with your class. Talk to Denise. Talk to your friends. I'll be waiting.'

In singing class, I can't concentrate, and Denise has to call me by name a few times to make me pay attention.

'You're half asleep today, Ms Rose,' she says, as the class filters out. 'Anything you want to talk about?'

I sigh. 'Yes. So many things on my mind.'

'Then let's have a tea. I've made my own herbal brew today. Fancy a cup?' She flicks the kettle on.

'Yes please.'

She throws a handful of dried fruit, berries and flowers into two mugs, pours boiling water and hands me mine. It's bright pink and smells delicious – like strawberries and herbs.

'Hibiscus flower,' she says. 'Good for problem solving. Now. What can I help you with today? You look like you've got the weight of the world on your shoulders.'

'I have,' I say. 'I've got the biggest decision to make.'

'Go on.'

'Marc and I ... we've got closer. More serious. And I thought I wanted to have a proper relationship. A public relationship. Like normal people have. I knew it could never be truly normal, but I don't want to sneak around. For everything to be hidden.'

'Sounds perfectly reasonable,' says Denise.

'Marc never wanted things to be hidden, either,' I say.

'But he was worried about my reputation. How I'd be perceived if things got out.'

'That's just like Marc,' says Denise, with a smile. 'And I bet he doesn't give two hoots about *his* reputation, does he?'

'No, he doesn't,' I say. 'He's happy for us to go public. He's talking to his PR team this afternoon about how best to do it. How to limit the damage, and not have me painted in a way that might hurt my career in future. But now it's coming to it, I have to make sure it's the right decision. Marc has warned me over and over again what might happen if our relationship gets out. And ... perhaps I'm not as ready to face all that as I thought.'

Denise sighs. 'It's a difficult situation. I feel for you. I don't know what I'd do if I were in your shoes. What does your heart tell you?'

I take a sip of pink tea, and it tastes as delicious as it smells. 'It tells me I want to be with Marc. It tells me that if we're together, we can cope with anything. And it tells me if I walk away from him, I ... I don't know if I could live.'

'You could live,' says Denise, putting her warm, white hands over mine. 'I assure you of that. Many young women have walked away from the love of their life, and then found another love of their life a few months later.'

'Do you think Marc and I ... do you think we stand a chance?' I say.

Denise looks at me for a moment. Then she nods slowly. 'A chance, yes. Marc is crying out for a girl like you. Someone softer to bring out what he tries to hide. And I've never seen him fall like this for anyone before. If he takes this chance with you, he'll never let you go unless you want him to. He'll stand by you through thick and thin.'

'I know that,' I say. 'I feel safe with him. Protected. I don't feel he'd let me down. But it's whether I can cope with things. That's the question.'

'And I think only you have the answer to that question,' says Denise.

'There's something else, too,' I say. 'A photographer. He took our picture just now. Leaving my dad's house.'

'Right.' Denise takes a long sip of tea. 'That could be a tricky one. I'd imagine the tabloids will be falling over themselves, trying to prove a teacher student affair. It wasn't an intimate picture, was it?'

'No,' I say. 'Just the two of us leaving the house.'

'They'll be trying to make something of that, though,' says Denise. 'If you carry on seeing each other in secret, there'll be more photos before you know it.'

We talk for an hour, but I'm no closer to coming up with an answer. I'm walking through the college grounds, about to call Jen, when my phone rings. It's Marc.

'Hi,' I say, kicking a pile of orange leaves. 'How are you?'

'It's not good news Sophia.' Trust Marc to get straight to the point. 'The photo of us is already being auctioned to the newspapers. It'll hit the stands tomorrow – probably in more than one tabloid.

'My PR team are struggling to limit the damage. They can see the tabloids having a field day, and following you for months, maybe even years to come. Your reputation might be tainted if we stay together. If you won acting roles, it would be assumed that I'd pulled strings. I don't know if I can let you go through that. Not for me.'

'It's not just for you,' I whisper. 'It's for me too. But ... I hear what you're saying. I know things will be hard. I need time to think, okay?'

'Okay.' I hear Marc breathing. 'I wish I could be with you. I wish I could hold you.'

I feel tears coming. 'I wish I could be with you too.'

'There are photographers all around the gates,' says Marc, 'but you're safe inside – we have excellent security. Just don't leave until I tell you to.'

'Okay.'

Chapter 74

I eat dinner in the meal hall that night with Tom and Tanya, and tell them about the latest twist in my situation.

'We know,' Tanya says. 'We both got contacted on Facebook this afternoon by reporters asking us to sell stories.'

'Oh no.' I put my head in my hands.

'I take it that means you don't want your apple crumble,' says Tom.

'Take it,' I say.

'Isn't that a good thing, though?' says Tom, spooning up my pudding. 'I mean, don't you want your relationship to be out in the open? And now it sort of forces the issue, don't you think?'

'Yes,' I agree. 'It does. It forces it one way or the other. Have a public relationship and be followed by reporters for my entire time at college. Maybe have my reputation ruined. Or walk away from Marc forever.'

'Tough call,' says Tanya. She looks over at Cecile and Ryan. 'What are you two staring at?'

They both smirk, and look back at their desserts.

'I'm guessing reporters got in touch with them too,' I say. 'Oh, great.'

'It'll all come out in the wash, love,' says Tom. 'Tomorrow's chip wrappings, isn't that what they say?'

'We don't wrap chips in newspaper anymore,' says Tanya. 'It's unhygienic.'

'Yes, yes, but you know what I mean,' says Tom. 'Are you really going to walk away from someone you love, because you're scared about what the public will say about you? This is your life, for Christ's sake. You're the only one living it, so who cares what people say?'

'It's not just that, though,' says Tanya. 'If she's going to be an actress, her public profile is very important. Reputations are everything in this business. If people see her in a certain light, it might be difficult for her to get work.'

'That works the other way, too,' says Tom. 'Notorious actors get more work than unknown ones. Anyway, I think it'll all blow over. And Sophia's such an amazing actress that when people see her perform, they're not going to care about anything they've read.'

'That's if anyone will give her a part,' Tanya points out.

Chapter 75

It turns very cold that evening, and I switch on all the radiators in my room and light a fire in the grate, burning logs and twigs I've found in the woods. It makes the room feel cosy, and I get into bed and watch the flames dancing in the darkness.

My head hurts. There's so much to think about, and the truth is, neither I nor anyone else has any definite answers.

The worst of it right now is that I can't see Marc. And that hurts. Being without him is painful.

I watch the fire for a long time.

Around midnight, I hear a tap on the French windows that makes me jump. I get up and go to the balcony. On the concrete, I see a white stone clatter to a stop. There's another tap, and this time I see a stone hit the French window.

I go to the balcony and open the glass doors. A rush of cold air comes in, and I shiver in my pyjamas. The college is dark and quiet, and smells like earth and trees.

Down on the ground, I see a tall figure looking up at my window. His white face is alight in the moonlight, and his lips are red and bruised looking.

'Marc?' I whisper.

'Sophia.'

My heart shudders.

'What are you doing here?' I say. 'How did you get in without being seen?'

Marc smiles. 'I have my ways. I'm coming up.'

I throw my arms around myself to stop from shivering. 'How can you? If I come down and let you in, some of the other students might hear.'

'Stay where you are.' Marc puts his foot to the wall and climbs the metal drainpipe. He jumps up each bracket until he's inches away from the balcony. Then he springs across in one swift, easy movement, swinging himself over the rail.

He's wearing a black t-shirt, black cargo trousers and dark grey trainers, and his hair is flopping onto his forehead. I smell soap and cigarettes.

'Romeo, Romeo,' I say.

'It is the east, and Juliet is the sun.' Marc smiles, reaching out to stroke my cheek. His eyes are teasing, but intense. It feels like there's no one but us in the whole world when he looks at me like that.

'It's too cold out here for you,' says Marc, stoking hair from my face. He scoops me up and carries me inside, rubbing my arms and kicking the glass doors closed behind us.

It's dark in my room, but the fire embers create a warm glow. He holds me tight. 'I missed you.'

'I missed you too.'

He rests me on the bed and lies beside me, propping himself up on his elbow.

I rest my hand on my cheek.

'Oh, that I were a glove upon that hand,' says Marc, smiling that devilish Marc Blackwell smile. 'That I might touch that cheek.'

I grin back at him.

'I thought if things are going to end,' he says, 'they couldn't end without me seeing you one last time.'

'Who says they're going to end?' I ask.

'I just had a hunch,' he says, 'that you might decide the challenges aren't worth it.'

'Maybe it's you who's had enough of me.'

'Never.'

He kisses softly, feeling me with his lips. Then slowly he undresses me and himself, looking into my eyes the whole time. I put my arms around him, feeling his broad shoulders under my fingers.

Effortlessly, he slides inside me, stroking my hair, running his fingertips down my neck and body. It's Marc, but a new Marc. I've never felt him be this tender before. His eyes are wide, and the clearest blue I've ever seen them.

'I want to let go now,' he tells me, moving deeper. 'I want to let go with you.'

'You can,' I say. 'I want you to. It's what I want more than anything.'

He moves again, his blue eyes growing softer. He grips me tighter, and his breathing quickens.

'Oh god,' he says. 'Oh god, Sophia. Yes. Oh yes.'

I feel him come inside me.

He looks right at me the whole time, his eyelids fluttering and his lips falling open.

I don't look away. I can't. I feel like I'm seeing right into his soul. And it's beautiful.

I wrap my arms around him and pull him closer.

Marc falls onto me, breathing hard against my neck. After a while, he pulls himself up and whispers, 'I need to know. Are we going to do this? Or am I going to have to get over you?'

I look into his blue eyes, so full of emotion – power, strength and fear – and I know I made my decision months ago. 'Yes,' I say. 'We're going to do this.'

'You're sure?' he asks.

'Yes.'

'I love you.' He strokes my hair.

'I love you, too.'

'In the morning then,' he says. 'We'll leave the college together. Hand in hand. Let them take their photographs.'

'Okay,' I say, feeling his arms slide around me. 'Tomorrow. First thing.'

We fall asleep wrapped in each other's arms, our foreheads touching.

Want to hear what happens next?

Part Two of the Devoted trilogy, **'Where the Ivy Grows' is available on Amazon NOW.**

FREE SECRET SCENE FOR ALL READERS!

For a **free secret scene from The Ivy Lessons, visit: http://eepurl.com/xsYdz.**

Thank you for reading!

Dear Reader,

I'm the author of the Ivy Lessons, and want to thank you from the bottom of my heart for purchasing this book. Welcome to the devoted family – there are thousands of us now.

If you enjoyed it, please help your friends discover a good read by tweeting and sharing. I pay attention to tweeters and sharers and will often seek you out and give you free, exclusive reads. Xx

28500415R00183

Made in the USA
Lexington, KY
19 December 2013